THE ISLAND OF THE GREAT MOTHER

GERHART HAUPTMANN

THE ISLAND
OF THE GREAT MOTHER

OR

THE MIRACLE OF ÎLE DES DAMES

A STORY
FROM THE UTOPIAN ARCHIPELAGO

TRANSLATED BY
WILLA AND EDWIN MUIR

NEW YORK   MCMXXV
B. W. HUEBSCH AND THE VIKING PRESS

THE ISLAND OF THE GREAT MOTHER

I

ON a certain day when the brooding sun was directly at noon several boats drew near the shore of a superb island in the southern part of the still Pacific. This island was surmounted by ranges of mountains and glittered in complete desolation. The boats, too, were remarkable, for they were densely packed and rowed, not by the dusky denizens of that region, but by ladies wearing the latest fashions of Europe. The whole spectacle appeared not unlike a pleasure excursion, for, amid the apparently gay and ever repeated shrieks of the occupants, the tiny vessels went zig-zag and changed their course again and again, as if a capricious hand were at the helm.

It was not pleasure, however, that had occasioned the trip, which, thank God, was being conducted on a perfectly still sea; but the boats were ship's-boats, and the women, survivors out of a shipwreck.

After, amid much chattering and screaming, they had surmounted a narrow line of surf, they landed at last in a little bay with an immense babel of cries of joy, of anguish, of apprehension, of tenderness, of pro-test and of encouragement. And at last considerably more than a hundred pairs of slightly wetted ladies' shoes had by good fortune reached dry ground.

But now that the landing, the most immediate step in their rescue, was accomplished, and this was realised by the greater part of the mob of women, there set in a transport of released emotion and jubilation, which mounted to embraces, kisses, sobs and tears of joy, and here and there to dances more or less wild. Here some of the rescued were lying in a deathlike sleep induced by terror or fatigue; there others reclined in a state of physical helplessness; others again were in a dumb despair; while a number of the rest were occupied in giving the sufferers attention and encouraging words. Only one of the women, the daughter of a multi-millionaire, an eighteen-year-old married lady, on her honeymoon cruise round the world and at the pinnacle of happiness, and, on the top of that, suddenly surprised by the disaster while she was sitting at lunch, —only this woman, a German lady, having lost her dear husband, an English lord, became frantic in her despair, and ran into the surf intending to drown herself, or, dragged out and held down by many arms, broke into convulsive cries.

Standing on a cooled block of lava on to which she had climbed to obtain a hearing, a woman cried continuously into the tumult of voices the same words: "Ladies, what is to be done? Ladies, think of the chief question, what we must do for our further safety. What is to be done? What is to be done?"

This cry, with its shrill and piercing tone which mingled with the sound of the surf, soon united a number of women at the foot of the lava block, who began a lively discussion among themselves and between the cries of the speaker found an opportunity to become acquainted with her. She was an artist well on in years.

She stood in the chestnut-brown silk dress in which she had sat down to table in the dining saloon of the East Indian. The deeply cut corsage of her costly gown was trimmed with Brussels lace. Her hair, whitened with age, looked as if it had been powdered. And as it was curly as well, the whole figure gave a rococo impression. Her wrinkled skin and dusky complexion, her strongly projecting jaw and broad, negroid, blubber lips, gave her an individuality which was rendered charming by her flashing brown eyes. Her whole appearance had a singular charm, which owed nothing either to beauty or to ugliness.

"Ladies, we must take counsel," she said. "And not as we have done hitherto, where all have chattered at the same time, as if they were in a Jewish school, but with order and system, as men do in Parliament. Therefore let us proceed at once to the election of a president."

One could hear the words "Election of a President," "Election of a President," as they flew from mouth to mouth along the beach,—words now first heard on that shore since the creation of the world.

When the majority of the women had gathered round the old artist's platform, she begged a hearing for a few words.

"LADIES," she began, after they had shouted from all sides to her to speak, "what has befallen us, as concerns the shipwreck and the landing, has happened before innumerable times. But never before has a shipwecked company so well-dressed and so one-sided in its composition found itself on a South Sea island."

There was laughter at this, as the speaker had intended, for by showing that her sense of humour was unimpaired she sought to impart courage to the women.

"You will say that the whole thing is not according to programme, and that Cook is answerable. Each of you no doubt has had her calculations badly upset; yet I would advise you, at least provisionally, to abstain from lodging any claim for compensation."

They laughed more heartily, save for a few who began to be angry. Their anguish passed into indignation when they thought they saw the fearful seriousness of their position being belittled and derided. They were soon, however, reduced to silence.

"I find myself at an age," proceeded the speaker, "where broadly speaking I have enjoyed all that life can offer, and so have it behind me. Thus I am perhaps the only one among you to whom this pretty adventure is not altogether unwelcome. That is to say, I do not imagine that my fate has anything more in reserve for me.

"And now—my attitude to the chance which has flung us by one sudden jerk out of the civilised world makes me perhaps peculiarly fitted to give you an example, ladies, of philosophical indifference, and so to render myself of use to you.

"There is only one lady here who knows something of my name and reputation. She is the lady whose twelve-year-old son was saved along with us. To the others I wish to say that my name is Anni Prächtel. Many of you have no love for Germany, the land of barbarians. Still, for lack of a better fatherland, I will not conceal that in it and its capital Berlin I have built up a reputation as a painter. For the rest, Berlin is the seat of the President of the German Republic." *

A voice shouted: "No, no, my dear Prächtel, I, too, know you, and I am not the lady with the son, but Frau Rosenbaum, 8050 Unter den Linden, the proprietress of the well-known linen drapery, where in the past you have often been a purchaser. So there are more than one who know you; but please do not put us off with a string of bad jokes."

Fräulein Prächtel retorted: "You only need command, Frau Rosenbaum, and I will vacate the platform. I scarcely flatter myself in thinking that you will discover no other person trained so obviously to be the shepherd of a flock of women."

"But why? But why?" was called from all sides. "Give your reasons."

"Then I propose Fräulein Rosita as President."

On the heels of the artist's unanticipated proposal there resounded a loud shout of dissent. For Rosita

* This passage was written in the year 1916.

was a seventeen-year-old circus rider, and moreover the most beautiful woman of the five continents.

By this judicious hoax Anni Prächtel had every voice on her side, for it became instantly clear that there was nobody among the women who could feel herself thrown in the shade by the beauty of the artist.

Accordingly she was elected president by acclamation, and as a result of her adroit and rapid management a series of decisions as practical as the immediate situation would admit were come to without loss of time. The women were divided into bands of ten. After Anni had elected herself head of the first Ten, she chose those who appeared most intelligent among the women, and gave each the leadership of a Ten. All the captains together constituted the government, of which the artist occupied the chair. A general census, if only for the purpose of a rough and ready survey, was the first governmental measure to be put in operation.

God knows through what misfortune the *Cormorant* sprang a leak and sank. But had it, indeed, sunk? It had lain on its side, while the waves washed over its mid-deck, yet the women had continued to see it until it melted into the horizon. The disaster had happened in the most beautiful weather and on a glassy sea. The men had put the women and children in the largest emergency boats, thinking that a steam pinnace could then be requisitioned to tow them. In perfect order all kinds of utilities had been stowed in the boats; axes, rope, nails and hand-tools of all descriptions, as well as abundance of corn, with which the *Cormorant* was freighted.

After this, so far as one could guess by the position of the sun, there remained at least five hours before sunset. This interval Anni desired to use to its utmost. After some of the women had discovered a spring of excellent water in a neighbouring cliff, five of the strongest were chosen to scale, if it were possible, a certain peak, which, according to their and Anni's computation, could be reached in something like an hour and a half, and must afford a wide prospect over the island. Was the island small or great, fruitful or barren, inhabited or uninhabited? All these were important questions, and could not be answered there on the bay, at the foot of an almost naked craggy coast. One thing was certainly comforting: the climate of the island was that of a paradise.

As leader of the exploring band the beautiful Miss Page was chosen, a tall, slender American, a genuine Diana. To her was entrusted one of the available Brownings, for she was well acquainted with the handling of fire-arms. Anni's maid, who had travelled and been rescued along with her, was made adjutant to Diana. Auguste was equal to all situations and could work veritable miracles. Accordingly, she had already discovered a cave for her mistress, sun- and rain-proof, and had directly turned it into a habitation. And she it was who was to be thanked that the artist had saved all manner of handbags, caskets, yes, even a trunk, as well as plaids and camel-hair rugs. Soon there was a tea-kettle going in the cave, and the smoke of a genuine Havana crept along the walls.

To receive their final directions Miss Page and her troop now stationed themselves before the cave, no longer in an elaborate toilette, but in a costume which by Anni and her governmental colleagues alike was draconically enjoined on grounds both of cloth-economy and physical efficiency. Wearing tennis shoes and a chemise girt round the waist, and nothing else, Miss Page resembled more than ever a Diana, though Auguste in the same attire produced nothing resembling the same effect. Nor did the almost forty-year-old Fräulein von Warniko, a lady accomplished in every sport, who carried as weapon and staff a boat-hook. The last two members of the band were Lolo and Mucci Smith, two pretty children, German on the mother's side and English on the father's.

"Good! ladies," said the artist, issuing from her cave. She spoke already with an almost imperial intonation, but with an undertone of deliberate cheerfulness. "Good! ladies. We must remember that we are compelled to build up our life now on a completely new basis.

"Myrmidons," she continued then, suddenly assuming the voice of the orator, "you are chosen out for a great task; the first great task imposed on us. Banish from your hearts all fear, or gloom, or weak complaint over that which cannot be altered. Fear, anguish, parting, treachery, sickness, hunger and death—these lour too in civilised lands. There, too, every one must subdue life by herself, and we are in no other case. Imagine that we are landed to conquer this island. Think we are conquerors. Think simply that you are Amazons."—It should be said that Miss Page understood German, having studied singing for several years in Munich, Dresden and Berlin.

"You will obey Miss Page," concluded the speaker. "And see that no one gets separated from the band! Who does not obey will be shot dead!"

Amid laughter and encouraging shouts the five went towards the mountain.

ANNI's position was contested, as was natural, but not openly. And, as was natural, too, the artist immediately recognised her hidden antagonists. These she made as incapable of mischief as possible. Frau Rosenbaum was set at the head of the second Ten, Rodberte Kalb, at that of the third. And Rodberte was allowed, after completing her first commission, to have tea with the President in her cave, which in jest she had called the White House. Apart from the more remote symbolism of the word, it was not unsuitable, for the cave was of a kind of white marl.

Rodberte, too, was no longer young, though considerably younger than the artist. During the foregoing ten years nearly every European review had contained articles by her of an æsthetic, ethical or political tendency. A charming novelette written in French—she spoke and wrote English, French and German with equal ease—had even been taken by the

Revue des deux mondes. She had lived for eight years in England, but she was born in Frankfurt. Her mother was French, her father German.

Unnaturally thin, Rodberte was almost as tall as Miss Page. Her sole ornament was her hair, which she could with difficulty keep in order. Even Miss Page's crown of hair did not excel Rodberte's in beauty, though for the rest the American was far superior to her in youth, blooming strength of frame, and nobility of expression. Nevertheless Fräulein Kalb was a remarkable and significant woman. In all things she showed a certain superiority over everybody, not only over Miss Page. She could not be mistaken for an angel. Her thoughts, which were restlessly mirrored in her somewhat beaver-like face, did not draw rein before God's throne. More familiar to her than celestial hallelujahs was the fiery element which burned through and through her supple and slender body. The artist, who had known her a long time, who had even painted her and again and again had studied her, thought now, while she sat opposite her in such a ticklish situation: She has always the same tormenting hunger in her which resembles that single flame which lusts to eat up all around it, to aggrandise itself, or to prevent itself from going out.

"For this time oblige me by saying exactly what you think, dear Rodberte. What, actually, do you see in this situation where we are imprisoned?"

"Absolutely nothing," said Rodberte; "we must wait. Just now I have a feeling as if someone who had concealed and saved up a malicious revenge for an offence ten years old, had meted it out at last to the dregs. All at once, as it were, one is deprived of all that one imagined one could never lose. The tale may be tragic, but meantime I feel only a diabolical mockery at the diabolical trick we have been played. More than once they asked me on the boat why I laughed out loud. That I was laughing out loud I did not know, but within myself I could not get away from laughter."

"Come, now, my good friend, what did you find to laugh at?"

Rodberte puffed smoke from her cigarette, and leant back with closed lips in the salvaged deck-chair. Then she let laughter and smoke burst together from her mouth.

"Let it become clear to you, my good Anni, how and in what a drastic fashion the gigantic accumulation of subtle questions which used to cause us sleepless nights has all at once been dissipated. Quite simply, they exist no longer. Now, for instance, do you still take seriously such questions as: which is better, a republic or a monarchy, Free Trade or Protection, the emancipation of women, the vote or slavery? Whether the Jesuits should be admitted into Germany, whether militarism is a thing bringing a curse or a blessing? Whether Marées is a painter, and Böcklin none, or Böcklin a painter, and Marées none? And behind these the whole queue of art problems. Or again the desolating question: Shall I go in summer to Berchtesgaden or to Biarritz, or make an excursion into

civilis
wishe
often
the p
of th
in evening ____,
with the motion of the sea, but solely by ___ ___ the unutterably vulgar variété music? Did it seem worth a farthing then—that inflated, grossly pleasure-seeking, profit-greedy, brainless, cynical business-man's civilisation? Very good, we have overcome it. We have returned to the bosom of nature, and, if it is your will, to paradise. And now we shall not act shabbily, but rather show what is in us without the paint and powder of civilisation."

DURING these last words, in which Fräulein Prächtel had raised her voice, loudly resounding cries came from the shore. Frau Rosenbaum appeared and declared that most of the women had been overmastered by a great excitement at the moment of sunset. Many ran to and fro along the beach sobbing and whimpering, others wept aloud and lamented as if they protested against the disappearance of the sun and through their protests sought to hinder its setting.

Anni Prächtel rose hastily and invited Rodberte to go down with her and if possible infuse courage into the poor women.

"It is natural," said she, "that a feeling of forsaken-ness should come over them now, and that with the

North? Or where I shall put in the winter:
n, Paris, Florence, or Rome? Or whether I shall
r take a run into the Riviera? Or which is the
brand of champagne: Heidsieck or Ayala? Yet
e questions were acute yesterday evening at dinner,
re—along with a million other civilised problems—
went down with the thousand tons of the *Cor-
ant.*"

odberte concluded her gallows humour.
I have firmly decided until further notice to
neither to a theatre nor to a concert, nor to a cab-
t, nor even to an art exhibition, a museum or a lec-
e. Also I intend meanwhile to give my Baron the
-by."

The artist laughed. She liked to laugh. She had
stened with a look of sly enjoyment to her comrade
disaster.

"I am differently constituted," she said. "Although
have saved no books, and unfortunately little of my
painting outfit, I shall continue to rummage for a long
ime among the phantoms of civilisation, even should
we remain here forgotten. But merely in such a way
as one whom people have deprived of his estates and
driven from his castles still possesses in imagination his
fields, disposes of his fruit crops, shoots his deer, or
yoked or his stallion to be

descent of night they should feel the full weight of the
destiny which has mysteriously befallen them."

A brownish-red light fell into the cave and made the
marl walls glow. When they came outside the women
were overwhelmed by the spectacle, which in the cave
they had imagined to be an ordinary sunset. From
Cuxhaven they had left eight thousand miles of sea
behind them, and almost every evening they had
watched the sunset from the deck. But here it was
characterised by a new and fearful greatness and
seemed like the finale of a symphony played by a
demiurge of music who had hidden himself behind his
work.

"No wonder," said the President, "if faced by such
a portent a mortal, feeling his weakness, should be
overcome by apprehension and terror."

"Truly what we see now we have often seen, dear
Anni," said Fräulein Kalb, "and in the same threatening beauty and majesty. And the others are in the
same case. But never have our souls and theirs been
so naked to the experience, so starkly confronted.
Something emerges in us all now which was smothered
under the lumber of the warehouse of civilisation.
Perhaps the primal apprehension of the living creature,
who in dim light feels the terror of beauty and the
might of creation. But hark! What a noise goes up
there along the cliffs! The crying and screaming of
the birds seems to have a kinship with that of the
women below, and may well come from the same
source."

In truth a universal tumult had broken out among the animals and birds on the summit of the cliffs.

"Certainly we have been brought far nearer to a knowledge of the true position of mankind on the earth, and to my mind in the universe, through this astonishing turn in our fortunes," said Anni. "One might say, we have slipped, like captive fishes, through a mesh of the net of civilisation back into the free ocean. Or one might say: with the shipwreck of the *Cormorant* a greater ship has gone down—that is to say, the ship of civilisation. Nay, we have become ourselves an undiscovered, primeval sea, in whose deepest ground that civilisation sinks never to be seen again."

"I am curious to know," said Fräulein Kalb, "what our fate will draw up as substitute for the sunk ship out of the unknown sea which you believe us to be. Possibly something good. At any rate, I can hardly persuade myself now that I was once confirmed, sat on my bench at school, recited a little poem on my father's birthday, wrangled with the parson, drank coffee with cream and skimmed the fashion papers in the café, and so on. Nay, I feel myself already moved dimly by all sorts of strange and monstrous things, so that, God knows, I could break out in this noise of animal fear without the slightest affectation."

Anni Prächtel exclaimed: "Then break out with a good conscience, dear Kalb. It is probably the sheer appreciation of the task which lies on my shoulders which prevents me from feeling a disposition to shriek to the sun. But if you must howl, Rodberte, then really I would much rather go alone, for it seems to me that if we are to have the courage and strength which we need for our preservation, howling will only have an enfeebling effect. I say nothing against the primal apprehension of the living creature, of which you have spoken so pertinently. If our situation has led to an outbreak of primal fear, and this may be expected to set in generally in the evening, then I expect and predict that the same situation will lead to-morrow morning to an outbreak of primal joy. For as free fishes in the sea we have equal claim to both."

THE artist and President of the women's republic which was inaugurated in such painful circumstances enrolled by her expressed desire the leaders of the Tens in her mission of encouragement, so that she appeared among the agitated women with a following. As a ruler she showed already a certain gift in the way in which she imposed her will on the women, using jest or earnest, sympathy or coldness, kindness or severity, or where hard measures were necessary, treating them with the sharpest sarcasm. A lady whose appearance and toilette betokened a certain profession cried continually: "I shall go mad! I shall go insane!" And then: "Look, ladies, that is hell over there. Tell me, are we living or already dead? The sun is the door of an infernal furnace. See the brown smoke of the fire! The sea is black like liquid coal."

Anni said: "My good woman, why are you shouting? Think rather of chocolate."

The woman betrayed herself by becoming sullenly silent, as Anni had wished.

"After all," said Anni to her attendants, "the comparison with coal and coal smoke was not inept, and if it occurs to Lady Lambert née Lilienthal as well, we shall have a fresh attack of hysterics. Her riches, while she was still a member of high society, were derived from coal."

The crying and running about had ceased by the time the artist with her following reached the end of the straggling encampment. Gradually the majority came to realise that a constituted power was present who had assumed responsibility for them for weal or woe. The leader and her helpers were now the centre of a general storm of complaints, demands and questions.

It was not easy to stand firm against that tempest, and the questions especially, which fell thick as hail, were difficult to answer with approximate plausibility.

"Do you think that my husband, my father, my brother has been saved? Had we wireless on board? Where really did the disaster happen? How long is it since we sailed from Hong Kong? When should we have reached San Francisco? How could the disaster have happened? How dared it happen?

"Do you think they are searching for us? Do you think they will find us? Where do you think we are in reality? Is the island known? Has it a name? Is it possible or quite out of the question that there may be found somewhere a port, a town with hotels, or at least a little comfort? Surely we cannot live like the beasts? Apropos beasts—there are no wild beasts here? For instance there can surely be no tigers? In God's name, if there are snakes, tigers and lions here, what shall we do then?"

"There is only one thing to be done, ladies," said the President, "to be resolute, brave and steadfast."

But it was not this noisy and turbulent crowd which gave the President and her helpers the greatest anxiety. That was needed rather for a few women who lay isolated here and there, and whom a genuine and fearful anguish of soul had thrown into a state of total will-lessness and apathy. Among these was a German lady, wife of an architect, who had reached the island with her twelve-year-old son, but whose husband after helping her and her son into the boat had drowned before her eyes. After he had voluntarily taken his hand from the gunwale for the sake of Lady Lambert, who was pushing her way in, a wild confusion of arms of drowning wretches in the water had caught him and drawn him in their toils into the depths. Beside this unconscious and moaning woman, who appeared little more than a girl, watched Miss Laurence, a broadly and strongly built, nobly proportioned, Anglo-Dutch woman.

She spoke in German, clearly, but with a somewhat thick pronunciation.

"We have laid Phaon" (that was the son) "and his governess a little aside. The deep slumber he has fallen into proves his sound youth. It is not so certain what will become of this poor woman. I think her loss is greater than any of ours. The doctor says that she will recover. I have grounds to doubt it."

The President arranged that Rita should be taken to her cave. This was done immediately by the Anglo-Dutch lady in a very simple way. She inserted her arms under the unconscious woman, lifted her without any effort, and with her burden followed Rodberte Kalb, who was instructed to show her the way. Miss Laurence walked over the sand with a heroic ease in which there was no sign of strain.

The beautiful Anglo-Dutch woman had been almost universally taken for a matron, for on reaching the island she was carrying in her arms a child scarcely a year old. By and by, however, it became known that she had found the child (it was a little girl) in the steerage on the voyage out, and had adopted her, the mother having died.

Beside the sleeping boy whom the artist now sought, watched Miss War, who for seven years had been his governess. One could mark from the sullen contortions of her face that she had been weeping, and the abysmal bitterness of her rapidly whispered words could not hide the fact. She broke out in a violent stream of English:

"What right had that stupid female, that vain, conceited, dense animal, to spring in at the last moment and take the seat reserved for his father?"

It was Lady Lambert who was justified, if she wished, in regarding herself as the object of this outburst.

"That beast," continued the governess, "must have

noticed all the same, as each and all of us did, what service Mr. Stradmann had rendered us. Who among us would be alive still if he had not requisitioned the boat for us? Could this supernumerary, inflated, stupid goose not see that in the attempt to save someone he had fallen overboard, and that all of us in our boat had only one wish—out of gratitude certainly but also for our own interest—to see him again beside us? But no: this sham aristocrat would spring in instead. The vacuous doll has robbed us of our one man, deprived him of the reward of his sacrifice, and on the top of that, deprived this boy of his father."

Anni Prächtel was not unsympathetic with this outpouring of righteous indignation. She herself had little affection for the Berlin lady. Yet she strove to mollify Miss War.

"Your anguish is natural," she said. "We know too from eye-witnesses that your version of the affair has much to be said for it. But the instinct of self-preservation remains, and there comes a moment when that gets reckless and desperate."

"But do you not know that the woman left her husband on board? Did he not wave his handkerchief to her with the supreme sang-froid and heroism of a true Englishman? Could she not have stayed with her lord? Ought she not to have done so?"

Thus Miss War raged on in fierce undertones, until suddenly the boy was awakened by the sound of her voice. He awoke, however, only for a moment, rubbed two great blue eyes in a face surrounded by sunny curls, smiled with drowsy amiability, breathed deeply, and was asleep again.

The sun had long set when the artist and her band straggled back to the cave. A watch was ordained, and the emergency, thank God, proved that among so many of the nervously exalted, incapable and broken, there was a gratifying number of efficient young heads.

In a light through which the colours of the ocean and the coast glowed for a last time in a new, magical beauty, so that one could not tell whether it came from above where no sky was to be seen, or whether it flowed up from potencies of light in the earth itself, the conversation of the home-coming women turned on the fatherless boy and on the chance which trembled over him of losing his mother as well.

"This misfortune," said Anni, "and the new turn it has taken touches me very very nearly, and on its account too I must guard that self-command which is necessary for us."

"The boy is really beautiful," said Rodberte.

Anni responded: "In that late marriage of Stradmann truly all was beautiful. Their household happiness combined in one the narrow interest of the home and the wider interests of the world outside. They were like turtle doves and yet they were not Philistines. As an architect Stradmann had not his like, and experts treasure his book on Gothic as masterly both in content and form. And he was not in the least one-sided. He was animated by a thirst for culture which seemed universal. It took him to Japan, where he collected in

many fields and prosecuted numerous studies. From
thence he purposed to go to Mexico to complete with
his own eyes his studies of Mexican architecture. The
man had a colossal energy and power of work, and with
it such a sensitive and tender soul that during his
fifteen-years' wedded life he was hardly a day parted
from his wife, nor indeed from Phaon since his birth.
Everywhere Phaon and Rita must be with him. With
Rita it was the same. She seemed energetic, absolutely
unsentimental and self-contained whenever one saw her
along with Stradmann, or she knew that at least he was
near. Once separated from him farther, she was
simply of no account to any one."

Rodberte said: "The boy is really beautiful."

LITTLE by little, silence stole upon the shipwrecked
company on the shore. They were all overcome by
sleep, old and young, despairing and courageous alike.
Many were dreaming, in a kind of waking trance; these
were the less fortunate ones. But most of them, after
all they had experienced and survived, were physically
exhausted to such a degree that they fell into complete
unconsciousness. They suffered no longer, for they no
longer existed. They were neither maidens nor women,
widows nor orphans: they were not even human, let
alone shipwrecked. Around them the night-life of the
tropics unfolded itself in vain; it was non-existent as
far as they were concerned. The Southern Cross stood
in the sky a little above the horizon, and higher up
shone the Centaur; towards the north was Arcturus,

blazing gorgeously; stardust, the Milky Way, myriad worlds. And myriads and myriads of shining worlds swam in the sea, too, which advanced and receded along the shore in billows of light and surging mountains of shimmering fire which shed a magic brilliance along the coast. The sleepers were withdrawn from all that, and yet they lay, as it were, within it, as on a mother's bosom, bound to it only by their breathing.

THE artist was awakened early in the morning by a ringing shout in front of her cave. The exploring party had returned triumphantly.

"Your joyous cry," said the President, hastily wrapping herself in a fur as she came out; "Your joyous cry is a good omen for all our future destiny on the island. I was never more happily awakened than on this first morning of my exile."

A renewed shout of joy was the answer.

"Children," continued the President, transfixed as if by astonishment, "you are so divinely lovely, that it is beyond my comprehension. If I were still in the world of civilisation, I should now first become a painter with you as my models—" The gallant maidens stood there, breathing deeply, fresh, with sparkling eyes, triumph in every movement, and each of them carried over her shoulder a cluster of greenish-yellow bananas, weighing from ten to twenty kilograms.

"This for a beginning," said Miss Page, "but there is more to come." And Fräulein von Warniko added, "President, the question of food may be regarded as solved. We should have enough and to spare of bananas and other fruits if there were not a hundred, but a hundred thousand of us." The pretty, charming, twenty-year-old Mucci Smith, who was, in fact, a gardener, with an outburst of childish and joyful pride laid before the President some green and gherkin-like fruits which she had recognised as fruits of the durian tree. "Taste these fruits, President, and you will believe that we are in paradise!"

"If I did not know that my old father at home is anxious about me," said Fräulein von Warniko, "I should not regret for my part that I am shipwrecked. For only to behold this island is almost as good as turning over a new leaf, which makes the old one appear dusty, torn, and dog's-eared. This landscape must make the human soul better, lovelier, happier, and more peaceful. If only our friends and relatives could be sent out here, one might wish never to return to the world." Lolo said that those slopes covered with fruit trees, those exquisite valleys full of palms and pisangs made her feel sad. She could not help enjoying them, she found that her senses were glutted with the rarest loveliness; but then she would say to herself, if only so-and-so, for instance, my mother, were here to share it, then, only then, would the enjoyment be real and blissful beyond all conception. As it was, one enjoyed, and did not enjoy; and experienced the pain of finally reaching something which one had hoped for only in another world, to find that one could not grasp it.

"Well, ladies—or I should rather say, children . . . well, my lovely and valiant children, I congratulate you, and congratulate the rest of us on the unhoped-for success of your first expedition. There will be other and greater ones. Come and drink tea and share my modest breakfast with me."

II

ABOUT a month had elapsed since the shipwrecked women had happily accomplished their landing on the island. During this period they hoped daily for rescue, but under the strong leadership of Anni Prächtel they were occupied in practical activities which were often successful. Thus, they had discovered that the surface of the island was no more than three or four German square miles in extent, that it was mountainous, but fruitful in the valleys and plateaux, and culminated in two conical peaks. The island lay like a horseshoe round a wide gulf, which had only one outlet to the sea, a small rocky passage, at its western end. From one of the peaks at all times of the day and night there floated a thin vapour.

For obvious reasons the island was christened Île des Dames. The harbour where they landed was Port des Dames: it was the only harbour in the island. The rest of the coast appeared to be steep and inaccessible. For the sake of simplicity the mountain was called Mont des Dames, and a strongly-running stream which flowed to the sea through a lovely valley became Fleuve des Dames. Bamboo had been discovered on its banks, and employed for the construction of tent-like huts; not only because the bamboos grew there, but also because of the luxuriant meadows beside the stream, and more than anything else, because of the shadowed coolness of the deep valley, into which not even the noon-day heat of the equatorial sun could penetrate. The settlement was called, with a touch of humour, Ville des Dames, and the whole vale Vallée des Dames.

Île des Dames was resplendent with gaily-coloured birds. It was a matter for congratulation that in all the divagations over the island no one had come upon cannibals, or the dreaded tiger, or any other beast of prey. Besides the inner gulf there were also bights along the exterior coast, too narrow for ships, but accessible from the land. Their waters, often seven to eight fathoms deep, were so clear that the living coral could be easily discerned on the black volcanic sand— a whole fairy-like world of richly-coloured coral, over which darted swarms of blue, red and yellow fish diversified by the orange and rosy translucence of jellyfish. The loveliest of these inlets was named La Rade des Poissons ensorcelés.

The bamboo huts of Ville des Dames were constructed in three concentric circles. They were so big that each afforded room for three colonists at most. Many lived singly in their huts, which were withdrawn a little to the side, a comfort permitted by the President.

Her hut was divided into two compartments, as she wished Auguste to sleep under the same roof but not in the same room as herself. Among the solitary settlers were Miss Page, Rodberte Kalb, and Miss Laurence, whose full name was Laurence Hobbema, while the trio Rita Stradmann, Phaon Stradmann and Miss War shared one roof among them.

RITA was somewhat better, but unfortunately not sufficiently to give hopes of a full recovery. Every morning she was brought from her sleeping quarters, floored with bamboo and passably furnished, to the front of the hut, where in Anni Prächtel's deck-chair under the coco-palms she passed the day sunk in an apathy which was dispelled for short periods only by Phaon's visits, or by some activity in which he was concerned within her range of vision.

The boy, as Rodberte had said, was really beautiful. He was beautiful when asleep or half awake, but still more when he arose and ran about lightly and cheerfully. Miss War was as strict with him as her power permitted, and did her utmost not to let slip from her hands the bridle with which she had to lead this noble colt, who being on all sides spoilt, enticed, and appropriated, as can well be understood, was in great danger of running wild. For this the Englishwoman was much disliked, not by Phaon and his mother, but by very many of the other colonists: but although she knew it and had indubitable proofs of it in the sharp remarks she overheard, and in daily arrogance, she did not allow it to change her attitude, which she felt for her to be a sacred trust. She was besides a zealous teacher, faithful and self-sacrificing; but in addition to these virtues she did not possess that of compliance; which made her pugnacious, though not quarrelsome.

Rita knew what a treasure her son had in Miss War, and that he was nearly as dear to the Englishwoman as to herself. Miss War never felt herself opposed by Rita, except when, in the unavoidable little disputes between pupil and teacher, she took Phaon's part in a soothing and motherly way. Besides Rita, the President herself, Rodberte Kalb, and Laurence Hobbema, always supported her when anything like this came into question. Phaon was certainly not kept on a tight rein; for Miss War sometimes slackened it liberally, and from time to time the colt was left to run free. He shared in the hunting expeditions which had become customary. In fact, no one could have hindered the unruly boy from doing so, and he was allowed, of course only in the company of Miss War, to take part in these and other expeditions within limits not too wide. But especially in the martial games, exercises in which they threw clubs and bamboo spears which they had fashioned. These exercises took place chiefly under the eye of the President in the morning or in the cool of the evening, on the wider clearing enclosed by the circle of the town of huts.

Phaon was not yet big enough to equal or to surpass in the primitive arts of hunting and war a Miss Page or a Fräulein von Warniko, and much less a certain Alma, a slim and sinewy mulatto. He took these serious games too much as if they had no purpose.

But he ran in front of the budding Amazons with passionate emulation and never wearied delight, so free from all undercurrents of sorrow that in his neighbourhood they were apt to forget that they were deserted by all the world and cast away on an island in the South Seas. In short, the whole essence of Phaon was assurance. So long as he felt no severe physical pain, and was not behind prison walls, no sorrow could overpower him for more than a little while. Thus his fiery spirit, blissfully intoxicated by life, had changed his sorrow at the loss of his father into a hope bordering on certainty that he had been rescued, and thus too the thought of possibly losing his mother never even occurred to him. There had certainly been a catastrophe, in which a ship and several hundred human beings had disappeared into the waves. But meanwhile, strangely enough, that did not in the least shatter his confidence in a practically immortal and indestructible life for himself and his mother. This steadfast and firm certainty of happiness helped the spirits of the colonists like a never-failing restorative, and everybody felt it. This cordial was frequently necessary. Although they had to some extent familiarised themselves with the situation in which they were, and could depend upon it that they would neither perish of hunger nor bleed to death under the knives of cannibals, nor be torn to pieces by wild beasts, yet they were cut off from everything which had formerly surrounded them and for which they had lived, and were as good as buried for the world of humanity. Yet

Île des Dames was certainly no tomb. One might call the island a paradise. But even Anni Prächtel, for whom a kind of mission in life had arisen out of the flotsam of the shipwreck, felt often that she was imprisoned, at least, if not buried. This mood would suddenly contort the laughing blue of the sky into a hideous sneer, or present it as the heartless and stonily pitiless face of a dungeon vault; the screams of parrots would become the mocking cries of demons, and the shimmer of the bays, the clearness of the deep water, an agony. All beautiful things would seem to become lies, the harsh and painful phantasmagoria of delirium.

Though the artist knew how to deal with these spasmodic attacks in her own fashion, other natures less gifted and resourceful succumbed to them, often in despair. There were days on which weeping, shrieking, and crying for help, infected the colony like an epidemic, and could only be checked by much effort and patience on the part of the President and her assistants. But the guard, which was changed every two hours, and which paced round the settlement from evening until dawn, heard much whimpering and weeping and lamentation within the walls of the huts; and accents of misery, homesickness, estrangement, desolation, all the wretchedness of exile, fell night by night on their ears.

The President could tell at once, in the daily assembly, whether the bygone night had been a good or a bad one in this respect. She ran her eye over the circle of lovely girls with the penetrating and observant look of an artist, and if swollen faces, inflamed eyes, sleepless and weary looks, were in the majority, she took the occasion not only to encourage as much as possible their fortitude and their hopes of rescue, usually by a lengthy exhortation, but also to counteract the demons of boredom, listlessness and melancholy, by announcing special orders for the day.

These measures had been thoroughly canvassed beforehand by the President and her intimates. Some were designed as prophylactics to prevent the evil, others to deal with its symptoms. A strict observance of the calendar belonged to the former class, as did also the keeping of Sunday as a holiday. Of the secular festivals, the President's birthday was the foremost; but they celebrated everybody's birthday, and it was Phaon's which aroused the gayest anticipation. A church tent and a reading tent had been constructed or were being constructed. Miss Laurence, who (with her serious disposition) had rescued a Bible, was profoundly versed in religious matters, and in her nobly shaped head with its severe frame of black hair carried a knowledge of Brahmanic and Buddhistic teaching; she was created Vestal of the Temple. It was called Notre-Dame des Dames, since this community felt justified in preferring the feminine to the masculine personification of the godhead.

Measures to overcome unexpected outbreaks of melancholy generally originated in a sudden inspiration of the President, if they were not taken from the list of possible diversions which had been drawn up. One of these inspirations was the arrangement for performances to be given, at which each of the ladies who was mistress of any artistic or dexterous skill displayed her powers. The beautiful Rosita was a tight-rope dancer, and had therefore to dance on a tight rope. Miss Laurence sang. Fräulein Gerte Bergmann, the violinist, who had saved her Italian instrument, gave a concert, and so on.

Of course the vapours were chiefly overcome, and that automatically, by necessary work, by the compulsion to eat and drink, to live a settled life, to remain healthy, and to unite in improving the standard of life in every possible way. Certainly there were no newspapers; but, instead, the day had another climax, which was awaited with eagerness: the evening hour, when the ten shorewatchers came home with the latest news from the coast. For every day there sprang up anew the hope of seeing a ship which would bring rescue.

BATHING in Fleuve des Dames was so attractive that it was indulged in every morning, and sometimes several times a day. The fresh water of the stream was more refreshing than the warm and relaxing waters of the bay. Each of the Tens had a separate bathing-place. It was not difficult to find bathing-places of more than earthly beauty along the river's winding banks, among the groves of pisang and acacia-like mimosa: and, indeed. could a civilised man have chanced to catch a glimpse of the Vallée des Dames about the bathing hour, he would have thought that he had fallen into Paradise.

At these times the valley rang with unrestrained mirth, except when some unusual depression weighed upon the spirits of the colony. The universal jubilation, laughter, and cries of pleasure, the thousandfold utterance of a joy heightened into ecstasy, echoed and re-echoed among the basalt cliffs of the ravine. To delight the eye, again, pictures of incomparable charm were revealed. The grand style of Gaspard Poussin and Claude Lorraine had apparently come to life here in a tropical world. That landscape, at once heroic and lovely, could well have been taken for a garden of the gods, and the bathers for Hesperian nymphs guarding the Tree of Life and the apples of the Hesperides, the golden gifts of the earth to Hera.

It was not the artist, with her more modern consciousness, who hit upon this analogy with the Greek myth, but Miss Laurence Hobbema. Her father was, of course, not the older Hobbema, but a modern painter who had only his name in common with the other. He painted pictures full of light, men and youths clad in the Greek chiton, Greek women white-robed and lightly girdled, the sunny sky, the sunny air, the sunny marbles of Greece, and from his London home had won to such eminence as a painter that his pictures were sold at huge prices all over the world. His daughter was not so free from shadows. In her spirit were deeper depths and higher heights, deeper shadows, therefore, and sunnier peaks. Although she was no artist, attempting only in secret certain poetical experiments, she had by far the richer nature. At the age of twenty-seven, her serious and religiously coloured spiritual life possessed the same ripeness as her body; but both body and spirit were still those of a seeker.

She accounted it a piece of good fortune that divine Providence had dropped into her arms the little orphan who had been baptised Dagmar. Miss Laurence said, however, that she regarded the baby as a gift from Heaven, as a daughter given her by God, and instead of Dagmar chose for her the name of Diodata.

The adoption of this child, and the courage to assume duties and responsibilities which the act postulated, are alone sufficient to reveal the character of this lady; but throughout the whole catastrophe she had shown herself wise, far-seeing, fearless and capable of self-sacrifice.

SINCE the hour when she had supported Rita, Phaon's mother, into the artist's cave, she had made it her business to look after Rita and Phaon. Her services in this respect were accepted without jealousy even by Miss War. The two ladies were on such good terms that even a little difference of opinion, which arose over the question whether Phaon should take part in the general bathing parties, did not antagonise them.

"No, he must on no account do so!" said Miss War. And, with her characteristic incapacity for giving way, she persisted in her veto. Laurence said: "You will only achieve the opposite of what you intend, Miss War. In the first place, the boy quite rightly regards these communal bathing expeditions as public festivals. He feels it an undeserved and painful slight to be the only one excluded. For that reason alone he will keep on rebelling against you, as he has often done already, and there will be scenes, and, as now, all the women in a body will take his part against you. Meantime, if your will prevails, Phaon, who, as we know, is an intelligent boy, will want to find out the why and the wherefore. I imagine, indeed, that he has already done so. He will ask me: 'Laurence, have I done something wrong? Is my not being allowed to bathe with the others a punishment? Why must I bathe alone in the custody of Miss War like a criminal?'" "Why? . . . Because! Why? Because! That is the answer I am in the habit of giving him," said Miss War. "Why? Because! And that is sufficient." "You are mistaken if you believe that is sufficient," replied Laurence. She continued: "I am astonished at Phaon's occasional capacity, even now, for original and relatively mature thought. I believe that he hides many a thing from you. He will not rest, believe me, until he knows the real reason for your action. And then his very simplicity, and, as we can well say, his innocence, will have been destroyed by what was meant to preserve them." "It is all one to me," cried Miss War; "In any case I shall have done my duty."

"She is like a donkey or a goat," said the President,

with her short dry laugh, after she, too, had vainly interceded for Phaon. That shrewd, experienced lady had no objection to any kind of morality, provided that it did not limit the freedom of the senses. Still less did she object to any religious denomination, whatever its basis, so long as it did not pretend to meddle with morality: for she held it to be one of the divine attributes of the true universal religion that it had never desecrated its purity by a vulgar union with a system of punitive morality. This point of view seems particularly worthy of mention since it was affirmed by an elderly virgin.

She was loved most, perhaps, by Rita, and, strangely enough, by Phaon, who ran to her at every opportunity and spent hours in her society. She was always glad to see him, for she loved his quick and ever active spirit, his divine assurance, and his ready answers. She had in herself to contend with a tendency to malicious wit of a kind which made her generally more feared than loved. But nobody questioned her position; for however she might let herself go in private, in her official dealings she always preserved the spirit of impersonal justice. So even in that respect, quite apart from her tireless labour for the welfare of the colony, she was the best and most suitable leader that could be thought of.

TIME, or the succession of events of which it is entirely constituted, according to the philosopher, did not stand still. And so on Île des Dames as everywhere else the second month followed the first, the third the second, the fourth the third, until the sixth month was at an end.

Then came the day on which Phaon's mother, as Miss Laurence said, passed over.

She had lived for long in a kind of twilight state, and for the last month was almost completely overshadowed; awakened to passing consciousness only by the radiance which fell into her darkness from the proximity, the voice, and the kiss of Phaon.

As the end drew nigh a strange vivacity possessed her, which the inexperienced took to be an improvement of her condition. The will to live, interest in her surroundings, and hope, seemed once more to be awakened in her.

Doctor Egli, the President, Miss Laurence, and Miss War, did not deceive themselves about the real significance of this apparent turn for the better which had set in. Miss War, indeed, was bathed hourly in tears.

Rita declared suddenly with an unspeakably touching and secretly triumphant smile that she now knew to what a strange illusion she had been subject. But that was of course inevitable, and was so planned by God. For the pain of separation was necessary to the joy of reunion. "How could I ever have been sensible of such happiness as this," she said, "if I had not believed that Erasmus (that was her husband's Christian name) was drowned before my eyes. Of course it was clear that his guardian angel must save him. His guardian angel stood behind him always, not only in his study, but also when we travelled, in the hotel, at the table d'hôte, in our room, on the Rigi, in the cell of St. Francis, at the tomb of Sebaldus in the Church of St. Laurence. Only when He bore him away to the Island of the Blessed under the high trees did I not see him, only then. I did not see thee, sweet and heavenly angel, and now all at once thou soarest again on golden pinions to and fro between us. Thou art no smaller when thou art far, and no greater when thou art near. When I see thee on high yonder, in converse with Erasmus on the rocky terrace before the purple tent. . . ." In this way she span her illusory fantasies. It was as if she had undertaken to swim a broad and rushing stream, had been swept away by the current, half drowned and unconscious, but finally had been washed up on the other bank; awaking there, she seemed to have attained a new, a higher existence.

"Your mother is very ill," said Miss War. But Phaon denied that outright. He was among those who saw in this dangerous renewal of vitality the beginning of convalescence. He had lived the last few years with his mother almost like a brother with his elder sister. She had readily accompanied him into the fantasy-world of his best-loved books: not only into the worlds of Cooper and Robinson Crusoe, but also those of Dante and Ariosto, whom he had devoured in Italian. Out of these, and other elements, some of them self-created, under his direction a mutual world of fantasy had arisen for him and his sister-like mother, to which most of their conversation and their strange, sometimes incomprehensible jargon, referred. So it happened that now when his mother lay on her deathbed in a waking dream, he mistook the disordered utterances of her spirit for that language, especially, indeed, as it was composed of elements known to him of old.

Moreover, the mystical exaltation of his dying mother resembled his own invariable state of mind, which could be described as a healthy exaltation, springing from true vitality. For these reasons the riddle, as it were, unriddled itself to him, and bliss encountered bliss, and the more completely as he was inwardly bound to the invalid by ties of blood and of love, and was entirely unwilling to admit that she could die.

"Guardian angel, sweet one, take me by the hand." As Rita said this to Phaon, and he clasped her hand, the last minute of her life struck. "Angel, sweet one, hold me." Phaon knelt and put his arm about her to lift her to a sitting posture. For this, it seemed to him, was what she wished. He was successful; she bowed her head forward and her loosened hair flowed forward. The boy lifted his face up, and Rita's slowly sank down on it. She breathed: "My darling! My sweet angel!" In Phaon's arms hung a burden. "Carry me, golden angel." Then it was as if a mountain sought to crush Phaon. A sound droned in his ear as if someone were greedily inhaling the fragrance of his hair. Then they took the burden out of his arms, away from his face, from his shoulder, and from his breast.

And Phaon stood up. They saw him grow white to the very finger-tips. Then the blood started suddenly to his head. And before anyone suspected his intention he dashed out.

THIS event, Rita Stradmann's death, was followed by a period of the deepest depression on Île des Dames. At the funeral an actual frenzy of despair broke out, and these Europeans, wailing like hired mourners, beat their breasts. The President called it crowd hysteria, and qualified it further by the adjectives disgusting and insincere. At all events it was troublesome to control. This immoderate and abandoned condition was by no means the result of insincerity in every case; only with difficulty could some of the women be restrained from suicide. Others went black in the face and fought convulsively for breath, a dreadful sound which could be heard far and wide, until they regained their natural colour, and wept a while, and finished either by falling asleep or by brooding huddled up, with fixed and vacant gaze. A mourner who had wept and sobbed continuously at the grave suddenly broke out into low-pitched spasms of laughter, which grew ever louder until they infected others, and before any measures could be taken to remove the victims, led to a horrible and almost universal attack of hysterical laughter and screaming which was disquieting. "Like you, we shall all die desolate and alone, and shall nevermore see the world." That was the thought and that was the cry which sent them all out of their senses.

"Dead woman, you are better off than we are, for we are buried alive."

Fortunately Phaon's obstinate resolve to stay away from his mother's funeral had not been shaken. Some time previously the boy had already prepared for himself a bamboo hut, away from Ville des Dames, higher up the river. When he fled in horror after his mother's death he was sought for there, but was not found. He was found instead in a hut as secluded, which Miss Laurence Hobbema had constructed, busying himself with the little Dagmar-Diodata.

SOME fourteen days after these events a new Assembly House was inaugurated, the ground plan and elevation for which had been drafted by Thorgerd Grimm, who had been in an Arts and Crafts School and had some skill in architectural design. This pavilion, erected under the artist's guidance, had turned out not badly, since another had been taken as model which that prince of painters, Miss Hobbema's father, had constructed in his London garden, and a photograph of which his daughter possessed. Instructed chiefly by Mucci Smith, the gardener, and also by what they could nearly all remember of their school lessons, they knew the value of the coco-palm for civilised purposes. And since it had been soon discovered growing here and there on the island, they not only drank the milk of the three-cornered nut, which was the size of a man's head, but were on the way to exploit the other properties of the tree. They tapped the gum, ate the

-€ 42 }-

palm leaves, and soon learned how to prepare the palm wine also. And now they had progressed so far as to use the trunk of the palm as building material.

As has been said, the emergency boats had been provided with well-furnished tool-chests, so that there were plenty of saws, planes and gimlets, as well as hatchets and axes. There were nails, too, and all kinds of things indispensable to a joiner and carpenter. And so they had been active in felling trees, had sawed, chopped, planed, rammed stakes into the ground, used the spirit-level and the plumb-line, laid and put together cross-beams, set up pillars and so forth, until in a truly surprising fashion a flimsy but yet fairly spacious and pleasant building was completed. It was christened at the opening ceremony: Maison de la Bonne Esperance. Among other things the President said in her address:

"Heaven has been good to us too in not taking away our beloved friend at any rate before our work was completed. I fear that otherwise it would have been discontinued and perhaps never finished. For I have observed with sorrow that the active, zealous, confident, joyous public spirit to which we owed the inception of this Town Hall has given way to indifference and feeble depression. That must be changed, my friends. I implore you to show once again your old, I will even say your inconquerable, youthful freshness.

"Was it not a wonderful thing to feel the spirit that inspired us when the bold project of this Tabernacle was suggested? In proportion to our resources and our number have we not done at least as much as the children of Israel?" . . .

And the speaker now described the joyous zeal with which each of the women and girls had contributed her mite to the success of the whole. "How gloriously," she said, "rang the axe of Miss Laurence! How the chips flew under the widely swung hatchet of dusky Alma, whose straight slim figure is yet so supple and soft, and whose sinews seem to be made of iron! How efficient and omnipresent was our excellent forewoman, Fräulein Warniko! Rosita, the world-renowned sylphide of the air, who is never dizzy—how she queened it between heaven and earth, walking calm and erect along the beams when the roof-supports were constructed. I would never come to an end if I were to appraise singly every service rendered by each of our colonists. Lolo Smith has revealed herself as a genius in handiwork, and you have her to thank for the pleasant and comfortable bamboo-chairs on which you are sitting, ladies. And it is Lady Lambert, as I must tell you, who has demonstrated how the fibres of the coco-leaf can be woven into these pliant, durable and elastic seats for the chairs. Frau Rosenbaum, our caterer, has provided for all your bodily needs. You have always found the table well-furnished. You have enjoyed bananas raw, boiled, baked, and candied, roast meat, game to your heart's content, and a mouthful of palm wine at the right time in our goblets of coconut shell, which Thorgerd Grimm has fashioned so beautifully. The lovely fish in all the colours of the rainbow we do not wish to forget, which Gesine, the sturdy Icelander, has angled for in the bays; and not only Gesine.

"Ladies, Frau Rita is dead. If I wished to recall the funerals of intimate friends and relatives I could count up to seven and twenty. Do you think that it is only here that people die, and that perhaps in New York, Paris and Berlin they live for ever? Travel by automobile through any civilised country, and in every tiny spot you enter you will see an undertaker's shop and the familiar stone-mason's yards in which those familiar atrocities, black and white marble slabs with golden inscriptions, rude crosses, and rubbishy angels, are cut and kept in store. So death is here, and death is there. You see, I am quiet and serene, and yet, considering my age, it should be definitely my turn next for Death's scythe. In comparison with me, ladies, you are all children still.

"You are impatient because you think that your youth may slip away unfulfilled in this paradise of a wilderness. I admit that we women have no real present and no real future in the absence of men. But have patience yet for a little while. Ninon de Lenclos was seventy when a youth shot himself for love of her, and because she did not love him in return. What do six months matter at your age? or one, two, three . . . yes, what great matter would it be for you if we had to spend four years on the island? The beauty of every single one of you, which has already increased so noticeably after six months, would then be at its most completely overwhelming for these slack scoundrels of European fops and dandies."

There was great laughter, and again it was obvious that the artist knew how to humour her people. And at the end of all the ceremonies, as more than a hundred sat down in a separate long room to a festival banquet at a real table, they felt in a highly beneficial way that they were again in touch with the larger world of civilisation, and that the pain of exile was considerably allayed.

The dining hall had been fitted up by Sister Hertha, a sick-nurse, who before entering on her profession had lived in Darmstadt, and had done practical work with the masters of its artistic colony.

But her helpers, too, were inspired by that spirit, so fruitful everywhere in handicrafts, which the deeds and words of Van de Velde had evoked in Germany. She had decided the size and shape of the table, of the wooden dishes, and other table requisites; she had decked the table with a fine mat, and the mat with embroidery; had provided beautiful jugs of coconut shell filled with the choicest orchids; and she had spaced in excellent proportion the doors opening out of the hall. These led onto a gallery which ran right round the house and was covered by the overhanging roof; it was completely protected by lattices made of mats, to which the graceful feminine talent for design, aided by the discovery of a coloured clay, had given a red-brown colour.

An unobtrusive frieze, which came from the hand

of Anni Prächtel, ran round the walls of the new refectory; on it she had represented allegorically the construction of the building, depicting naked women with axes and saws, and all the other activities of the task; but, curiously enough, she had repeated constantly the figure of a guardian spirit standing above or behind the workers, leaping, beckoning, leading them on or calling them back, bringing bananas, dancing, playing the flute, or aiming with a bow at one or other of the women; a spirit resembling Phaon, who was the only person who had taken absolutely no part in the enterprise.

As, with the help of the palm-wine, the banquet grew noisier and noisier, the guests discovered that Phaon's rôle in the delightful frieze was not quite comprehensible, and urged the President to explain it. "Oh dear! What next? Only a stupid fancy," she laughed.

III

THE artist and Rodberte Kalb sat facing each other, clothed, it is true, only in chemise and girdle, but otherwise much like other Europeans, at table, in a pleasant room of the pretty little bamboo and coconut house which by this time had been erected, also, for the President. The second of February, the first anniversary of their landing on Île des Dames, was close at hand. The ladies discussed many things, including the proper way of celebrating it.

"Let us be honest for once, my dear Rodberte," said Anni. "Tell me seriously and in confidence what you really think of the whole amazing adventure. We have now been actually a year on Île des Dames. But I have still a feeling of incredulity about the whole affair. This feeling has not decreased but rather increased in strength since we first landed on this coast, a fact which is extremely curious considering all that we have experienced and accomplished in these twelve months." Fräulein Kalb said drily: "Give your nose a fillip." The artist laughed. That she had done already more than once, she responded, and always in vain. She was still unable to decide whether she had not as usual done herself too well on smoked salmon for supper, and was now bearing the consequences in an intricate and extra-vivid nightmare. If that should turn out to be true, the decision should at once be taken to set down this fantasy on paper immediately on awaking. . . . "Then," said Rodberte, "you had better begin at once."

"And," she went on, "according to my estimate of this new and extraordinary Robinson Crusade, it is full of reality. But if you want to take it as a dream, you must at least reckon with the fact that there is no awakening from it except perhaps in the hour of death." "What the devil!" The President broke into her customary expression, and smote the table with her fist. "As far as I am concerned," she continued, "why not? But what the devil! The dream is becoming tiresome."—"Well then, try taking it as a reality—" said Rodberte. "I cannot. This rubbishy women's colony remains unreal for me. And what could it be but a trite reality when it is already so dull and boring as a dream? Tell me, how could that immense ship, the *Cormorant*, go down at all?"—"Perhaps through a piece of wreckage from Rozhdestvensky's fleet," was Rodberte's opinion, "or a drifting mine from the Russo-Japanese war; or perhaps all that floating ark of civilisation with all its pottering cargo of painted and shallow civilised ware, fell to pieces of its own accord because it was flimsily built and eaten by corruption."

"Well, dear Rodberte, in confidence," so the President concluded this part of the intimate discussion, "I must admit that I am beginning gradually to grieve for that giant ark full of shallow pottery which has drifted away from us."

At this moment the room was darkened by the entry of Miss Hobbema, who shut out the brightness of the tropic garden as she stepped over the threshold.

Her enormous hat of bamboo-straw was removed as she came in, revealing the proud face of the theosophist, crowned with thick black plaits, and her large soft eyes in whose depths shone both goodness and wisdom. She wore a sleeveless chemise of raw silk girdled in the middle by a wide belt woven of coco-fibre, and bast sandals fastened by bast straps. Her body was like a living statue, and the stuff of which it was fashioned, like living bronze embodied in flesh. Like another owl of Pallas, a parrot sat on the naked shoulder of the lovely apparition. It had been for years her companion, and had been rescued by her from the shipwreck. She loved ornaments, and, in consonance with her nature, usually gave them a mystic interpretation. The crown of yellow orchids with which she had decked her hat gave proof of this, and still more the spiral of heavy gold in the form of a serpent, which coiled round her beautiful upper arm.

"Am I disturbing you, President?" asked Miss Hobbema. "A goddess is never a disturbance," was the answer she got, "when she enters the hut of a poor mortal.

"Approach, most welcome one!" The ladies laughed, the parrot shrieked in chorus.

When it had been quieted and Miss Hobbema had entered a decided protest against her elevation to divine rank, Anni none the less could not deny herself the pleasure of defending this step—perhaps she promised herself an amusing quarter of an hour:

"I have often asked myself: By what ways and means is our rescue likely to be accomplished? We have, of course, discussed this question often, and all together. Among other things, it has been suggested that chance must be our best ally, or that we must succeed by some means or other in acquainting the distant world of civilisation with our position. And for this purpose we have employed some of our rescued bottles as a bottle-post, that is to say we have entrusted them to the Pacific Ocean.

"We have also caught sea-birds and fastened medallions with inscriptions to their legs. Our somewhat overstrained Fräulein Babette Lindemann, whose talents I do not at all wish to disparage (as you know, she worked her way up from general servant to lady's maid, and from lady's maid to well-read travelling companion), well, our Fräulein Lindemann has even shut herself up in a pitch-dark room and tried through a Swedenborgian telekinesis, or thought transference, to make our situation known to an old aunt in Lübeck, and to suggest to her what she should do in order to rescue us. I do not set much store by this attempt. But at least it occupied the attention of our colony for several weeks, sustained their spirits, satisfied the impulse to self-deception, and above all kept hope alive.

If Babette Lindemann's method were a practicable one, I would have tried to establish contact not with an old aunt in Lübeck, at any rate, but with somebody quite different—preferably the Sultan." Here the parrot, excited by the ladies' laughter, began again to squall in an appalling fashion.

"I only wanted to say," continued Anni, "that we should not be left alone for another fortnight if only some influential and suitably talented representative of the world of men could get an idea of the throng of beautiful and helpless women, young girls and young widows, which is gathered here. Expeditions went in search of Nansen and Emir Pasha. Could not a Peters, a Stanley, or a Sven Hedin be found, or shall we say a Sardanapalus, if it were known what an unheard-of haul could be made here?—not too bad, indeed, for the harem of a King of Kings."

The parrot flapped its wings and shrieked wildly with a thick accent which it seemed to have caught from its mistress: "Laurence, make coffee! make coffee! make coffee!" He finished with a clatter of his beak, through which rang the sound of a curious word, something like "Nemqueteba." All this noticeably increased the merriment. The President continued, while she stroked her brown knee, the thin knee of an elderly Indian woman:

"I have been made President. To that I was predestined because of my age, in which I surpass all of you, and because of another equally unrivalled characteristic of which, in my opinion, Miss Hobbema, you are the direct antithesis. It was you, and not Miss Page, nor the lovely sylph of the air, to whose aphrodisian and ripe charms I do every justice, nor was it anyone else, but only you whom I have always voted for in the imaginary beauty competition which I sometimes hold. It is so. You can laugh at me and rebuff me as much as you like.

"And because you are our high water mark of beauty, and since all earthly hope of attracting the world's attention is more than vague, I have in my dreams, which are slipping more and more from the rock bottom of reality, set my hopes on you; I see in you an Andromeda and am expecting the Perseus who is to rescue you."

Needless to say, the divine bird on the polished bronze shoulder of the Anglo-Dutchwoman nodded its crest, and in an ear-piercing tone answered these sentences, too, with its countlessly repeated: "Laurence, make coffee!"

"What do I care for Perseus?" said Miss Hobbema, "I would rather choose Hercules." And she came back to the favourite game of her imagination, in which she changed Île des Dames into the island of the Blessed, the garden of Hera, where Hesperian nymphs guarded the wonderful Tree of Life bearing the golden apples of Hera.

"Do not streams of nectar," she went on, "actually flow in this marvellous island of ours? Do not airs of heavenly coolness, mingled with the fragrance of the most enchanting spices, blow everywhere and through this very window? You know that I eat no meat, and am all the less inclined to be a huntress? That has not hindered me from penetrating already more than once to the very topmost peak of the crater of Mont des Dames. I hardly believe that Diana Page is so versed as I am in every particular of the topography of our island-gem, and in its mysteries, which often border on the supernatural. In my wanderings I have much richer experiences than merely outwitting and shooting wild creatures. Surrounded by the immense majesty of the ocean's blue radiance which expands as I mount, I am penetrated by a power, by a boundless loveliness in which I realise the most sublime visions in thought alone. I hold converse with Zeus. I have seen the cave where he couches with the youthful Hera. A half circle of trees stands round it, each of which bears within itself the strength and sap of immemorial youth, in its giant trunk the indurated wrinkles and bosses of an immemorial endurance, in the green world of its summit a world of colour, a world of exuberant blossoming ardour, a world of the most exquisite bliss, a world of celestial and unforgettable music.

"That is what is called extravagance, is it not? Good, I live on extravagances. For example when I am teaching my glorious Phaon, and we discuss that Greek mythology which, thanks to my parents, I drank in with my mother's milk, I often forget who he really is. It seems to me rather that I am teaching the son of Hyperion, the youthful Helios who is destined later to illumine the world. I wait for the day when he

shall take his flight to the Ethiopians on his golden
couch, where that lovely plaything, the sun's chariot,
with the fiery steeds of the sun, stands in readiness
for him. It is this myth of the Hesperides that most
of all satisfies my soul and lets it breathe. I perceive
and see that island which lies like ours secluded from
the world, hard by the Gorgons, on the very confines of
eternal night. I take pleasure in imagining that this
mighty sun which daily sheds light and heat upon all
of us alike is not the old sun of the earth, but the
sun of our Hesperian island only, and I look upon myself for my part as Hygeia, one of the most intoxicated
with light of the daughters of the Night. You may
think, here we have again the crazy Englishwoman.
As a matter of fact, I am more Dutch than English,
as you know, and as my name bears witness. But go
on thinking what you must, I do not see why here,
freed from every connection with the old world, I
should not seek the highest inward pleasures of which
I am capable. I have by this means achieved so much,
that I am perhaps the only one among us all who is in
full accord with the fate which has befallen us."

It was well known into what states of exaltation
Laurence was frequently transported. The higher
circles of the colony could take no exception to them.
The President felt herself always stimulated and re-
juvenated as if by a bath by these exaltations which
fired Laurence's eye as if she were drunken with light.

"Well, I was absolutely right," she asserted, "when

I began by calling you a goddess. We others—I am not jesting—" she continued, "are infected with the blight of triviality, from whose destructive influence no inhabitant of a great city can ever escape. And I find that England, Europe, America and so forth, are only overgrown great cities, as it were. My wings are becoming stiff; their muscles are shrinking. And when that has lasted for some time I shall have to use them at the very best as feather-besoms to sweep away dust. But you have phœnix-wings, Laurence. And if you do not occasionally take me by the scruff of the neck and whirl me off with you, you will see me perhaps in a short time creeping on the ground like an earth worm. I was saying to Rodberte before you came in: The dream is becoming tiresome. I meant the dream which we are all compelled to dream here. Now, my dear Laurence, it is entirely owing to you that I begin to see it again in a new light."

"I can tell you, Anni, why you have fallen a victim to the horrible demon of boredom, whose coffin-lid, by the way, is shut down upon the whole of the United States. To escape suffocation the Americans will probably plunge some day into some idiotic war or other."

It was Rodberte who said this, pausing a moment and then beginning again.

"You had plans. You wanted to make something positive out of us and the situation which once and for all presented itself. You wanted to express your creative power for once in flesh and blood, instead of merely in colours and on canvas. You wanted to seize the opportunity for an experiment in communism. To be our doctor, our deliverer, our law-giver, our Moses, and besides that, our father and mother in one, and finally our redeemer.—But although in many respects you have succeeded in calling out the best in us, in accomplishing this thing and that with us, and at any rate in preventing us from declining into corruption, yet on the other hand in this island land of Cockaigne life is made much too easy for us to foster a strong morality. A rigid organisation either cannot be maintained or else is proved unnecessary. The women are blooming and ripening like fruits, even though their spirits are depressed. They need only to work a little when they feel inclined, for if they do not even wish to lift a hand the apples of Paradise drop into their mouths But what are the feelings of a doctor, deliverer, supporter, law-giver, Moses, father, mother, redeemer when nobody is ill, or needs to be delivered and supported, and all are so meek, prosperous, lazy and peaceful that a law-giver or even a Moses has not a single act of transgression, disobedience, or violence to reckon with? What are the feelings of a father or a mother when Nature is both father and mother?

"Doubtless, as I have said," she continued, "your untiring efforts have spurred us on to something. Ville des Dames with its Town Hall and its pleasant pavilions is witness to that. But you can go no further now. For you lack precisely the two things which would be necessary for a work of redemption, even in an earthly sense.

"This is how the matter stands: in the midst of national and cosmopolitan societies even civilised man regards the earth as a vale of tears, and yearns for a better existence. By his religion that is guaranteed to him under certain conditions in a future world, in the beyond. But the beyond for us is the great comity of civilised states. And the certainty that we shall attain to that very real and well-known land you cannot or will not give us. Like Moses, to lead us out of exile back into the promised land—that you cannot do. In the chief aim of our settled desires you cannot be our redeemer, and that makes you peevish and is a burden to you. Besides it is possible, nay likely, that our chief aim, the goal of our deepest desires, is not yours. There remains the other matter, in which unfortunately you are equally powerless. You can procure for us outcasts neither of the two things requisite for redemption: neither our fatherland, nor the other."

Anni and Laurence immediately enquired, "What do you mean by the other thing?"

"Ah, what do I mean by the other thing? Adam, it is well known, was living in Paradise when God conceived the notion that it was not good for man to be alone. What could that mean except that Adam was unhappy, alone in Paradise? He would have been unhappy and lonely, too, if God, there and then, had moulded another thousand Adams out of clay, breathed life into them, and set them in Paradise beside the first. To dispel his unhappiness Eve had to be created. As a matter of fact until then he was nothing but a sterile monster, a piece of barren, breathing clay, a pot as it were filled with breath which his Creator could draw back again at any time. And then he would have been an empty pot, nothing more, significant only for its emptiness. But Adam became the image of God and came into possession of the mystery of creation, truly *cum grano salis,* when he acquired Eve. As everybody knows, from that time he too created men, quite independently."—Again the parrot shrieked and squalled fearfully.—"In short," concluded Fräulein Kalb, "think of Eve in Paradise as the first lonely pot of the Potter. If Adam had not arrived she would either have been an empty or a full pot, but always nothing more than a single pot, denied an equal or more than an equal share with Adam in the creation of the human race. Even if a thousand other Eves had been set down beside her."

"I understand," said the artist after a brief silence followed by a mirthful chuckle which betrayed the fact that some of the ideas aroused by Rodberte's remarks delighted her sense of humour.

"I understand, indeed I understand it very well, Fräulein Kalb," chimed in Miss Hobbema very seriously, not at all as if the theme were merely a witty jest of Rodberte's. Laurence continued: "I really do not know how it has just occurred to me. Turning it over in my mind I can find no connection between it and what you have been expounding. Yet I shall unbosom myself of it. Of course a condition such as ours is unsound, and becomes the more unsound the longer it lasts. I am sorry to say that I—being in a sense the spiritual adviser of the colony—meet with many indications of this. That we are dead to the world, though living, is not after all the worst feature of our case, and it is idle to think of it. We have passed over into our better land. And dead though we may be for the world, who doubts that in spite of it we are in ourselves alive?—The matter you have touched upon is in reality much worse, Fräulein Kalb. Say what you will, without the prospect of a real and as it were infinite future existence humanity can have no rounded and complete present. A social community which cannot propagate itself is like a sailing ship which lies becalmed in some windless zone of the Pacific and rots to pieces. Or it is like a grove composed only of flowering branches cut off and placed in water: it can neither strike roots nor bear fruit. Certainly we should be in a different case if that possibility were open to us. For then we might live to see the day when the lost heritage of civilisation would be established again, and by our own efforts. The feeling of being deserted by God and man, this feeling of damnation, would be dispelled by the mere consciousness of genuine progress.

"Yes. After all I have discovered the train of thought that led me to Fräulein Lindemann, whom you yourself mentioned, and of whom I now wish to speak.

"Fräulein Lindemann frequents the little temple committed to my care, which we have somewhat ambitiously styled Notre-Dame des Dames. I must admit that she often usurps a great deal of my time. I put my services gladly at any one's disposal, and I conceive it after all to be my vocation to assist by word and deed any one who feels the need of confessing to me her spiritual afflictions and difficulties, and claims my help. But if I gladly give up a great part of my time, it is for the good of all and not merely of one. And, as I said, Fräulein Lindemann seems often somewhat far-reaching in her demands.

"She came on board ship at Bombay. Her mistress was a member of Annie Besant's circle. Somewhat limited, of course, and uncritical. I have made her acquaintance, too. At any rate, the influence of Indian mysticism as practised by this lady and the circles of Bombay and Benares has been far too powerful for Babette Lindemann. She is like a furnace which glows almost to bursting point with chaotic internal fires. One might say of her what Buddha says in his Fire Sermon: 'Ye monks, everything burns, the eye burns, appearance burns, the ear burns, sound burns, perception with the ear burns, comprehension with the ear burns. The nose burns, smell burns, perception with the nose burns. The tongue burns, taste burns. The body burns. Contact burns.'—So it is with her. I myself have felt all that in her, and, by contact from her, when to my sorrow she has clung to me with both arms, sobbing. And I know, too, that her mind is fevered, and all her thoughts. As Buddha says:

-< 61 >-

'With the fire of lust, the fire of sin, the fire of error, with all kinds of care, grief, sorrow and despair they burn.' "

The artist said: "She has these fevered eyes." Rodberte: "She is unintelligent and over-strained."

"Often I do not know," Miss Hobbema continued her explanation, both slim brown hands tucked into her coconut fibre girdle. "Often I do not know what is the truth about her condition, although I must acquaint you with something which seems to confirm your fairly clear explanation, Fräulein Kalb. That is to say, she affirms nothing less than that something of the same kind has happened to her as was announced to the Virgin by an angel in Fra Angelico's lovely painting on the wall of San Marco in Florence. She can come to no other conclusion, and this is the only possible explanation."

Anni was enormously shocked.

"I have suspected something of this kind for a long time," she said, "for I am not blind, and I see what a childish, over-strained, ridiculous and scandalous state of things is already prevailing in spite of all my un-ambiguous and sharp remarks. Only yesterday—may God preserve me! but, if I may use slang I think I am beginning to smell a rat—well, only yesterday I heard there behind a hut a lullaby, sung God knows how tenderly: 'Hushabye baby, in the tree top.' I stepped over. And there was a red-haired, stockish Rubens type of a countrywoman, bursting out of her clothes, so far as one can speak of clothing . . . a creature healthy through and through, rocking a cradle she had fashioned of reeds with, I fancy, a duck-bill in it. A girl from Berlin is running about in trousers with a false moustache stuck under her nose. Madness is, of course, contagious. I am only waiting now for one of the hussies to come to me and declare outright: 'President, I am a man.'"

"Why should not these poor women, at any rate those whose nature is like that, resort to illusion in their life-and-death struggle with sensuality?" said Rodberte Kalb. "Why make such a great to-do about it? What are we to reserve ourselves for, in any case? Or what grounds have we here for remaining absolutely sane if madness makes us happier? If Babette Lindemann flatters herself that she is pregnant with the future Buddha, well, leave her that satisfaction. Or what can we offer her by way of compensation? In the very heart of civilisation do we not deliberately make little girls crazy with joy by giving them dolls?" she continued. "For my part, I wish that Babette's doll would suffice for all of us. I should certainly be no spoil-sport. And only think, Laurence, what possibilities for Notre-Dame des Dames! Why should not the faith in Babette's doll become strong enough to remove mountains and bring us all to Europe?"

Miss Laurence said:

"I wish you would just make the attempt to talk Babette out of her Buddha, if only to convince yourselves that it is impossible. But at last she has of her own accord taken a step which must deprive her of her hysterical illusions if there is still a grain of sense left in her. She has called in Fräulein Dr. Egli."

"*Lupus in fabula*," said Fräulein Kalb, for at that moment Fräulein Egli entered.

Fräulein Egli was two-and-twenty, of medium height, with broad hips and shoulders. She seemed the incarnation of a type very like the women of Basle drawn by the younger Holbein. Her hair was of an indefinite darkish blonde but almost as abundant as Fräulein Kalb's and Miss Hobbema's and was swathed around her head in the same way as theirs. Her face was large, broad and covered with freckles, but a very perfect example of the Alemannic racial type. The brutal strength of jaw and cheekbone was accompanied by the most extreme fineness and regularity of nose and eyebrow. Her profile was very finely chiselled, and the extraordinary fineness and thinness of the nose was in strong contradiction to the powerfully moulded chin, the chin of a youthful Berenice. Her whole head in its noble and yet rustic contours was reminiscent of a Gudrun in captivity, a princess and yet a slave. This impression was heightened by a customary knitting of the brows and a kind of gloomy fire in the eyes, veiled, but not completely hidden, and by the wilful and passionate mouth, usually shadowed by a painful seriousness.

"Come, give us your report," cried Miss Laurence to her, "give us your report!"

"There is not much," said the physician, "to report:

-: 64 :-

according to my finding, I can only say that Babette Lindemann's suspicions of her condition are not mistaken."

THE impression made by this communication betrayed itself first by a moment of silent amazement. Then they all tried to pretend that they knew quite well it was only a joke of the doctor's. The grave surprise, however, of the Swabian, who was not far from being offended by this behaviour, put an end to that: but thereupon the girl had to stand a cross-fire of questions. Did she believe in miracles? Had she forgotten that they had been twelve months on the island all but a week?—Or that with the exception of Adam and Eve every human being had two parents? And where did she think of looking for the father of the child, since it was common knowledge that there was not a man upon the whole island? Obviously annoyed she rejoined in a tone of cool objectivity that she had established a physiological fact which doubtless had its natural cause. That was the answer to the medical question which had been put to her. The other questions arising from that she must beforehand decline to consider; they did not come within the province of medical science.

Fräulein Kalb wanted to know for how many months the enigma had already been an inhabitant of Île des Dames. In the doctor's opinion, for over two months: and once again they put her through an examination in which their doubts of the trustworthiness of her diagnosis could not be altogether concealed. As it was soon clear that she was seriously upset and offended in her professional honour, they assumed an appearance of being completely convinced that her statement was true. Fräulein Egli meanwhile remained monosyllabic, and quickly withdrew after first asking if there was anything else they wished to know, and being answered in the negative.

Hardly was the physician gone ere the scepticism broke out anew, not Laurence's, for she had taken but a small and a consistently tactful part in the whole discussion, but the artist's and most particularly Rodberte's. The scepticism grew into complete disbelief.

"I think," said Rodberte, "that this young woman who, as she has told me, passed her final examination scarcely fourteen days before embarking, is seizing the opportunity to make herself a little important with her newly-minted knowledge."—"That I do not believe," interjected Laurence. "That German girl is hard-headed and thorough: I have sufficient proof of it; and although I am completely at a loss to account for the situation it would be difficult for me to doubt any fact sponsored by Fräulein Egli."

"Then there is only one remaining possibility," said the artist, "either among ourselves or somewhere else on the island a man must be concealed."

"Permit me," said Laurence; "I shall find out the rights of the matter from the patient herself." She went out and returned after a short time accompanied by Babette.

"WELL now, what is the matter, my dear Babette?"
was the President's greeting. She was constraining
herself to the utmost amiability in the substance and
style of her remarks, the tone of her voice, and the
play of her features, with the intention of evoking
confidences by appearing confidential.—"Well, my
dearest Babette, what news are you bringing us?
Come along, take a seat, Babette. I must begin by
paying you compliments. You are growing younger
and prettier. Has she not literally a festive air, Rodberte? If we had a postal service I would swear that
the postman had brought you some wonderful news
today, either that a rich old aunt has died and left you
a legacy, or that your sweetheart is coming to carry
you off. How she smiles! What a light, what a happy
light is in her eyes. Confess, Babette, unbosom yourself to us."

"So you do not know it yet," said Babette, blushing
with downcast eyelashes, bashful and yet ecstatic.
"The noble Miss Laurence told me that you knew it
had been confirmed."—"Yes and no," said the artist.
"Indeed, I can only say yes and no. You will admit,
my dearest Babette, that the whole situation is not
only unusual in the ordinary sense but extra-unusual
in an extraordinary sense."—To this Babette assented
with solemnity. "O yes, indeed, most certainly it
is."

"Now can you and will you tell us how you account
for it?" continued the President. "I can and I will,"
was the answer, "that is, in so far as it does not affect

-C 67 ϡthe Holy of Holies, the ineffable mystery." Sunk in a reverie she repeated: "I can and I will."

With great care they now made ready a seat for the miraculous maiden, and recognised that she was transfigured by a kind of inward ecstasy. Still in a reverie she laid her hand on the back of the chair and lowered herself into it in a way which proved her attention to be directed towards something hidden in the deepest recesses of her soul. Then she suddenly raised her eyes and looked straight at Anni.

She said: "I have long expected it. Already in Benares after I had bathed in the Ganges I guessed that one day it would happen as it has happened. It might have been about the beginning of December that the world altered for me. I noted, quite in secret, that I had become endowed with new senses. Or perhaps it is better to say that each of my senses seemed to be heightened and multiplied. All at once I believed that I knew how every sense—sight, for example, and hearing—represents an infinity of senses with an infinite number of organs of perception. From all sides, almost too strongly for me, too powerful for your poor servant, new things pressed in upon me through new senses."

After saying this, Babette gazed before her with a thoughtful smile. She possessed that charm which is peculiar to emotional natures. Although her rather delicate body had attained a certain fullness in the warmth and peace of that fortunate climate and her face, a lovely oval, was graced with charming dimples, yet a languishing pallor lay upon her which indicated consuming longing and midnight vigils. She wore the customary chemise, and over it a blue one-piece dress, taken from the little store of possessions which she had rescued. It was as if she wished by simplicity and amplitude of attire to make a stand against the picturesque scantiness of what had become the ordinary styles. Her dusky hair was loosened and fell in a mass on her bosom.

They refrained from interrupting her silence so as not to give an impression of urging her which might arouse mistrust and opposition. So she began to speak again entirely of her own accord.

"Well, I know that I am face to face with the noble and good Laurence, with our noble and good Mother President, and the cultured, penetrating, noble and good Rodberte Kalb; why, then, should I not tell them of the divine grace I have experienced? I was suddenly aware of the mysterious and divine force, the cosmic force, the extra-cosmic force which has brought me to this miraculous island. And only think, I recognised it at once. For long before I landed here in the body I was here of nights in the spirit, with a clear presentiment of what has now befallen me."

She held her trembling hands in her bosom, twined in the flood of her hair; and now tears fell upon them.

"If I weep," she said, "it is from joy. You must believe me, you dare not doubt that I am an initiate. I have known all this darkly since my childhood. The clouds of incense from this island of my destiny enveloped me even in my cradle. Ah me! I saw its beauty already in my dreams, wandered happily in its pleasant groves, and swam blissfully in its rivers and bays. True, when I went on board ship with my mistress on a journey round the world it seemed to be only a chance arrangement. Except for a mysterious shudder which often came upon me, the plan of sacred predestination suffered nothing to be so soon revealed to my heart. In short—" she opened her eyes to their fullest brightness—"I carry in my womb the son of a God, the Prince of Peace of the world."

"My dear good Babette," said the painter, "you must feel yourself that what you have told us is for us simple mortals, well, a hard nut to crack, as the saying is. I admit cheerfully that I am not an initiate. In my youthful dreams the cherished Island of the Blest certainly played a part, but it was by no means precisely this island, with its mysterious destiny. Therefore be so good as to help out my very average understanding."

"You must know that I rejected the ardent overtures of an elderly lord in England, and those of a young man in France who did not wish to disclose his name. But a countess said to me: 'Babette, the Prince is brokenhearted about you.' A famous poet in Germany left his wife for my sake. What could I do? Even then I did not show him the slightest favour. I was sorry for him. But what could I do in face of my destiny?"

"Good, good, you have told us that your destiny is

already accomplished in the most exalted sense," interrupted Anni again, with a slight touch of impatience, since she had a pitiless loathing for everything that she classed as hysteria. "To prevent us from making a mistake in your case it would be advisable for you to give us a clue as to how this supernatural occurrence became a reality in the world of natural fact. In plainer language, Zeus showed himself to Europa in the form of a bull, to Semele as a beautiful youth, before she was consumed by the fire of his real presence, to Leda as a swan, and so forth. In what shape did he appear to you?"

Babette shook her head with decision. Then she said firmly and earnestly: "No, Mother President, it was not Zeus." While she said this the smile on her lips was almost contemptuous.—At that moment her hearers were practically convinced that she was out of her mind. The diagnosis of the physician was once more discredited, and they wished only to find out what particular form Babette's madness assumed. The question was put: If it was not Zeus, who was it, then?

"It was Mukalinda," said Babette.

The President and Rodberte Kalb stared at each other almost stupidly while Miss Laurence listened with earnestness and attention. The President asked: "But who is he——?"

Babette's breast heaved with a profound sigh, then she answered with formality: "At the time when the Perfect One, the completely awakened Holy One, proved in wisdom and in wandering, was still upon the earth, he was wont from time to time to meditate under the Mukalinda-tree. Seven days he sat there with his legs crossed. But there came great tempests and black clouds which showered continuously storms of snow, hail and rain upon him. Then it was that the serpent-king Mukalinda left his dwelling, and made seven protecting rings with his body around the Sublime One and lifted his great head as a shelter over the head of the Sublime One. Therefore was Mukalinda blessed when he came before the Sublime One in the shape of a beautiful youth. And what is Zeus compared with Mukalinda the blessed?

"And thus, friends, did it happen. Deborah, the young Jewess, sleeps with me in the tent. Because the air in the tent was too stifling for her—there were hot winds blowing at that time—she took her bed away and made it up under a tree on the banks of Fleuve des Dames. In this wise the door of our tent was open and I was left alone. And then a mighty unrest seized me. Oh, my friends, I had never felt an unrest, an expectation, like that. The light of the moon was shining through the door. Then a bird cried close by in the forest. That cry was a sign for me—so much I already understood. Oh, good and noble ladies, my heart fluttered as if it were in my throat. Then something whispered: 'Know thou art a woman.' And already I had sprung to my feet in a terror more sweet than terrible. I did not know whether I was still dreaming or newly awake. There was the river, a broad, silver, scaly serpent, hollowing out the valley, glittering as it crawled along. A moment before I had heard its rippling and rushing, but now there was not a sound. Suddenly the sound broke out again almost deafeningly, then as suddenly was cut off. I listened, tensely, like one who waits for an approaching joy and must die if it turn aside and deny itself to the pining, wasting lover. I whispered, 'Divine One, come and satiate me.' All remained still, though I waited for any sound. Again I sprang up. My whole body glowed with scorching light. I burned inwardly, my whole frame was consumed with heat. The glow, the thirst, I thought, thou wilt quench, the scorching light thou wilt quench. The tiny demons, the silver snakelets that dart like hissing flames from thy skin. Go, I thought, quench thy burning flesh.

"I do not know if I bathed then in the river or only thought I would scatter into it the stored up sun-heat of the day. Whether I was waking or dreaming the river flowed round me, and there it was that Mukalinda in the shape of a youth took me by the hand. But how strong was that hand, though its possessor appeared only a boy! And how terrible his strength as I lay once more on my bed in the tent, not knowing how I came there, unable to move, to breathe, to cry out. I groaned: 'Mercy! Loose thy seven rings, Mukalinda! O Mukalinda, loose them!' Oh, Mother President, how terrible was the suffocating, surging strength of the seven divine rings round my whole body, round all my limbs! I thought my last hour was come. But then—O, Mukalinda, O Muka-linda! then he broke with me through seven heavens. And in the seventh a purple, flower-strewn couch opened out, and there the mystic wedding took place."

"There is nothing more to be said about it," declared the artist when Miss Hobbema led Babette away. "We have here an attack of hysteria, in which an unsatisfied organism imagines that for lack of which it sickens."

"That brings us directly, Anni, to the deficiency which I touched upon before," rejoined Rodberte, "through which, unfortunately, your work—our all too chaste Amazonian state—is doomed for all time. If it were only this deficiency the problem might finally solve itself. But it provides a lasting source of disease. We have but now seen an example of it; and look out, others will soon follow. For everybody knows how easily delusions of this kind spread and lay hold of those who have the same predisposition."

"It is difficult to put a stop to that kind of thing," said the artist. "If danger threatens us from the side, truly I do not know at present what steps to take against it with any prospect of success. The poetic bent of the amiable Laurence's mind, and her influence generally, will at best pour oil on the dangerous fire, or, put in another way, her mythological infatuation, her intoxication with beauty, are not likely to inspire greater powers of resistance in the *locus minoris resistientiæ* of our colonists.

"I think we should leave the whole matter alone for

a time, and regard it only as something to enrich our chronicles. I hope, my dear Kalb, that you have listened well."—Rodberte alone, because of the scanty store of ink, pens and paper, was permitted to use these materials in writing, but in return she had taken over the duty of recording the life of Île des Dames from day to day in an exact history.

IV

INVENTIVE as ever, Thorgerd Grimm had fashioned a tom-tom out of a colander which Auguste, the President's maid, had succeeded in making. A piece of the tanned hide of a dwarf kangaroo was simply stretched over the top of the kitchen utensil, and in the beginning this was beaten with a spurtle, but later with a carefully made drum-stick. One day the pretty mulatto, Alma, beat the drum in the manner which had been agreed upon as a summons to the captains of the Tens. Soon afterwards there gathered in the Town Hall Frau Rosenbaum, Rodberte Kalb, Miss Laurence and Miss Tyson Page, where the President and a few other ladies awaited them. The enquiring glances of passers-by who would have liked to know what was the occasion of this unusual measure could not penetrate the composed mask of the President, over which, it is true, a smile flitted now and then—a hint at least that nothing tragic had happened. The five commanders seated themselves round the oval council table, at which the others present also took their places, namely, the physician, Thorgerd Grimm and Gerte Bergmann, the violinist.

Anni began: "Ladies, I have called you to an

extraordinary session. Since, as you must know, I disturb your peace by such measures only in case of the most urgent necessity, you may reasonably assume this to be an occasion of that kind. It is not. All the same I have to make a communication which is very unusual, at least, considering our position.

"In order not to keep you in suspense and to spare you the trouble of making wrong guesses, let me tell you at once that nothing you are likely to think of at this moment has anything to do with what has actually happened. No ship has been sighted, nor has the postman brought us a letter from Europe; nobody has fallen sick, or come to grief, or perished. Nor has anybody seen a cannibal, or a tiger, or a rattlesnake. If you suspect a rebellion of some kind, be assured that never was a well-founded state more peacefully run than ours. Even a coup d'état, a revolution inspired from above, a plot to establish a monarchy on Île des Dames, is absolutely out of the question. I think you are sufficiently acquainted with me to know that I would rather cut off my hand than stretch it out to grasp a crown. Île des Dames remains free. That is as certain as if I had solemnly sworn ten thousand oaths to preserve the republican constitution."

The ladies smiled, but with a touch of bewilderment. They could not understand what Anni was driving at.

"I have still more to say by way of introduction," she continued. "When you have heard my communication, do not allow yourselves to fall into the error of thinking I am an imbecile. You laugh. It is anything but a laughing matter. I have asked myself more than once whether I have still all my wits about me. For it is a very, very hard nut that they have ·to crack. My wits would have been all broken by this time if they had been a set of teeth! I wager you will agree with me when you yourselves have tried to crack the nut. Nevertheless, I am not crazy. You must absolutely rid yourselves of the tempting idea that I have a slate loose somewhere."

Naturally the tension of the audience was heightened by these words. But it did not yet seem great enough to satisfy the President. She began again.

"Keep firmly to that, then, ladies; in all circumstances keep to it with adamantine firmness, my friends and comrades, that I am completely sane and not in any way wandering or crazy. Besides, what I have to disclose is an actual fact. But precisely the circumstance that it is an indubitable fact makes my position a dangerous one so long as you have only my simple word for it. For it is a fact of such a nature that until you confirm it by the evidence of your own eyes you can only be convinced of my madness. So take good heed, ladies; I am not mad. Take further heed, lest the mere presumption of your President's mental instability react upon you, and even make her really abnormal. It would not be the first time something of that kind has happened. Satan himself often begins his base designs by a sham attack, by suggesting a condition of unsoundness which is accepted as an inevitable fact and so actually becomes real. No, I swear it, I am not mad. But the whole affair is all the madder."

"Is it the fish portioning again, President?" asked Frau Rosenbaum. "I can only say that I am now looking after it myself, and nobody can complain."

"If it were that, my introductory speech might be much shorter."

"Is it, then, the scandalous conduct of a few of the women and girls," interjected Miss Page, "who, as they allege, being overcome by an irresistible frenzy, betook themselves to Mont des Dames and spent four or five days and nights in a continuous orgy of palm-wine, dancing and rioting, before they came to their senses?"

"I have already told you, my dear fellow-citizens," cried Fräulein Prächtel, "that every attempt to guess the nature of the event, and to anticipate my revelation, is fruitless, and doomed to failure. Only hold fast to this: I am not mad, and we must all keep our wits about us. There is evidence at hand which makes this perhaps our most difficult and important task.

"We have now been on the island for one year and six months. Women, only women, remember that. The fits of mania which you mention, my dear Page, are only one among many signs that a process of insidious decay has set in, or if not that, at least an undermining of our colony's 'psyche.' Spiritual inbreeding does not agree with us. As a matter of fact, one cannot even call it that. For spiritual as well as physical creation requires men and women both. We are falling sick of a spiritual shiftlessness. And, much as we had to keep several continuous fires burning before we got our fire-drill set a-going, we have to keep our spiritual life alight. It is a fire which has been burning from time everlasting. We have nothing akin to the fire-drill which might make accessible to us the sacred source of its terrestrial or celestial primal fire. We have no drill, no friction, no struggle—naturally, a spiritual struggle, please do not misunderstand me—I mean the struggle between man and woman."

"I should like to ask the President," said Miss Laurence Hobbema, rising to her feet in tall and noble beauty, "I beg of her, to state briefly the matter under consideration, and to do so as directly as possible, especially if immediate action is necessary."

"Immediate action is not necessary at present. Besides, the new fact will clear up nothing; it will rather throw us all into bewilderment. If any one is expecting definition and lucidity, she can only be disappointed. What I have to impart is certainly an unambiguous fact, but its very unambiguity is a riddle of the sphinx, sheer and insoluble."

SHE cleared her throat and seemed to gloat over the expectant faces of the ladies.

"Doubtless," she began again, "you still remember the flight of poor Babette Lindemann about seven months ago. The good-hearted but over-strained creature was impelled to that step by an idea which she unfolded to me in a note she left behind. She wrote that she was following a higher call which once and for all had come to her, although her neighbours could not believe in it and wanted to talk her out of it. The Voice that she obeyed had given her a clear description of a path leading into the interior of the island, and also of a lofty and solitary sacred spot where she would be able to fulfil her destiny secure from hostile forces   We were not to trouble to look for her, for it would be to no purpose, since she was certain of divine support.   The cave which she would inhabit until in the fulness of time her high destiny was fulfilled would be in the normal course of things easily found, but not in these extraordinary circumstances, for a divine vapour would conceal her even from anyone who chanced to stand beside her.   I leave the divine vapour out of the question," said Anni Prächtel.   "At any rate something had much the same effect, since, as we know, all attempts to trace the fugitive were unsuccessful.

"We had given Babette up, as was only to be expected after an absence of more than seven months. Personally, I assumed that she had been drowned while bathing, or had perhaps fallen a prey to some shark. Here then you have the new event.

"Babette came back tonight.   She has descended from the smoking volcano like an Isis, a mother of the Gods, a mystic radiance round her head and at her breast Osiris, a Son of God not more than fourteen days old."

THE first effect of this revelation was to strike the

leaders dumb. Then Frau Rosenbaum, who sat beside the President, quickly shot out her hand and grasped that honourable lady by the wrist in order to feel her pulse. She even stood up and laid her left hand on her forehead. This action as if by general consent provoked a burst of laughter in the Council Chamber, a kind of nervous relief which could not be controlled.

"But I beg of you, ladies," cried Anni as they continued to laugh, "I am not mad, I am not out of my senses; it must be understood that I am in full possession of my faculties and not at all feeble-minded.

"I call now upon Gerte Bergmann to speak, since it was first over her threshold that this actual miracle passed tonight."

THAT lady said in the broadest of accents:

"Weel, I canna tell ye onything except that Babette cam' to my hoose this evening wi' a wee bairn in her oxter, but whaur she got it frae, I'm sure I dinna ken."

The free and easy tone of this statement aroused more shrieks of laughter.

"Ay, leddies," continued Gerte, "wi' the best will i' the warld I canna gie ye ony ither answer, for to my knowledge there's no' a man in the colony, unless one has joukit in disguised as a wumman."

Frau Rosenbaum cried: "Nonsense, that would have been found out a hundred times in bathing."

Fräulein Prächtel expressed herself more bluntly. "I should like to see the man," she said, "who could keep his incognito even so long as fourteen days among such a throng of women as we are in this tropic heat. A dead ox would come to life among such a herd of cows."—She added: "On the other hand, there have been large man-like apes perceived in the interior of the island. Can Gerte, or Fräulein Dr. Egli, or Thorgerd Grimm, who have seen the infant, give us any information, if, for example, it is hairy, if the hair is long or short, if it extends over the whole body, including the face, and of what colour it is?"

"Shame, shame!" sounded on every side.

"To cry shame, shame, will not alter the fact, if it should turn out to be so. The sons of God, that is, the angels, have wooed the daughters of men, as you know, and why should not an animal standing one step lower on the ladder of development, let us say, a genial chimpanzee, conceive the notion of elevating his race, with the help of a super-ape, to the dignity of super-super-apes? And as for the lady who becomes his partner, is there any irregularity in this wide field which has not already happened? When you are dying of thirst you drink out of any puddle.

"Once more then to my point. Can Doctor Egli give us any information about the shape of the infant's skull? There is a small text-book in our library which contains a diagram of the skull of *pithecanthropus erectus,* which was dug out of an alluvial deposit in Java. The child I am thinking of would probably closely resemble such a creature, about three-quarters human. It would be an interesting comparison to make. Of course, I am not thinking of a mandrill, for example; an orang-outang would be more likely, or a chimpanzee, or perhaps some ape still higher in the scale. Have you examined the child's feet? One ought at least to discover how far they conform to those of apes, which are so characteristically like hands."

At this point the craft-worker, Thorgerd Grimm, a fine and sensitive nature, broke into loud sobs. In answer to enquiries, she explained, still weeping bitterly, that with all due respect to the President she could not endure to hear a sacred matter treated in so frivolous a fashion, and a member of the colony who was her friend besmirched with such a suspicion. Babette was perhaps somewhat inclined to excessive romanticism, but she, Thorgerd Grimm, had, on the other hand, proofs of her supernatural powers. She did not wish to discuss them further at that time. How Babette came to have her child was certainly an insoluble mystery. But there were more things in heaven and earth than were dreamt of by any worldly wiseman. And for at least one thing Thorgerd would answer with her life, namely, that Babette was the purest, most unspotted, chaste and virginal creature on the earth, far removed from any suspicion of an ignoble, or even of a conscious, love affair.

During the first part of this somewhat hysterical apostrophe the tide of feeling had turned almost entirely against the President. But Thorgerd's concluding statements lost her again the sympathy she had won. In such a circle the idea of an immaculate conception could be regarded only as the sheerest nonsense. So when Thorgerd finished there was nothing but an embarrassed silence.

Suddenly Doctor Egli rose to speak. She refrained, she said, from all hypotheses about the origin of the infant. She had been informed by Gerte Bergmann of Babette's arrival, had found the mother asleep, and had established without any difficulty the existence of the child. She had examined the boy closely, and could not only answer for it that he was sound in wind and limb and was a fully developed viable male child, but also that only on his head did he have a few downy hairs. Unfortunately, she added with quiet irony, there could also be no question of a four-handed child, and the boy would have to be content with two hands, like the rest of the colony, even although four were twice as many as two. "In short," she concluded, "the child is a beautiful and well-built human child, and wherever he comes from we have every ground for wishing that many other such fruits will fall into our laps from the same source."

Doctor Egli's conclusion was ratified by a burst of applause, and the subsequent speakers all insisted that the colony owed the deepest gratitude to Babette, no matter what way the newcomer's existence was to be explained. For Île des Dames had attained something like a present, and more completely a future, reality, through the very birth of this its first indigenous citizen. Whether his birth was miraculous or not, Babette was absolutely in the right to maintain that her child was a kind of Messiah. He was really a Saviour, a Redeemer of the colony; and this would become more and more evident. The seventh of August, the day on which the child appeared, would be celebrated as the greatest national festival, yes, a thousand years later. It would be said, and with complete justice, that on this day the first foundation and keystone of a new and promising State had been laid. And of a new and powerful nation too, it was to be hoped, whose essence would be drawn from the fine flower of the great peoples of the world. Indeed, it was evident already that the new event had invigorated the spirits and stimulated the imagination of the colonists to a fabulous degree. Although they were unable to account for it, they regarded it as a grace from Heaven which proved that they were neither forgotten nor doomed to destruction.

As the affair became generally known, it provoked an orgy of joy which surprised the Council and first really convinced them of its enormous importance. For scarcely ten minutes after Anni Prächtel had concluded her speech with its dramatic climax, the Town Hall was rushed by forty ladies at least who wanted to know how much truth there was in the wild rumours which were flying from mouth to mouth in the town. And these women, when the plain truth was roundly affirmed, flew into the same kind of frenzy which had seized the colony at Rita's funeral, but out of joy this time, not grief. They skipped and screamed and clapped their hands. They seized each other and whirled round in circles. They fled with streaming hair into the open air, because they felt the Town Hall too confining. They ran around with shrieks, laughter and jubilation, and many threw themselves on the ground in ecstasy. The outbreak culminated finally in a round dance of a strangely wild and yet solemn nature, in which were mingled the movements of well-known international dances. This time too there were howling as well as dancing dervishes, consisting of those colonists whose feelings of joy were transmuted into fits of weeping.

"Here we have another famous how-d'ye-do!" said the artist with a sarcastic laugh, when she was left alone in the Town Hall with Rodberte Kalb and Miss Laurence. "But I admit," she continued, "that to-day's performance is much more entertaining than the first one at Rita's funeral. Only look, my dear Laurence," and she pointed through a window, "is not that a literally godless spectacle? Is it not like a dance round some invisible fetish, some heathen abomination or other, exactly as if we were living two thousand years before Christ? As a matter of fact, I also must confess," she added, "that recently I have often felt quite uncertain as to the era I am living in.

"My historical consciousness, based on the epochs of past European civilisations, is becoming less real daily, and so is my own individual past. I can believe in it if I wish, but I cannot prove its existence to myself.

We have absolutely no means of convincing ourselves and others that an occurrence of yesterday really happened, and was not merely a dream.

"But to return to our muttons," she interrupted herself. "You will admit that the party of sober intelligence, or rather, of healthy common sense, will not be exactly strengthened by today's events."

"President," replied Miss Laurence, "I am glad of it from the bottom of my heart." She went on, developing her theme at length; "The origin of God, the origin of the world, the origin of man, of the individual, your origin and mine, is veiled in mystic darkness. Prove me the contrary, if you can, when I assert that not only the origin of all life, but the whole of life itself is mystery. We are surrounded by it as fishes by the sea. Even though the fish is provided with practical instincts which sustain life, which make him a thoughtless and selfish hunter of food, and enable him to distinguish and to entrap other forms of life which serve his needs, yet he remains dependent on the salt watery element, on the great mystery of the sea. He is born, he lives, he dies in this mystery, whatever credit he ascribes to his fishy common sense for his practical success. I do not know if fishes are aware of this. In any case, awareness of this is a higher state of being. You will say I am inclined to edifying sermons, and should reserve them for Sundays. Yes, and no. I think that you yourself, intellectually advanced as you are, and with you the whole colony, may benefit by my meditations. A higher state of being I call that wherein temporal and spatial limitations certainly exist, yet where the illimitable, beyond time and space, is not cut off from the imprisoned soul, but is infinitely accessible to it.

"Even a child so beloved and sheltered as I was may yet have often a feeling of desolation in the very middle of London or Berlin, even among crowds of friends. This feeling expresses the true state of the individual, and, when it is shared by mankind, the true state of mankind. Our peculiar destiny, our exile, strengthens this feeling. Our destiny, however, has only made our situation more clearly visible, it has not altered it. We are still captives imprisoned by time and space. Only, our heightened consciousness of it increases our yearning to press into the eternal, the illimitable, into the boundless and free mystery.

"Therefore I find it natural that theosophical doctrines, Rosicrucianism, somnambulism and other similar tendencies, should be gaining ground in the colony. At the worst they are illusions which purport to open paths for us into the infinite, and to renew our relationships with our dear ones. But true paths into the infinite can also be discovered. We complain about the swarm of spiritualists and hypnotic mediums. Are we not fundamentally all mediums, and can anyone be blamed for even imagining that she is an instrument for the revelation of divine wisdom? Life, in so far as

-꒰ 89 ꒱-

it enters consciousness, is a state of feeling. It ranges not only from pain to the uttermost bliss, but from one pedal note to the broadest, to an infinite, symphonic harmony.

"The founders of Rome are said to have been discovered and suckled by a she-wolf, and so kept alive. I salute with all my heart the mystery in the shadow of which Babette's son has been born. The myth surrounds him from the beginning, and has not first to conquer him. I do not care to invalidate a belief in miracles, if it is fruitful and gives an impetus to the forces which make for life. To do so, and to substitute for the miracle only a petty scandal, would be to annihilate an essential impulse towards higher things which is a sheer necessity for our state. If we hold fast to the miracle we see ourselves as chosen vessels, and can easily accustom ourselves to the thought that we are the blessed mothers of a people called to the highest destiny, perhaps even the redeemers of the whole world."

"Your optimism, as usual on the whole, hits the right nail on the head, Miss Hobbema," said the artist. "I am even so convinced by it that I am determined to form a triumvirate with you and Rodberte as a kind of conspiracy for the maintenance of invaluable illusions. Girls, give me your hands on it; let us further this profitable swindle in every way. I foresee that we shall need the broadest interpretation of it, since things are bound to occur which must degenerate into coarseness if they are not raised to a high level of beauty and nobility.   We shall therefore establish a new myth, and invite the co-operation of the whole colony. Paradoxically expressed, we are spreading over our island an invisible and mighty dome on which in shining constellations and noble mosaics we shall project and symbolise our beautiful and sublime lies, whether we are to call them emblems or reflections of our destinies on earth.   In this way we shall arrive at a new religion, a new sanctity, a new science and art, a new culture, and, last but not least, a national god."

She concluded: "Help me to construct this dome, dear Rodberte, dear Laurence, and we shall ourselves all three of us blaze as constellations in it hereafter."

"Assuredly I must, but I should like to refuse."— With these words Laurence laid her hand upon the clasped hands of the other two.   The President and Rodberte Kalb had taken hands with a certain solemnity, and yet with the secret smile of augurs.—"It vexes me," said Laurence, "to hear such words as swindle and lie, when I must believe in beauty and truth."

"Oh, my dear Laurence," said Rodberte Kalb soothingly, "what does it matter if only we are at one in our aim?"

"Yes, if only we are at one in our aim," repeated the artist, "and the strength of our dome will be founded on the fact that, publicly at any rate, we shall take our stand most firmly on the principle of the Napoleonic Code: *La recherche de la paternité est interdite.*"

"WELL and good, ladies," the President began again after a short silence during which the mingled cries of parrots and women re-echoed in the room. "Well and good, ladies; but what further position do you intend to take up regarding the main point?—I mean, is it your opinion that for the future also we are to ascribe everything of this nature to the Unknown God, or do you think it important that we three Fates, at least, should not humbug ourselves, but should rather postulate a completely natural act instead of the divine one, and supervise its administration like wise women? For in any case it will be on the natural act that we will have to build our future. We could only count on the repetition of a divine act of grace every three thousand years at the most. That would be of no practical use at all."

"But in the name of God! That is impossible!" cried Miss Laurence.

"What is impossible?" asked the President. "What could be impossible, in God's name, seeing the impossible has become possible?"

"President, you will never convince me of that! Never, never will you do that!"

Anni Prächtel returned: "You mean, of the natural act. How extraordinary! You believe instead in the other, which is only vital as a symbol and completely contradicts the laws of nature. But He! Can it be impossible? Then there must be another male human being concealed on the island."

V

PHAON was now in the first third of his fifteenth year. He was too young to be regarded as a youth, but on the other hand he looked more than a boy. Phaon was beautiful, as Rodberte had rightly observed. In giving him the name of a favourite of Aphrodite his father had a presentiment that he might be at least a favourite of the gods. Phaon, the pure child of love, had already opened his divine, solemnly joyous eyes before his parents were married. He had not the permission of an official or a priest to thank for his existence, but the most sublime Eros himself, who had incarnated his omnipotent power in two favoured children of men for the sacred work of creation.

The constellation under which Phaon was born was a fortunate one. The sun and Venus were predominant in his horoscope: when the womb of his mother was lightened the sun stood at noon on a day in midsummer. The royal star in Leo was proportionately near the sun. The astrologer saw no disturbances from quartile or opposition aspects. Later it would have to appear what reliance might be placed on the splendid aspects which the position of the sun indicated. In any case it was possible already to describe

Phaon as a beautiful light glowing with intelligence, a *Phos noeron* which had been thrown off by the glorious *Phos noeron* of the Neoplatonists. His complete horoscope was found in a handbag of Rita's and deposited in the archives of the colony entrusted to the President.

Miss Laurence Hobbema saw him as Helios, as she had declared with noble enthusiasm to the President and Rodberte. He was for her the son of Hyperion, whom the Hesperian nymphs instructed and prepared for his sacred destiny. Next to Miss War she was his chief preceptor. Although her grafting of the myth of Helios and Hyperion on to Île des Dames had only sprung from her need to give a poetic turn to their isolation and distress, yet Phaon's part in it was justified by her real belief that he was born for greatness. She was convinced that even should none of the women ever see the world of civilisation again, he at any rate would return thither, following his high destiny. What glad tidings, what new message or healing he would bring to mankind she could not have said for the time being.

Miss War, who had completely taken the place of Phaon's mother, was unanimously elected to this office by a plebiscite of the colony. The President, Frau Rosenbaum, Rodberte Kalb, Laurence Hobbema and the physician, formed an educational council. It was decided in every possible way to satisfy their fosterling's insatiable hunger for knowledge, but to guard the darling of the colony himself like an irreplaceable jewel.

FROM the first Miss War's problem was not easy. . . .
To have to fill a beloved mother's place is itself a
thankless task, and if it is not carried out with the
greatest delicacy it is usually resented bitterly by the
orphan as an attempt to dishonour the dead. But Miss
War possessed delicacy. Yet in spite of that, whenever she wished to enforce a measure for his good
against his will, she was always compelled to recall the
memory of the mother who understood him so much
more completely. The absence of his father, of men
in general, and of masculine authority in the colony,
to which appeal could be made, weighed still more
heavily on her. The final and best means of compulsion were lacking. Phaon's waxing bodily strength
and clear intelligence soon surpassed all the others.
Accordingly Miss War's sphere of influence became
narrower and narrower; especially when the honest
woman could not prevail by craft or moral suasion, and
had to resort to commands and threats of punishment.

Her educational duties fell into two divisions, physical and moral, halves which certainly could never be
completely sundered. With great firmness she insisted
that Phaon should be well groomed, like a perfect gentleman. She meant by this, scrupulous care of the
hair, skin, nails and teeth. Daily battles on this count
became unavoidable. Phaon had no aversion to physical tidiness, he was rather predisposed to it; but he
burned every morning with a furious impatience to be
out and about in the open air, untrammelled. The
manners of the boy and the growing youth were charm-

ing by nature; so Miss War had little trouble with them. Also his innate good-breeding excused her from the duty of instructing him how to eat and drink.

To her pupil she harped with obstinate monotony on the necessity for punctuality, thinking thus to acquit herself of the moral part of her task. But it was an undertaking of the utmost difficulty to tether the wild thing to the minute-hand of his own chronometer. He seemed to be made for the timeless existence of the gods; it gave him endless trouble to understand the breaking up of time into hours. And finally, Miss War's worst plague: Phaon was completely inaccessible to the idea of work. Not a plough would have been dragged through any field in the world if it had had to wait for the taming and breaking-in of this wild colt of the prairies. . . . What he undertook he undertook as a game. He must appear to have entered into the matter of his own free choice, and its accomplishment had to be equally spontaneous, and above all enjoyable. Whoever attempted it and however often, no one ever succeeded in tying the boy down to work which he thought work. Every time he freed himself unmarked, like a conjurer who slips easily out of the most skilfully tied knots.

MISS WAR recognised and fought with all her strength against this dangerous talent. But the idea of responsibility and of duty was simply not to be hammered into Phaon. On the other hand, it was not little that he accomplished by way of pleasure and mastered in play; for example, all the languages spoken in the colony, in which he expressed himself fluently and freely. He knew, too, all the literature which was available, except what bored him or was withheld from him.

The growing youth had a sense of humour. His great talent for imitation enabled him to mimic in a most surprising way the movements and accents of men of all nations, classes, and professions whom he had observed on his travels. He had caught from them their pet themes, stories, tricks of speech and weaknesses. From time to time he gave himself and those ladies of the compulsory Amazon-State who had a taste for it the pleasure of an exhibition of this talent; which, combined with his inexhaustible joy in life, always secured Île des Dames from a complete lack of gaiety.

In this respect, too, however, Miss War put the brake on Phaon's sun chariot whenever she could (a favourite expression of Miss Hobbema's). "You are not a Bajazzo," she used to say, "nor a clown, nor a merry-Andrew, nor a general buffoon."

It was not easy to read Phaon's real nature. The boy, careless, open and confiding as he was, showed indeed no inclination to secrecy, but from time to time he fell into moods which did not tally with his usual ways of life and action. Periods of reserve and solitary silence alternated with times of extreme sociability. And little as Miss War, who would have liked to keep her pupil safely in the golden mean, approved of the second extreme, she even less succeeded in dealing with it. She had to be content to leave Phaon unmolested now and then in his bamboo hut beside Fleuve des Dames, the first time for a few days, and later for a week at a time; for once an attempt to unearth him had driven the fugitive to a farther flight into the unknown interior of the island, where he remained hidden for a long time.

About the time of the arrival of the little island marvel, the first native of Île des Dames, Phaon was nowhere to be found: he was not at Miss War's, nor at Laurence's hut, where nearly every second or third day he spent hours in playing with the quaint, lovable Diodata, now more than two years old. When later her foster-mother desired for some reason to see and speak with the boy, and looked for him in his bamboo-hut and his customary haunts, he could not be run to earth. It was not entirely the thought that she must encounter Phaon at any price that sent Laurence next day up the mountain.

Her step seemed much too pensive for that. The noble creature, whose inner goodness and nobility of soul expressed itself in every movement, and in the bearing of her whole body, found herself in a state of the deepest abstraction. From time to time the proud lady shook her proud head, crowned with the natural ornament of her rich, dark, well-plaited hair, as if she were dismissing a thought which ever intruded itself anew. But from time to time again the beautiful woman heaved a deep sigh.

None of the island-dwellers had been so profoundly and universally aware of the fate which had befallen them as she. On the other hand, none of them was able to meet it with such firmness of character. That is to say, her capacity for thought and feeling was apparently far in excess of the other women's, so that she was bound to penetrate more deeply into the riddle of the world than they, and to be more sensible of the peculiarity of their condition in happiness and wretchedness, pleasure and pain, indulgence and renunciation, hope and fear, because she was morally fitted to be so. While she was still in England and still came into contact with the best minds in Europe, she had not succeeded in finding that which could satisfy the vague desire of her soul. Neither in musical, nor in literary nor in scientific circles. She relapsed more and more into precisely that state of loneliness which she would have liked to avoid. She then tried to get rid of it in other ways, and with more success. For several years she, the brilliant woman of the world, dwelt in voluntary solitude among woods and fields. She lived in a cottage far from every other habitation, and occupied herself with gardening in the time she did not devote to the study of religious and philosophical questions. During these years, when for many months she spoke to nobody, she enjoyed a happiness very like Thoreau's in Walden. But like him she found herself one day thrust back again into the whirl of life.

So in a certain sense she was already prepared for a life of exile. Also, the life-task which she had sought

in vain among the realms of civilisation stood now un-
avoidably before her. And so Laurence Hobbema had
never really felt her own value so much as here.

She had entered upon this journey round the world
for the same reason that she had first gone into the
world, then into solitude, and again into the world;
wishing and hoping to experience something which
should give to the whole of existence its real meaning,
justification and value. Instead of that, the shipwreck
intervened. Even during the catastrophe Miss Laurence Hobbema felt that this journey had been no
chance one, but predestined for her, and that some of
the great and obscure expectation of her soul was now
realised. At least, the slight touch of spleen which
she had until then always felt in herself was wiped
out with one stroke and sunk in the sea together with
the international banqueting-halls of the *Cormorant*.
The tormenting boredom which had overpowered her
among stupid or brutal seekers after pleasure, with
their thin veneer and insipid uniformity, was all at
once routed, so that the very shipwreck during which
her own life was in extreme peril, appeared as a necessity and a redemption. She had an inward certainty
of this, for she had felt calm and free as she looked in
the face of inevitable death, neither seeking for rescue
nor imagining it possible.

The outcome of the adventure, with the landing on
Île des Dames, meant now for Laurence really and
truly a great renewal and rejuvenation. She had been
swept along against her will by the mighty, turbid

stream of Civilisation, and now at last she knew that she was drawn out of it, apart.

She saw herself standing on her own feet; she obtained a consciousness of herself, and rejoiced in the increasing value to which she dared lay claim, both for the colony and herself, and in her own spirituality which was still richly unfolding like a blossom. With quiet joy, even with ecstasy, she observed how she was becoming more and more a part of nature, a part of the paradise surrounding her, how new powers and organs were developing in her, how each of her senses, sight, hearing, smell, taste and feeling, was extending its range and power of discrimination, and how her consciousness was growing more and more to resemble a too-fortunate householder, scarcely able to dispose and make use of the wealth poured upon it by its never-resting slaves, the senses. When she compared her present with her former condition she often said half aloud to herself, like a disciple of Buddha to the Master, "Wonderful, Lord, wonderful, O Lord! As if, Lord, one were setting up again what has been overturned, or unveiling what was hidden, or showing a wanderer the path, or bringing light into darkness." Laurence had an occasional wish for things, chiefly books, from the deserted realm of civilisation, but she would as soon have thought of wishing herself back there again as a boy would have wished to return to a cell in a hospice for old men, or as one who was quenching his thirst by full draughts of crystal clear water from a mountain spring would have yearned to drink from a stagnant puddle. As far as she was concerned there was no need for a ship to land. If it should happen, however, she was determined none the less to go on making her permanent residence in Ile des Dames.

UNDOUBTEDLY the lovely Laurence was suffering to-day from a slight uneasiness. For besides the fact that she sighed now and then and shook her head, she sometimes stood still for a long time, and several times she altered her course. But yet in the depths of her soul there lay a high and solemn joy because of the grace that had descended in such an inexplicable manner on Île des Dames through the birth of a boy. This way or that, whether an immaculate conception was to be assumed or natural procreation, the birth of a human being was for Laurence the highest mystery of all, which not even a miracle could overshadow. And recollections of her own childhood, of baptismal ceremonies and family banquets after the birth of her younger brothers and sisters were associated with this, so that the lovely island seemed to bask in the warm radiance of a Sabbath light. Moreover she was soon to baptise in the church of Notre-Dame the little island first-born for whom the name of Bihari Lâl had been chosen. So it came that, in addition to the rest a consecrated feeling of anticipation, a great and joyful but profoundly religious experience, was projected by the virgin priestess upon the groves, forests, beaches, valleys and headlands of the island. With its smoking mountain peak it seemed to Laurence to be a mighty sacrificial altar.

Chance willed it that after some hours of meditative strolling she should meet Phaon gaily wending his way downhill. After he had been for a few seconds in her field of vision she acknowledged with a certain surprise and yet with a certain relief that he must still be spoken of absolutely as a boy. This conclusion was not to be shaken by the alternately deep and shrill tones of his voice, which naturally did not escape her notice as the youthful Stradmann greeted her with joyous shouts and gestures. He imparted to her that he had discovered all kinds of new things on his wanderings, above all a lake which was as if enchanted, and deep hidden in the forest, and, beside the lake, a great bird of such fabulous magnificence in colouring that it could not be described. The bird, so he said, had quite certainly made its escape thither from the Islands of the Blest. For, only to judge from this bird, there must have once been such islands, and they must have disappeared. Miss Laurence said: "My boy, what need have you of blessed islands?" With a laugh he replied that he certainly felt quite pleased with himself. But not only the bird with the indescribably brilliant plumage, but also a peculiar feeling which he had, were sufficient proof that other marvellous ecstasies existed, and it was to be hoped not only in a past which would never recur.

IT was a peculiarity of the growing youth to accept the unexpected without surprise as something to be taken for granted, and so he did not stop to enquire the hows and whys of this sudden encounter, but began at once to speak of things they had discussed at their last meetings. "Hello!" said Laurence after a while, "I have not seen you for eight days. Something has happened meanwhile, which I suppose you have heard of already. You have got a new playmate." He was disconcerted. Then she tried a ruse, and teased the boy with the story of Adebar, the stork. Had he not observed that one or two storks had circled round the island and then settled upon it?—"Storks?" He laughed out loud. Yet he looked searchingly at her with wide eyes, and, Laurence thought, a questioning uncertainty, even mistrust. "Well, Phaon," she cried, "it is quite true, a new citizen of Île des Dames has arrived. Friend Adebar has been here and has brought a tiny little boy in a tiny little parcel!"—She went on, so as to be quickly relieved of all her task: "And only think, he threw the parcel with the little baby down the chimney to Babette Lindemann."

THIS mythology did not at all fit into the usual frame of Laurence's exalted soul, but she could often be naïvely merry like a child, and especially with Phaon. She liked, also, to tease her pupil, often only in order to amuse him and, through him, herself, and to refresh herself with the opposition of his never-failing exuberance and especially his laughter. To-day there might have been another intention in her exposition of the children's fable, for with her great dark eyes she followed intently the effect of her words on Phaon. The result satisfied her. True, the boy's hesitation, his subsequent laugh of superiority, and afterwards the way in which of his own accord he added to and heightened the absurdity of the stork-legend betrayed that he had outgrown that fairy-story; but his supplementary and completely indeterminate contributions left her scarcely a doubt of the vagueness of the ideas which for him took the place of the childish tale. Also he found the arrival of the baby quite natural, and so he seemed to be utterly in the dark about the nature of conception in the mother's body and its necessary presuppositions. Thus there was no way of making him comprehend the high excitement in the colony or of drawing him into it. He dropped the whole affair very soon, and began to speak of other things in which he himself was interested.

Laurence made use of this turn of the conversation to speak of Mukalinda.—"Who is Mukalinda?" asked the boy. He did not know. Miss Laurence wanted to know if he had really never heard of Mukalinda. She pretended to be much astonished at his ignorance. She was of the opinion that she had herself sometimes told him about Mukalinda, in the hours when she and Phaon had studied together the wisdom of the Hindus; and she especially wanted to ask "if he had not somewhere encountered the Serpent-King Mukalinda with his seven rings, perhaps by the Lake of the Bird of Paradise?"

"Of course," cried Phaon eagerly, and began now to dwell upon the fiction of a Serpent-King in a high-spirited and completely unembarrassed fashion. With imagination and inventiveness and gaily ironic exaggeration he described how and where he had met Mukalinda, how he had been received by him, what the god looked like and how he moved, and how he ate only earth and had set himself to swallow all the five continents piecemeal. He asserted finally that he had said "You will be frightfully thirsty, your Majesty." But no, Mukalinda thought, it was only a hunger for land that he had. Besides, there was all the sea . . . and so on.

The beautiful Englishwoman was genuinely glad that her beating about the bush had been so completely without result.

VI

About the end of August Bihari Lâl was christened. On the fifteenth of September Deborah, the
handsome Jewess, was delivered by Doctor Egli of a
healthy little girl. In October the same thing happened to Alma the negress. She bore a completely
white male child. Then a longish pause ensued, until
in December Rosita, the enchantingly lovely rope-
dancer, contributed a boy to the tale of the colony's
citizens. From now on the mysterious creative power
extended its operations to most of the ladies of the
colony, so that finally only Anni Prächtel, Frau Rosenbaum, Miss Tyson Page, Miss War, Miss Laurence
Hobbema, Fräulein Dr. Egli and a few others stood in
isolation as barren fig-trees. "We must confess," declared the President, "that we are neither called nor
chosen, but are rather ready to be plucked up and cast
into the fire."

Since Babette Lindemann at the beginning of the
second year after Bihari Lâl had already given birth to
her second, a girl, and Deborah later to twins, and in
exact rotation Alma as well as Rosita had a second boy
each, at the end of the second year after Bihari Lâl's

birth the new Eden could point to an increase of more than two hundred souls, which were duly entered in the register of births kept by Rodberte Kalb.

La recherche de la paternité est interdite. This principle was still firmly upheld. And whoever it was, whether Mukalinda or some other god or hero, that was implicated, it would not have been easy to track him down and prove his complicity in such a delicate affair. One can imagine how everything was changed, especially Ville des Dames, whose name was no longer so appropriate as when the colony was founded. Strangely enough more girls than boys were born, but already there were many boys crowing and tumbling about among the bamboo-huts. Ville des Dames formerly bore the stamp of a shipwrecked settlement. Its leaders had really no other preoccupation than how to sustain the hopes, the faith and the courage of the colonists, and how to keep at arm's length hopelessness, despair, and even madness. This department of the Government was considerably relieved of its burden. The spirit now reigning on Île des Dames was much more that of a settled and still satisfaction. No more were poor exiles and homesick wretches to be seen brooding by the hour with teeth clenched and eyes wet, but everywhere was a fresh and healthy activity. Necessary duties which used to be performed with reluctance were now done with apparent pleasure. Irritating silences, loud quarrels, and a tendency to burst into tears at every opportunity had given way to a secret gaiety which found an outlet in roguish mockery and often in outbursts of mirth which sometimes spread through the whole town.

Since these strange drops of manna recurred with the same constancy and regularity as the moon's phases or the revolution of the earth upon its own axis bringing alternate light and darkness, all the wonder gradually ceased to be wondered at. The artist had not succeeded in carrying her proposal to examine the mystery thoroughly, and to put it, as it were, under supervision; especially since the one natural possibility pointed in a direction which the discreet investigations of Miss Laurence, Rodberte Kalb, and Fräulein Dr. Egli proved to be quite out of the question. The first blow against it was struck by Miss War, when it was indicated to her that before a supernatural origin could be finally assumed for the children with which Île des Dames was blessed, it would be necessary to consider the possibility of Phaon Stradmann's responsibility— a mere conjecture certainly. The lady flew into a terrible passion, and after she had abused in the most severe and sarcastic terms all those whose minds were filthy and miserable enough to entertain such a low and shameful suspicion, she answered for Phaon's innocence with the most sacred oaths. But this was not sufficient for her. She catechised her pupil by himself. And with regard to the central point, after stalking it from all sides like a cat round a bowl of hot stew, she had thought out for her oral examination a subtle system of encircling advance, which she put into practice without forbearance. With its help the boy was really so thoroughly probed to the very marrow that finally even the most hidden corner of his soul must have given up its secrets. The result of this was that Phaon's complete ignorance and innocence were clearly and irrefutably demonstrated.

It was impossible for a child of nature, like Phaon, if he had anything to hide, to survive Miss War's examination for two hours and longer without betraying it by half a word, a glance, or a gesture. She began with warm and simple confidences, and sought, by interjecting harmless questions, to lure him on to the ice while he was in the full flow of his narrative. But in vain she waited for the moment when he should lose the thread of his story, show confusion and betray himself, in short when he should slip on the ice and fall. No, what should he betray when there was literally nothing to betray?

One would have needed to be more stubborn than a mule to doubt Phaon's innocence further. And indeed there was no one who now did so; not even the artist-President, who in the beginning had leaned to the contrary opinion, and who was always such a realist. She had rather helped to destroy the last remaining shred of suspicion. For since Phaon often came to visit her of his own free will, she being the only one, as he said, with whom he could rightly speak German, she also had sounded him in her own way and had confirmed the fact that he was doubly both literally and symbolically, a veritable orphan boy.

So the closure was applied to this enquiry, and with

profit to Île des Dames: for it was quite definitely known now what was not to be reckoned with. As one may speak of a great wave of death which devastates a continent like a plague, so here one might have recognised a great wave of coming-to-life. It had overwhelmed the colony and enriched it with an incredible and wonderful experience. And, as wailing and sorrow follow on the heels of a plague, so on the heels of this wonderful process of growth only joy and great jubilation could break out.

The lasting effect of this great supernatural fact, apart from the blessing of children, was seen variously in particular ways, but in general in a new and higher mentality. Under the shadow of this sublime wonder how could they speak of themselves any longer as an exiled, forlorn, forgotten and outcast congregation, or be capable of feeling themselves such? It would be unnatural, and ungrateful besides, were they to regard themselves other than as a body of Chosen People, were they other than proud and happy to have been considered worthy of such an unheard-of proof of favour from the unknown powers of Heaven.

A long time before the expiration of the second year after Bihari Lâl's birth, the idea of supernatural procreation was already recognised as possessing great value for the general happiness and improvement, and was elevated into a dogma inviolable, because orthodox. This was just; the flourishing serenity of Ville des Dames was an irrefutable proof of its justice. Moreover, without the shadow of a doubt, it would have been believed in even if one or other of the island women had been caught *in flagranti* with a man. The dogma had established itself, and any endeavour to upset it would have been fruitless.

If they were really a Chosen People—and nobody dared doubt it any more—they had sufficient reason to be thankful for the shipwreck, since it was only a bridge leading to the sacred soil of Île des Dames. Every single one of the elect had a right to be highly pleased with herself and to think much of herself. But only those, of course, whose offspring, crowing or toddling in leading-strings, were living witnesses that the wonder had cast its shadow over them. Those whose creative power was still in abeyance found it by no means easy to maintain their prestige. But they endeavoured to do so, and succeeded partially by supporting the dogma with double emphasis, and egregiously flattering the prevailing spirit.

The most frequent topic of discussion and the greatest stimulant to the women's pride, which it heightened even to triumph, was perhaps not so much these hypothetically divine births as the incontestable and proven fact that motherhood was possible without men. And indeed with this proof Man was dethroned, and Woman entered upon the sole supremacy of the World.

The realms of civilisation in which they formerly lived had been designed to suit the surplusage of men who were, in any case, completely superfluous; it was a men's civilisation! Kings, knights, citizens, peasants, artisans and wage-earners it was who played the part in it of pillars and representatives. Woman was not even recognised. She was regarded as an inferior appendage. That state of things would never have been altered had not the hour come when women could be entirely independent of men. The turning point of the world had now been reached on the sacred soil of Île des Dames. What evils would thereby be destroyed, how much injustice and nonsense swept away! Man had formerly been mankind. Man and mankind were synonymous terms. But to-day one would like to see the man who could shut his eyes to the fact that mankind and woman were the same thing, that there was no other human being but woman.

THIS fundamental change in the communal spirit of the colony was naturally bound to alter Phaon's position completely and for the worse. He very soon observed that it was not merely by the crowd of little children that he was displaced from the centre of interest; in that case he would certainly have met with less sympathy than before, but he would not be diligently avoided and disdainfully treated as now, whenever he visited the colony. The real reason for this conduct he could not guess, because of his youth and light-hearted trustfulness. He had lost by growing up into a man; and this loss had come upon him quite reasonably as a natural consequence of the new spirit which, once for all, had become dominant. But as the only half-grown man on the island he had to bear not only his share of public contempt but the whole burden of despite that should have been laid equally upon millions and millions of masculine shoulders. This state of things caused him more and more and at last almost completely to avoid the centre of Île des Dames. Thus, what Miss War, following her educational principles, would have had to enforce, came about quite spontaneously. For the loyal woman could not be turned aside by these enigmatic natural phenomena from her project of educating Phaon to be in every respect a perfect gentleman. And in his present stage of development, which was, as she knew, the most dangerous, her greatest care was directed towards keeping unconscious as long as possible those passions which lie slumbering in men and youths, and which become dominant when they are awakened. This unconsciousness, which makes a youth the most unembarrassed comrade and playfellow of young girls, this purity and childlike innocence, was the all-captivating charm of Phaon, the young European now nearly a man. It was this treasure, this peach-bloom, this radiant state before the Fall, which had to be guarded from the slightest hurt like the very apple of one's eye; for even the slightest touch would have been sufficient to scatter the blossom. Rodberte Kalb and Laurence thought much the same. All three ladies welcomed the fact that their pupil of his own free will was beginning to avoid the precincts of Ville des Dames.

"What should the boy learn here," demanded Rodberte Kalb, "where the women feel themselves so completely at one? Now more than ever that they are having children without knowing by whom, something essentially primitive has come over them. That is itself to be welcomed as a sign of warm, happy and increased vitality. Already our ladies would no longer fit into European society. But naturalness is a necessary concomitant of this return to nature. And as for the naturalness of our ladies, that is more and more leaving nothing to be desired. Why, even our broadminded President has felt herself compelled to check their excesses by a decree. Our ladies have become positively brazen. But their brazenness arises from exuberance, and that again is caused by the fortunate soil that nourishes us, the fortunate sky over us, in short, by all the wanton and careless abundance in which we live. All our senses have daily the richest and sweetest satisfactions. And so the women's glances are by turns sleepily satiated and ardently desirous. For it is clear that amid this perpetual satiation desire itself is insatiable. But as for morality, it has little prospect of playing any part in this hot and fearless instinctive life, which as we see brings us to this, that we already get children without the help of men. Indeed, we have a kind of spontaneous generation, and it is reasonable that we should be absolute man-haters in our pride at the patronage of Zeus, who has been prodigal of children from all time. Yet I could not pledge myself for the loyalty of our ladies to Zeus if an Achilles or a Hector or even only an elegant lieutenant of marines were to appear. And our Phaon in beauty will soon come no whit behind an Alcibiades."

"According to my experience," said Laurence Hobbema, "all the colonists have decided that Phaon, the child of our colony, is taboo. I do not believe that any one of them has anything more than a motherly feeling towards him. On the other hand, we cannot blindfold him. Our ladies have developed in very different directions; some are as wild and supple as panthers, others, and indeed these are in the majority, are like luxuriant plants. They show no modesty either in their dress or their undress. Wherever one goes children are openly given the breast. Truly a stroll through Ville des Dames would have given great pleasure to Rubens. And yet the taboo is inviolable. Only, as I say, we cannot blindfold Phaon. In the long run that would have a bad effect on him."

Laurence, who was by common consent called simply the goddess of the island, shared Rodberte Kalb's thoughts, but she added her own, and these revolved round the higher ideal incarnated, as she thought, in Phaon. The purity of the youth, which Miss War as well as Rodberte revered and wished to keep safe, was to her more than mere childish innocence. She harked back rather to what she had once said to the President, when she allotted to Phaon the rôle of a youthful Helios destined later to illumine the world. That was certainly an ideal quite distinct from Miss War's perfect gentleman; and it was this ideal which "the goddess" saw endangered.

She it was whose delight in myths, and tendency to transcendentalism, had chiefly created the new spirit in Île des Dames. She had immediately attributed to the enigmatic phenomenon of Île des Dames a miraculous nature in the sense implied by Babette Lindemann, and her capacity for enthusiasm had attached to this miracle the lofty connotation of a new orientation of the whole human world. She had become the creator of that new consciousness which made the exiles of Île des Dames regard themselves as a Chosen People, yea, as the redeemers of the world. Thus she had become the creator of a new faith, a new love, a new hope. But certainly the motives which induced her after Anni's discourse to help in the construction of the mystic dome of the new cathedral in Île des Dames were worlds asunder from that which led her to see in Phaon not Phaon but a Helios, a Lucifer, a *Phos noeron,* a Lightbringer, a Saviour.

Compared with that which Phaon evoked in her, the faith with which she had endowed the colony was artificially manufactured. Her enthusiasm for Phaon was unsocial. The riches of his spirit, the beauty of his whole appearance, had bewitched her as Socrates was bewitched by Phaidros. And as Socrates wished to guard the beauty and purity of Phaidros, so she wished to guard Phaon's.

Thus she had persuaded the President, and without any trouble, it is true, to build for Miss War and Phaon, on an airy and healthy site less than an hour away from the settlement, a fine wooden house, which possessed, in addition to their living and sleeping rooms, several schoolrooms where Phaon was instructed.

The idea was that this building would be still more valuable later on when the next generation of Île des Dames would have attained school age. Often for hours, even for days at a time, the President herself fled to this place of refuge for which the title of Academy was adopted. Miss War, or whoever it was who sojourned in the house, could at once assume on seeing the artist that the doings of the Chosen People had once more proved too highly coloured for her.

Her last visit had occurred when the dogma of the orthodox feminine cult had, as it were, shown its teeth for the first time: for the fact that Phaon was looked at askance as a male being was, after all, a trifle. Besides, the boy himself, with his really divine disposition, was not in the least influenced by this. Now, however, the dogma arose with bristles on end and bared tusks, like a powerful black boar in a fen, and whetted its curved weapons in readiness for child-murder.

For, in all seriousness, one day the majority of the women who had given birth to girls took objection to the existence of the boys, and in public assembly brought up for discussion the question how the purely feminine state of the future was to be defended from the danger threatening it by the birth of males. With woman-like inconsistency the mothers of the boys were goaded to madness by this perfectly justified and logical question, for they saw only the danger which threatened their beloved offspring. The essential weakness of their position, however, could not be strengthened by mere outbursts of anxiety, rage, and indignation: on the contrary their opponents turned these to advantage. They proved that if the question were disallowed as unfair the dogma would be betrayed. And their pressure was so strong, for they too were passionately roused by the agitation of the boys' mothers, and were moreover in the majority and in the right, that the ticklish question was actually discussed.

There could be no talk of a future women's state even if only half as many boys as girls were born. Among the Amazons male children were slain in order to keep the state pure. They were exposed upon the mountains immediately after birth, since that was the most humane form of elimination.

The mere mention of this was enough to split Ville des Dames for the first time into two hostile and raging camps.

WHEN, after the occurrence of these events, the President betook herself to the Academy in a fit of annoyance and rage, a stream of practically incomprehensible words flowed from her eloquent mouth: words, of which the beginning, the burden and the end was the word, nonsense!

Had Miss Laurence been at hand there would have been one of those encounters which often arose between the two ladies (who were in most respects not ill-disposed towards each other), but this encounter would probably have thrown all the former ones into the shade. However, she found only Miss War, to whom she could speak freely without any constraint or fear of contradiction, when the topic was the consequences of the miracles on Île des Dames.

"These hussies," she said, "are all without exception over the border-line. They completely lack the correcting influence of masculine society. I feel the lack of it myself, and am falling a victim slowly but surely to the prevailing madness.

"The so-called civilisation of Europe," she continued, "is also founded on openly acknowledged lies. Several more or less witty books have been written on the subject of the conventional lie. There are very few creative truths, but that makes all the more creative lies and errors." There were, she went on, countless canonical examples of this. But, as a spectator, to have actual experience of how such a huge, swollen and rank error may luxuriate and flourish in the middle of a wilderness, rooting itself more and more firmly and spreading its top over the heavens, and to have to look on without doing anything,—that was no easy task for a nature like hers.

At this point Miss War's mind either strove vainly, or refused, to comprehend the meaning of these words. She was wont to turn her head aside whenever Anni Prächtel's eye caught hers directly.

"The world, too, is full of quixotry," went on Fräulein Prächtel. "And it is all to the good that we have rescued from the shipwreck a full measure of it: why not? In the lovely Laurence to be sure, we have, on the one hand, a goddess in strength, goodness and humanity; but on the other, she might quite well be a La Mancha. She makes us crazy. She drives madness to its extremity.

"How these children originate, is fundamentally a matter of indifference to me. Sometimes it seems to me as if all these brats crept, tumbled, and flew straight out of the pregnant womb of this ridiculous island. Why should not several hundred thousand children be conceived yearly in the fiery belly of Île des Dames and be shot out into the air? Just in the same way, there may be demons of hell living here who come up at night through the craters and smoke-holes to lie invisibly with the daughters of men. As I say, I am quite indifferent. But if an enquiry into the origin of the phenomenon is to be set aside for definite reasons, it ought to be remembered that there exist other and not less important hypotheses than these nonsensical conclusions we have jumped to, about a purely feminine or supernatural procreation, which lead to criminal acts."

It was the supreme council and the other thoughtful elements in the community which were to be thanked for hindering from becoming law the crime of a systematic slaughter of male children. A strict separation, however, of the superior and inferior sexes, girls and boys, was enforced by the establishment of a settlement for boys only. Thither the masculine olive branches were taken immediately after being weaned, and for the time being were well looked after and supervised; later a further decision would be made.

VII

ON the third of March in the third year after Bihari
Lâl's birth a coast-watcher ran through the colony
brandishing in her fist her bamboo-spear and crying:
"A ship! a ship!"

After the breathless runner had been somewhat
calmed and it had been ascertained that this time the
alarm was not a false one, as it was often by Phaon's
instigation, Laurence, Tyson Page and Rosita, the
former dancer, accompanied her to the place from
which the ship should be visible.

The news burst upon the colony like a thunderclap.
It was yet early in the day and so all kinds of maternal
duties had to be performed before other groups could
join the first. Meanwhile a great concourse gathered
before the Town Hall.

The steamship was said to be a huge one with three
or four funnels, and to be making directly for the
island from the west. So it was credible that they
might be taking four o'clock tea in a magnificent saloon,
perhaps on one of the gorgeous German Orient liners,
and that a few hours later Île des Dames might vanish
for ever in the great ocean!

Naturally a feeling of joy broke out immediately with

elemental force, and combined with tempestuous hopes which, apparently dead, had only slumbered, and now arose with double vitality. On the other hand feelings of another sort were also perceptible, which added to the draught of joy a clearly recognisable aftertaste of bitterness. A quarter of an hour after the publication of the great news one might easily have drawn the false conclusion that it had been construed as a herald of devastating ill fortune rather than of approaching joy, since the general emotional upheaval found vent chiefly in weeping and wailing.

LAURENCE, turning with her troop into the palm thickets where Ville des Dames was hidden from sight, heard these sorrowful sounds and said: "I understand you, my dear people." And when, like the others, she had climbed for a while in silence, breathing deeply, and with serious mien, she began to hold a kind of soliloquy with herself which she continued so far as the exigencies of the path allowed.

"Yes, yes," she said, "my good sisters, you are once more catastrophically poised between gain and loss, and the loss is really the only certainty. All that by your own efforts you have become, created and acquired, will be riven asunder in a few seconds as if by an earthquake, washed away as if by a flood. Once more a glorious epoch will be cut short by a kind of shipwreck. I wager that not only are you untrue already to the great ideals of Île des Dames but that the new soul which you have acquired by your own strength during years of need is already thrown overboard. You are already ashamed of your proud and courageous will, of your proud and courageous thoughts, your free and independent deeds. Most certainly your doll's clothes are now waiting for you and you will don them again with pleasure."

"There is no choice," said Miss Tyson Page. "If the ship lands we are both rescued and lost. I shall be absolutely compelled to continue my studies with Artôt in Paris, as I had intended. If it lay in my power to decide now whether the ship should land or not I should be silent, my dear Laurence, and for all time say neither yea or nay."

For a while they were silent and thoughtful. Then the dancer said, with a slight cough: "We shall certainly make a sensation. I fear it will begin at once, when we come on board with all our belongings they will scarcely be able to hide their laughter. Well, I know a very trustworthy woman in Brussels who will look after my children."

Laurence, who was all the time striding upwards drawing deep breaths, not unlike a Pallas Athene accompanied by Venus and Diana; Laurence had said that, in what was approaching, the only certainty was loss. And certainly it would be in itself a loss to have to give up this young and promising world for the trivial round of an outworn civilisation. In it the individual was but a drop in the ocean. The maidens and consecrated mothers of Île des Dames who had been accustomed to the great freedom of action and movement of goddesses, would become mere drops in the ocean of common humanity, when they were thrown back into society, and would be lost in it. And more than that, they would have to leave behind them the real and concrete paradise of riches and beauty which was Île des Dames.

In the full four years of their residence the colonists had made great progress in the discovery and employment of these riches. Rodberte's scrupulous chronicle kept an exact record of the fortunate days of discovery, of the discoveries, and the discoverers. The most illustrious name there was that of little Mucci Smith, who had delighted the President with the glorious fruit of the durian on the morning after their landing. Very soon after that she had identified, on hills more than a thousand feet high, thickets, yes forests of date-palms, Phœnix Dactylifera, a tree of which Muhammed said to his followers: "Honour it as your sister." And she had shown them how bread, wine, vinegar, honey, flour, and all kinds of plaited work, could be obtained from it, and how even the date-stones could be utilised. At the suggestion of the goddess Laurence, Mucci was universally acclaimed as Thamar, that is, the palm. But after that the indefatigable Mucci, now Thamar, made what was really her best throw.

One day, on a botanical expedition of discovery, Thamar had wandered as high as 3,000 feet. Her sister Lolo accompanied her. Lolo had carelessly broken a twig laden with red berries from an evergreen bush. Thamar, however, did not notice it until they were long past the place where it grew.

The bark of the twig was greyish-white and rough, the leaf not unlike the leaf of the lemon-tree. White fragrant blossoms grew beside red fleshy berries. Some berries were of a deep purple colour. Pretty Thamar became reflective, and made Lolo go back with her to the place where the branch had been found.

They discovered it soon in a ravine open to the west, which widened into a finely terraced valley, and when Thamar had examined the broken branch and the whole bush, a glance over the breadth of the valley convinced her that similar bushes grew everywhere. Shrubs of the same kind clothed all the terraces with an undergrowth in the shadow of the palm trees. Thamar's behaviour seemed extraordinary to Lolo; she seemed in the grip of an almost overmastering excitement. Neither of the virgin mothers could remember ever to have gazed on such an enchanted and enchanting corner of the earth. Clear and fresh springs everywhere guaranteed coolness and fertility. It seemed as if the invisible gardener of this kingdom, probably never trod by the foot of man, had carefully guided refreshing currents to the very roots of the trees. Then Thamar said: "Unless I am altogether mistaken, this gloriously fragrant paradise will enrich us in an unexpected way, not with gold, but with something which is a thousand-fold more valuable to us."

In a few minutes Thamar had reached another bush and had taken from it white and strongly scented blossoms and berries both fresh and old. The old berries were dried up. From each brown, wrinkled and bitter-tasting capsule there rolled out, when Thamar opened it, two green and fairly hard kernels, which even Lolo recognised at once as coffee beans.

So there was no longer any need to go without that precious beverage, coffee, in Ville des Dames, and this was of the highest importance for the life of the colonists. Merely through the consciousness that they were drinking coffee and that they were able to enjoy it at any time they liked, they saw themselves again initiated into the great community of civilisation, and thus the feeling of exile was lessened; but the actual enjoyment of the drink increased their daily comfort, and quickly showed its effects in a warmer sociability and a more ardent spiritual life.

The other treasures discovered in the island and utilised were tobacco, hemp, the pepper-vine, several kinds of cinnamon trees, sugar-cane which was pleasant to chew, various fruits and ornamental woods. (Among these, one of extreme hardness, beautifully veined, and of a chocolate colour, which served as a looking glass when polished and was so used by the ladies.)

In certain places on the shore there were natural salt pans caused by the influx of sea water which quickly evaporated in the shallow pools. Whole provinces could have salted their daily soup with it, and not merely the scanty numbers of the Chosen People.

Miss Page, Rosita, Lolo Smith, the mulatto Alma

and other ladies, and Phaon as well, brought home daily from the hunt peacocks, pheasants, snipe, quail, woodcock and sometimes even large and small dappled deer. And fishing in the brooks, streams and bays was every whit as profitable.

There were clay deposits which made it possible to fashion and fire jugs, plates and cups, and many other utensils had been invented which were a credit to the dexterity and taste of the colonists. And yet the riches, the charm, the amenities of the island, were by no means exhausted. It possessed countless obvious and hidden beauties, hills, ravines, valleys and dells, lowlands and plateaux of exquisite variety, a veil of heavenly mimosas and orchids, enchanting springs, blossoming thickets of unusual magnificence; and it possessed, too, noble columnar masses of porphyry, whose summits melted into the shimmering blue sky. Dreadful chasms and rifts yawned in it, and, finally, over everything towered that ever-fuming peak which could well bear comparison in its majestic beauty with the sacred mountain of the Japanese, Fuji-no-yama in Nippon.

Halfway up this mountain a herd of grazing zebu was one day discovered. They almost gave one the impression of being domesticated by some previous colonist or other, rather than of being indigenous products. This idea found support when a cave was discovered with what looked like the ground plan of an altar, round which were lying parts of a basalt figure from which, with little trouble, an exceedingly primitive female image about two feet high could be reconstructed. The learned Laurence at once spoke with enthusiasm of the youthful home of Dionysos, which Herodotus had set in the tropics: "What a glorious thought that perhaps the Greeks have lived here before us!"

Miss Laurence was right in saying that to abandon the island was to make loss the only certainty. Besides all the other things, the loss consisted in the sum-total of labour, invention and practical capacity which had been exercised on this exquisite field of exile, an already flourishing and dividend-paying capital which would have to be abandoned unused.

It was necessary to climb to a certain pass in order to espy the ship on the horizon, to the north-west of the island. The coast-guard affirmed that it sent out a great volume of smoke. Laurence wanted to know by whom, and where, it had first been sighted. First by Lolo and then by Phaon. "Were Lolo and Phaon together, and what were they doing so early so high up on the mountain?" Lolo and Phaon had been conducting the Holy Mother Babette to a certain place where all the trees and grass ceased and there was only steaming slag. Laurence wanted to know what was it, then, that Mother Babette intended to do there? A fleeting glance assured Laurence that a scarcely perceptible smile curled the full lips of the accompanying goddesses. "Oh, Mother Babette," cried the watcher, "had some mysterious purpose in hand up yonder by the enchanted lake, where the water exhaled sulphurous fumes—a purpose of which she dared not speak freely."—"And what have Lolo and Phaon to do with it?"—Lolo and Phaon had nothing to do with it.

Meanwhile this much was gradually elicited: the steaming lake had been discovered by Phaon, and he had found a serpent there.

They had reached the entrance to the lovely valley of coffee bushes, from which the first view north-west was visible. The smoke of civilisation could still be seen, but according to Phaon, Lolo and Thamar, who were busy on the coffee terraces, it was farther away and not nearer, so that the hopes of a landing were growing less every minute. The disappointment of the women was after all great, while Phaon, as Laurence among others perceived, only joined in it out of compliance. Apparently, he had some quite different idea in his head which he was pursuing with characteristic perseverance and which made the threatening event merely a disturbance to him.

When Miss Laurence sought to penetrate his mask, he readily threw it away and declared with gay enthusiasm that he actually felt no inclination to leave Île des Dames, where he had never enjoyed himself so much as now.

Phaon relapsed, however, into monosyllables. He seemed to feel a constraint in the presence of the continually arriving colonists, and to be unpleasantly affected by their lamentable chatter. When the landing of the ship was finally out of the question he vanished all at once.

The lovely Laurence, however, had observed how he slunk into the brushwood. She, too, was pleased with the decision which Fate had taken. But that could not be the reason why she immediately left her comrades to follow the beautiful boy.

This wonderful Laurence, who officiated as priestess in the church of Notre-Dame des Dames, was highly venerated by the whole colony. Her personality radiated a serene goodness and an unapproachable purity and loftiness. She had established for the devotions under her charge a ritual which was gladly accepted by all denominations in the colony. And it was entirely owing to Laurence Hobbema that it was observed with such seriousness and dignity.

"Nothing can be done for the person who cannot comprehend the pointing finger of Destiny—whom the growth of this garden springing from the solemn necessities of the shipwreck does not enlighten, who has not a soul prophetic enough to realise that here the divine and pure mother earth is once more ours in which the golden grain of religion can be destroyed and raised up again, can grow in renewed and blessed beauty, can flower and bear fruits." This was what she asserted; and she said often: "Is it not like the story which the ancients used to tell about the moon, which they thought was composed of earth from Olympus? That earth was for them the purest in the earthly world, although certainly most impure of celestial substances; and the raptures which the blessed experienced there arose from the fact that the masculine and the feminine principles were united in one body, and penetrated each other unhindered, with endless mutual delight."

In the sanctuary of Notre-Dame des Dames records were being kept that were destined to be honoured as the sacred scriptures of the island. Here were described as eternal truths the wonderful incidents in Babette's adventure with Mukalinda; as well as record after record of the repeated supernatural conceptions. Everything was written down from the loftiest standpoint of holiness. Councils were held to sift the accumulating mass of mythology, and to canonise the selected portions.

"It does no harm," Laurence gave her opinion, "if absurdities are mixed up with it. Only, we must keep the imaginative side quite apart from the purely reasonable. We need an imaginative reality: the other is accessible to us at will. The ancients are again our examples in this; the moon was for them a heavenly body which they scrutinised scientifically. And, on the other hand, it was also the goddess Artemis, and the one conception did not interfere with the other."

Laurence enjoyed the highest veneration, and, in her own realm, an unimpeachable authority. She blessed the pregnant women and those in childbirth, and introduced a special island baptism which she herself performed; the esteem in which she was held mounted almost to that given to an actual saint. Strangely enough, as she and the others felt, it was increased by the fact that neither the procreative god nor any sacred hermaphroditism worked on her, and she was looked upon as more than merely childless—as the chaste vestal.

Laurence herself hardly knew what had happened to her when she suddenly found herself again quite alone and tracking down Phaon. Assuredly she had not decided to do so. Rather something of whose very existence she was hardly aware, some mystic force, had driven her to it blindly. As she observed the quickness of her breathing, and realised the eagerness with which she was following up her human prey like a huntress, she had to smile and shake her head several times in astonishment. Why was she climbing after Phaon whom she could safely expect to see to-morrow in the so-called Academy at the lesson-hour? Why was it all at once so unbearable to think that she would not see him again till to-morrow, and not at once and on the very spot if possible?

Laurence had never once suspected the existence of what now so completely overmastered her, until it had swooped headlong upon her. It was an emotion of such intensity that it left no room in her soul for anything present or future, for anything else at all. As if her life depended upon it this lady usually so self-possessed, was dragged over stick and stone after Phaon and lured on by his image.

"It is simply an insurrection in me," thought the lovely Laurence, still on the track of her youthful quarry, her royal shoulders now gleaming a little with an olive sheen. "Has this sudden rebellion of my whole nature," she continued to think, "any connection with the possibilities that came within arm's length through the threatened landing of the Orient Liner? Should I not have been one of the few who are cheated by themselves of the real prize, the real harvest of Île des Dames, and who have therefore lived in vain through this epoch so rich in blessing?

"Truly what can you do, if you have not been deemed worthy, like the others, of being overshadowed by the mystery of this magic island? And how can your pupil help you in that, who although you have been with him nearly every day, has not been able to help you, and indeed, for that reason, has not helped you?"

Laurence perferred not to answer these questions. Nor any of the others which crowded upon her, and which were all concerned with the question in how far her present behaviour could accord harmoniously with her priestly dignity and her position as Phaon's tutor. All these questions were overshadowed by a strange and heady rejuvenation. This beautiful artist's daughter stormed with royal strides and bounds through the paradise of palm and pisang trees, rousing up swarms of araras, and a European who had seen her would have believed that he had encountered an Artemis of Peter Paul Rubens, girt to the knee and glowing with Olympian fire.

She was seized with a longing comparable to the deadly thirst of a fainting and weary wanderer, and around her played a Fata Morgana similar to the mirage evoked by languishing thirst. To be sure, her longing was born of abundance. The sun and the soil which created the island's wealth of blossom and fruit, which set the warm sap of the palm and the spice trees flowing, which enveloped height and valley in clouds of incense, had matured this longing, too, like the wanton chalice of an orchid. "Yes," thought the lovely Miss Laurence, at once dismayed and blissful before her own transformation, "yes, yes, this is what happens to the proud and haughty. It comes home to me now tenfold that I have identified myself with Pallas Athene, the goddess cool and superior to everything. So I find myself in this state of complete defencelessness, which, if it were not filled with such resolution, such joy, such strength as could uproot trees, I would describe as subjugation or complete weakness."

While a trilling, joyous and bird-like sound escaped from her throat, let us say a kind of blissful warbling of the gods, she knew all at once that she was neither one thing nor another, but a nameless being of eternal youth. Her arms, breasts, hips and thighs filled her with ecstasy. She loosened her hair, and was enraptured by its touch on her shoulders, breast and hips. Every part of her body, even the smallest, thrilled with the purest bliss. She doubted no longer that she was nine-tenths composed of paradisaical earth. But certainly the remaining tenth was strong enough to carry away the other nine-tenths in a whirl of bliss.

Laurence gave a fleeting thought to Miss War. But what did Miss War signify, when one was led into the heart of the mystic cloud of marriage with the infinite? All her senses were transformed. What she saw, heard, touched and inhaled as fragrance, had never before been seen, heard, touched and smelt by her. And Phaon? That most gracious Eros she saw certainly for the first time as he vanished, marked by her, secretly in the bushes.

Ah, this impish, scurvy and cunning god! She felt every muscle tighten in her divine body. She would conquer him, quite certainly, were he a god ten thousand times as beautiful, and ten thousand times as beguiling. . . .

VIII

LAURENCE had introduced Indo-Greek elements bit by bit into the cult of Notre-Dame des Dames, because she followed Max Müller in conceiving the idea of a universal religion. This tendency of hers appeared more strongly than ever after the hope, or fear, that a ship would land, had been frustrated. . . . A few months after the event which embraced both the emergence and the disappearance of this hope, Laurence founded a temple on the spur of Mont des Dames that looked to the north, high above a mighty cliff beside the sea. The landscape there was as exquisitely varied as a natural park. It included, too, the site where the broken image of the goddess, the relic of a childish art, was found, that cave which proved that the island had been already inhabited thousands of years before.

Laurence now appeared less often in the Maison de la Bonne Esperance, and, strangely enough, had taken no further part in Phaon's education since the day of disappointed hope of the ship's landing.

It would be good for him, she averred, in his youth, not to be too deeply saturated in the particular style of thinking to which she herself was especially prone.

Miss War seemed to be but indifferently pleased by

this declaration, and deplored the fact that now Rodberte Kalb, who was, it is true, a learned kind of female Voltaire, would have to provide more of the instruction. Rodberte, the worthy governess thought, was encouraging Phaon in a direction towards which he was already too strongly predisposed. In vain the governess worried herself to find out the real reasons which had operated to make the noble Laurence break off her tuition of Phaon. Laurence seemed inclined to provide no further information, and even withdrew herself more and more from Miss War.

Besides, there was also this to be considered. During the erection, and after the completion, of the new sanctuary Laurence spent most of her time beside it. In the beginning she showed herself once or twice a week in Ville des Dames, but later scarcely once a fortnight, until four weeks after the consecration of the temple she made her last visit for a long time to the settlement.

This visit was remarkable in many respects. For the lovely Laurence came to ask formal leave of absence for about six months, and to appoint for that period a representative, a vicar, a substitute, whom she had selected in the person of Juliane René.

A ceremonial farewell and induction was held in the bamboo church of Notre-Dame des Dames, and Laurence gave the following address, which was stenographed by Rodberte:

"Daughters of earth and Heaven! But daughters rather of earth than of Heaven! A call has come to me. After succeeding, thanks to your unanimous decision and the practical help of our house-builders, in establishing two new places of worship, I have received a call to withdraw for a time into the highlands in order to meditate in stillness, more deeply than before, upon our position and our vocation. But by our position I mean more than geographical isolation, by our vocation, more even than the development of our new social order, in which women are to regain the due rights of which they have been deprived; although in regard to that also I await enlightenment. What I mean is the vocation of humanity in general, both in time and in eternity.

"Our settlement has already developed from modest beginnings into its present flourishing state. If we or our children and children's children are ever discovered, which is bound to happen, the whole human world will benefit from our labours. Without the blessing of our divine children we could neither have counted upon the day of discovery, nor been able to perform a real service to the whole of humanity.

"The fact that we can do so ennobles our actions. Because in every way we are working for the happiness of humanity and not merely for our own, in all that we do there is the joy of the ideal. Without that we should sink to the animal level, imperceptibly, perhaps, but steadily. The higher type of human being believes that only those actions are genuine whose completion affects in some way the happiness or woe of humanity, so that the immediate advantage to the doer is subordinated to a higher advantage for others in the future.

"I avow quite frankly that I have fallen into an extraordinary state of being. To put it modestly, my emotional life has gained in depth. I am even tempted to think that formerly my heart was deadened. The feelings I experience, the blissful presentiments, hopes, images and thoughts which surge within me, are sometimes so staggeringly new and strange even to myself, that I often believe that I am being born again, or at least that a new and far better soul is entering into me. And I would have to consider it literally as a crime against myself, against you, against humanity, and against God, if I were to pay no attention to this intimation and not give myself up to such a divine state, fervently and completely.

"In order to do so, in order to avoid any interference with this inner life, secret and holy—and only for this reason—I now seek solitude.

"I will not conceal from you that I tremble with ecstatic joy at the prospect of my quiet existence. I am not sure that revelations of the highest kind will not be vouchsafed to me in my retreat. In any case I am ready to hearken, to watch. And not only to hearken and to watch, but to set down in writing what I see and hear, if the new power within me will suffer itself to guide my hand.

"In the great world of civilisation there was much talk of spiritual fathers: but we want to be spiritual mothers. It is another reason for my withdrawal that

I wish to accomplish this for all of us. We desire to be mothers, and yet spiritual, not like those so-called Fathers whose fatherhood is only a lie. I have conceived the tremendous idea of using my state of grace for the creation of a new kind of human being, that super-woman who will replace the fundamentally misshapen and distorted types of the past, that divine material, so to speak, which will form the actual and ideal stones for the building of a new and perfect civilisation.

"The civilisation from which we have sprung is, in spite of all, a petrifaction. By that I mean that, although it is so active, it is only superficially alive. It ripens only a few people out of hundreds of millions whose life is deeply rooted. Europe once had a great period. I mean that in which the Romanesque and Gothic Cathedrals arose under the sacred domination of the Church.

"It was a great period, for it acknowledged the supremacy of religion. But it was also not great, and had to fall to pieces, because it had trampled upon, dishonoured and brought into utter contempt, the human basis upon which it stood. One cannot found life upon a contempt of life, nor human happiness upon a contempt of humanity, nor human brotherhood upon a contempt of woman, the mother of humanity.

"*Mulier taceat in ecclesia!* nay, rather, let her speak, let her fill the aisles of the future Church with the triumphal song of life. For there is one eternal truth;

-: 141 :-

that whatever paradise we hope to enter must be entered through the gate of life.

"The civilisation from which we have parted is still characteristically one in which the human race, and especially women, have not raised themselves from this state of dishonour. To what extent we have already accomplished this can be recognised by the discomposure, even the horror, that afflicted us, openly or secretly, at the approach of the ship. But it must be still more completely accomplished. I declare to you, and I call the Bible to witness, that you are gods! Let each one of us be the Church, and let each one of us rise to the estate of godhead.

"Once more—the civilisation from which we are parted! It has among other characteristics that of cherishing its sources of error, of sanctifying and perpetuating its defects. It is, of course, a masculine civilisation, and lacks the maternal mode of thinking which is closely allied to nature and fruitful. Women think less, but more essentially, than men. Naturally not the women who are ruined by civilisation, but the instinctive, unspoilt, maternal women. In a civilisation supported by mothers the noise of flails threshing empty straw, the deafening clatter of talking-mills grinding chaff, can never prevail as they do in a masculine civilisation.

"Christ himself was born of woman. His teaching of love for one's neighbour would have been completely realised long ago in an empire of mothers. Love, too, is born of woman. Not only because she gives birth to everything, and thus implants love in the boy, but because she carries and shields the developing human being within herself for nine months, and because during this period, in this relationship true human love is first effective. Solely out of this mystery was the high and pure *Caritas* first produced from the womb of time.

"Only much later, it seems to me, was man infected with it. Primitive society consisted of mothers and children. The first social impulse arises from the nursing mother, guiding and shielding her young. Let us consider, in this respect, the analogous relationship of a mother cat to her kittens. There is simply no bond of this kind between the male cat and the kittens, nor could one describe his relationship to the female as one of *Caritas;* it is much more like enmity.

"I make no attempt to discuss the state of affairs between men and women in the realm of masculine civilisation. You know that there, too, an enmity between the sexes, indeed, an ancient enmity, is affirmed by important men and judges of the human soul.

"Thus the *Caritas* which issues from our souls has by itself become the motive that links human society. Or do you think, merely to mention an instance, that man would have cared in the slightest for his children if we had not succeeded in transferring our *Caritas* to him, and had not influenced him in every conceivable way? But what is he who does not care for his children? He is at heart unsocial. Proofs of that can be found in Europe alone by the million.

"We live here, in many ways, in a state of wonder

and happiness. On this island-jewel in its sapphire setting of the sea, we are preserved in unending mystery. We are undergoing the most profound change that ever human being has undergone. There is no priestly caste among us. For priesthood of every kind and degree is a spirit-deadening waste product of the masculine drone. In this garden of a new soul there is thus nothing to hinder the soul's development. Remain united during my absence, let each one of you meanwhile strengthen her self-confidence and preserve her faith, even her credulity, for the future immeasurable advantage of the whole world."

After this address Laurence inducted Juliane René into the office of priestess, and disappeared immediately from the settlement.

AMONG the many lovely spots on the island one of the loveliest was that chosen by Laurence for the upper shrine. It was called the Bona Dea of the Stone. The stone referred to was not the entrance to the basalt cave, which was covered with flowering creepers, nor the cave itself, but the broken old statue of meteoric or moon stone which had been found in it.

The wall of rock in which the cave was hollowed fronted a flat open space which had the charm of a spacious and exquisite garden. Its western boundary was the cliff-edge where from a giddy height one beheld the sea boiling with surf, as it gnawed away the scarps and crags of the island.

The new temple precinct sank to this cliff edge with

its natural pulpits and balconies, by a series of flat terraces on which stood single holm-oaks thousands of
years old. Not far from the entrance to the cave fell
the rushing, bubbling or trickling waters of a spring
which had found its way out over the hollow cliff, after
dropping gradually down to it through a deep fissure in
the rocks. It dowered the place not merely with
heavenly verdure, but in the heat of noon with heavenly
coolness. For a long time this natural park had been
a favourite resort of the divine Laurence Hobbema.
She loved the magnificence of its overgrown rocky bastions, its giant trees, and its infinite horizon. How
gloriously the summit of Mont des Dames rose to greet
the eye everywhere between the masses of cliff and
foliage! She loved the deep damp shadow of the
thickets and bushes and the exquisite veil of flowers
and grasses which seemed not of this world, and which
covered the banks of the watercourses. Soon after discovering it the fair lady had kept this region especially
in mind, and had not only planned to do much with it,
but had very soon begun to cultivate it.

The first thing was to lay down paths in all directions: this had been done a long time ago, volcanic ash
being used instead of gravel. Stairways and open
spaces were introduced into the network of paths according to a general design. "What was required,"
Laurence had said with the ultimate approval of everybody, "was to create a place which should be beautiful and holy, rather than useful. In order to feel at
home with Nature one needs a garden as well as a

house: the garden, helped by Art, is what first brings nature, so alien and distant, near to us, and makes it familiar. But," she went on to say, "we do not need only a pleasure garden of earthly and heavenly delights; our joy in it must also be associated with a change of scene: let us therefore establish this cave and terrace garden as a place of pilgrimage."

Not very far from the waterfall, so that its noise was no longer deafening, a little wooden house fragrant with resin had been erected in a homely style, which reminded one of a small Japanese temple. This was the place in which Laurence settled after her departure from Ville des Dames.

SHE was not completely solitary there; not even when there was nobody near her. She had brought with her the little Diodata, her foster-child, whom she regarded always with a shade of pensive melancholy. The nobility of her soul was a guarantee even to herself that she would never withdraw any of her love from her fosterling. It was precisely her deep maternal passion, unexpectedly intensified by what she carried in her womb, which led her to feel that Diodata was after all an orphan. Lolo Smith looked after the child, and put herself by day and night at Laurence's disposal. The great garden also with its forests and rocks, besides providing much work for Mucci Smith and her band of youthful gardeners, was daily visited by some of the Daughters of Heaven, who came to perform their devotions in the cave of the Bona Dea or merely to take a pleasant stroll upon the volcanic ashes of the pathways.

Phaon's visits, too, broke in upon Laurence's solitude. But it was not apparently on her account that the boyish youth, whose step Laurence could already distinguish from afar, knocked so frequently at her door. He still displayed a truly touching attachment to the little Dagmar-Diodata. A close observer might often have noted a deep though fleeting blush on Laurence's lovely cheek at Phaon's arrival, if he turned first not to her, but to the child.

Laurence's attitude to Phaon, since she had been honoured by the god's favour and had entered upon her sacred mission, seemed no longer that of an adult to a child, much less that of a teacher to her pupil. One might have perceived in her an infinitely tender and almost shy respect, a demeanour which would have deeply affected any initiated onlooker who saw the proud and noble woman with the childish youth. True, there was no initiated onlooker, unless it were Phaon himself.

MENTION has already been made of Laurence's attempts at poetry. More than a decade and a half after these present occurrences a number of her poems fell into Phaon's hands, among which there was one as follows:

> Here the god's steps lightly fall
> Within the sacred rustling wood.

I would not change my solitude,
I, who am happiest of all.
As the volcano's lofty frieze
Menaces with sudden might,
Flaring through the solemn night,
O'er the heavy-hanging trees,
Even so my heart's ablaze,
Feeding like a kindling brand
Upon the nights of this land
And its golden shimmering days.
And the guardian spirit striding
Nightly o'er the quaking ground
By my hands is shielded round
Skilfully his footsteps guiding.
He draws the passion from the dreams
That flutter in my trembling breast.
From the wide ocean's white unrest
Waver cool and watery gleams.

The fleeting red in Laurence's face, although it was
the expression of a slight disappointment when Phaon
seemed to have eyes rather for the little Dagmar-
Diodata than for herself, could not change her simple
and kindly feeling for the child. Phaon had shown a
liking for the child from the moment he discovered her
beside her sick mother in the steerage of the *Cormorant*. Of course at that time he was into every corner
of the beautiful ship, with one or other of the officers
or sailors. His affection for Dagmar, often merrily displayed, continued after she passed into Laurence's care,
and indeed was for Laurence a source of quiet joy.

Laurence's disposition, however, was not the kind to be disturbed by such joy in the good-heartedness of a boy.

Certainly the positive and lasting attachment of a youth so free and wild to a child then scarcely two years old, as well as some of the ways in which it was expressed, seemed at times rather strange. An exceptionally true and tender brother could not have shown more concern for her. He had put up netting over her crib so that she should not be plagued by insects. And when counsel was taken as to what would be good for her Phaon threw his advice into the scale. From his wanderings he brought her exquisite shells, lovely corals, coloured stones and crystals, and even one day a Bird of Paradise, which is also called Bird of the Gods, in Latin *Paradisea Apoda,* which is to say the paradisaical footless one.

> Why dost thou lay jewelled pledges
> In her lap who cannot see?
> They are but stones to her, and she
> Will cut herself upon the edges.
> Give them rather to my eyes,
> Thirsting for their loveliness,
> Which thee as their true lord confess,
> And from beholding thee can rise
> To gaze at suns unflinchingly.
> Thou art my sun, so let me gaze,
> Even if I perish in thy blaze,
> And I shall bless thee till I die.

This too is one of Laurence's little poetic efforts.

Laurence's solitude was interrupted as well by other

occasional visitors. Doctor Egli often sought her out. Miss Page appeared, Rodberte appeared, and once the President herself was engineered up the mountain, carried on a woven litter for the greater part of the way by young mothers.

As was her way, the President had not left her sarcasm at home on this occasion either, and her store, although she had scattered it lavishly from her litter, was still undiminished on her arrival. "Well, my dear Laurence," so ran her greeting, as she was lifted out of the litter and deposited on the ground by that slim guardian angel, Phaon, "Well, my dear Laurence, how have the tables of the law progressed? At any rate, I like your holy wilderness much better than Sinai, where once Moses, the male ambassador from God, discoursed with Jehovah."

Laurence could fall in with that jesting humour without in the least compromising her dignity. She was natural through and through, even in her loftiest moments. And so she never had to step down from a pedestal. She said therefore: "I will not contradict a woman of your style and importance, my dear President. But it would oblige me if you would make a note of one small point: I have no ambition to vie with Jehovah in thundering from Sinai. Not because that display of power had precisely the opposite effect from what was intended—think of the golden calf— but because I am opposed to every display of power, and all government by force. I think we shall manage without tables of the law, or judges, or policemen."

—"Yes, yes, I have been a policeman, I have been a policeman, dear Laurence," sighed the artist, "and therefore you will depose me. You will depose me, upon my word you will, my dear, have no doubts about it," she cried, as the lovely Laurence shook her head in deprecation: "You will depose me, and quite rightly. How could an old plucked crow hold her own with a swan?

"Jesting apart," she said then, "of a truth I feel slightly embarrassed in your presence, as if you were a queen. You were always beautiful, but what a strange, what an extraordinary—how shall I say it? —what a peculiar and wonderful change has come over you! I always thought that the celestial air up here must be vastly beneficial, but I did not know that one could become an Isis through breathing it. What if I were to try it too?"

Everybody laughed merrily.

Fräulein Prächtel continued: "Seriously, you are of such unearthly beauty, my dear Laurence, that I consider the Thusnelda of Piloty in the triumphal procession of Germanicus—the picture hangs in Munich—to be nothing in comparison with you. Rule over us, do, and let your outward and inward beauty flow over our colony. Conjure up a second miracle in Île des Dames, a miraculous garden of beauty such as would entice even a sea lion to live on land altogether!"

THE Lake of the Serpent, which Phaon had discovered, so called because of the serpent he found on its banks, was within an hour's easy climb of the cave of the Bona Dea. There Mother Babette with her son Bihari Lâl passed her days in a tiny wooden hut. She, too, often visited the lovely Laurence.

To be sure neither Babette's facile enthusiasms nor the unreality of her religious world were to the taste of the more austere Anglo-Dutchwoman. But the good heart and kindliness of Babette, and her extraordinary inner certainty, overcame that inward resistance. Babette lived apart from the mothers like an anchorite, although she had Bihari Lâl with her. She gave herself up to Buddhistic meditations and trances, and whatever she communicated to others was couched in the language of the legends which have grown up around Buddhism. She was of no use for anything else. The reasons which led Laurence to increase her zeal for transcendentalism were as obscure as all first causes in life and in religion.

Very soon Laurence was regarded by most of the women as a being of a still higher order than that in which they were wont to place themselves on account of the miracle of Île des Dames and its consequences. After only two months of seclusion she ranked as a saint, or rather as one of those wise women skilled in magic runes, who were so highly esteemed among the Nordic peoples. Babette, a little over-strained as usual, had seen her floating high over the tree-tops, and lower through the thickets, and over the meadows, as a light and disembodied spirit. But other visitors as well affirmed that she glided over the garden paths without touching the ashes and, like a Botticelli figure, flitted over the tips of the meadow grasses.

Laurence's daily life in that paradise of cliff and forest was really of an unsullied purity and holiness, which were determined in their expression by her essential character. Her character had fundamentally the same components as that of any civilised European. Ancient and Christian elements, including not only Indian but much other lore, both sacred and profane, were associated in her with what was specifically feminine and generally human. Only the vastness and all-embracing nature of her isolation fused them together in an unusual and excellent degree.

The recluse, who was anything but a penitent, lived in such a manner that she must infallibly have been mistaken for one by those who did not know her. She rose before dawn. Her friend Lolo was not allowed to disturb her in any way at that time, nor even to speak to her. She betook herself out of doors into the open, where she remained until about an hour after sunrise. Lolo knew quite well what she did in these solitary hours, for Laurence made no mystery of it; but it had soon been understood that she must be left entirely to herself during this morning period.

Her first visit was to the waterfall. One of its streams was broad and strong enough to refresh her with a mild and pleasant shower-bath; and with that she began her day. Before she came back to dry land it was her habit to spread her arms out against the descending shaft of water. The hour before sunrise she then spent in deep meditation, in the closest feeling of unity with nature, in whose manifold and holy nearness, however, she saw only the symbol of an inconceivably lofty cosmic destiny. In this hour before the day, she often said, "I am, as it were, still in the bosom of Mother Night, although awake, and I get an inkling through all my sense of her deepest mysteries, and at the same time experience the childish bliss of security in the mother's arms." In this intermediate state Laurence awaited the awakening of the universal sun. As she waited, whispered words escaped her, as: "We await thee, thou pure and mighty light!" or: "After bathing in water I yearn trembling for thee, thou holy bath of fire!" In this intermediate state of waiting for the sun, in which dreams were still dominant, she had daily new and yet related ideas about them, and still more about sleep and its relationship to what the sun, which she called the most blessed star of all, must soon herald. She was of the opinion that even in a state of complete wakefulness sleep is only partially routed. Sleep is always fundamentally present. "If I may use an image to illustrate my meaning," she said to Lolo, "sleep is a wax-candle of vast dimensions, and waking is a tiny burning wick. The idiom of our language speaks of people as more or less wide-awake. Sleep is always one and the same thing, but there are countless degrees of wakefulness. To make a research into these would be of tremendous importance for humanity."

For the reception of the sun-god as he blossomed into splendour Laurence always descended the garden terrace and stepped at the right moment onto a certain rocky pulpit. Here her heart always expanded with the same sense of majesty. And looking into space she felt every time: Verily, spaciousness is joy, and joy is spaciousness. Laurence said of herself that she did not believe that any priest of Bel in Babylon had more rarely missed the rise of the day-star, the sun-god, than she had.

When the sun came, now like an inverted water-lily, now like a purple sea anemone, a rose-coloured mushroom, a tulip of fiery vapour or a ruby chalice, flowing with mysterious power up from the sea-level, it was as if an iron band were loosened from Laurence's breast. She felt as if her limitations, the limitations of humanity must be surpassed. The bowl of fire rises from the deep waters, streaming like a second sea into the world. This birth of the sun is the daily re-birth of mankind. Compared with this waking dream just beginning, she thinks, even the pleasantest waking dream is a torment. But what would it be if the sun of a still higher awakening were to rise some day over this awakening and this sun? But she dismissed this recurring thought as unsound. She thought that it was the sign of a lost innocence when one was not completely on the actual spot where one stood: it signified a divided soul. Therefore she practised repression in order to be sure above all of the sane singleness of her spirit.

In the sunrise she saw the great awakening. She recognised an obscure connection between the sun and consciousness. The sun's awaking power is in many ways a veritable creator. When the sun had swung into the sky, greeted without fail by the feathered world, Laurence followed with holy joy the release of all creatures and souls, the out-flowing of all conceivable power and of the creative forces of the morning.

A moment ago, perhaps, she had seen the still and silent moon, but now the mighty light of the sun had burst in like a conqueror, fighting every inch of the way, seizing, plundering, but above all bestowing, and always triumphant and clear.

We live on the sun as much as, yea, more than on the earth, thought Laurence; more in the sun than in the earth.

The rocky pulpit on which Laurence was wont to await the sun had with its surroundings gradually become her favourite resort. Near it a gulf opened into the sheer and inaccessible cliff, a gorge hollow with caves into whose depths the surf was strangely sucked and as strangely spewed up again, echoing at regular intervals. It was as if something or other were brewing and seething for somebody down below there in a mighty cauldron of rock. When she looked into the gulf that scene from Goethe's Faust came into her mind where holy anchorites are disposed on the side of a mountain settled among gorges. And with her characteristic humour she called the boiling depths the Anchorites' Pot.

But more than that: the whole seraphic finale of the cosmic poem came to life for her beside this gorge.

CHOIR AND ECHO

> Woods bow the head to it,
> Cliffs make their bed of it,
> Roots anchor there at last,
> Stems crowding thick and fast.
> Wave tossing after wave
> Shakes not its deepest cave.
> Lions without a sound
> Peacefully glide around
> The sacred honoured seat,
> Love's holiest retreat.

And she saw Pater Ecstaticus soaring to and fro, she heard him sing psalms of the eternal fire of bliss.

> Fever of agony,
> Billow of ecstasy.

She saw too the Pater Profundus issue from the depths of the rocky chasm, and the Pater Seraphicus come from the middle heights. Then again the choir of blessed youths:

> Hand in hand clinging
> Joyously circle round.

The exhortation rang out:

> Soar aloft to higher circles,
> Growing ever unobserved.

The younger angels made music and then the full-grown angels. And finally before the highest and purest cave there sang Doctor Marianus.

> Yonder float women by
> Heavenward drifting.
> The loveliest borne with them
> Starrily crowned.

And she heard his ecstatic jubilation:

> Mightiest mistress of the world!

It was an almost hallucinatory evocation of the poem which sometimes well-nigh approached its supreme reality. That was not to be wondered at with Laurence, who had founded the cult of the Bona Dea, and who desired to realise in herself the idea of motherhood in its purity as well as the idea of spiritual motherhood. She it was who led the women in the cave of the Bona Dea as they sang the chorus of the Penitents:

> To heights thou art soaring
> Of realms eternal,
> Hear us imploring,
> Peerless, Supernal,
> Gracious, Maternal.

And how should she not have sung from her very

soul the close of the whole Chorus Mysticus, with its
sacred concluding truth?

> The eternal—feminine
> Draws us above.

To sanctify the day: that was the constant formula
according to which Laurence after breakfast described
in what she called her Sylvan Book certain of the inner
experiences of the morning.

When she had finished the entries in her Sylvan
Book she gave herself up for some hours exclusively
to her animals and plants. In her plans for their
welfare and proper care, as well as in the general
arrangement of the spreading pleasure garden which
was like a penitents' grove, she was completely matter-
of-fact and unsentimental; as also in the unwearied
discussion of her further arrangements and plans for
everything that could change this natural and varied
Eden into a temple precinct dignified by art, a kind of
temple city.

This did not exhaust Laurence's curious preoccupa-
tions. She arose by night every third or fourth day
to observe the starry heavens. There was an occult
strain in her. Not quite like Mother Babette's, but
still of such a kind that when she spoke of astrological,
magical and hermetic matters none of the island
mothers could follow her. Sometimes she was subject
to a brooding melancholy which persisted throughout
the day after her nocturnal meditations. In expression

and countenance she then resembled that grand severe meditative woman whom Dürer has endowed with symbolic wings. Like her she sat still the whole day, her open eye turned inward, in a condition of weary dejection which was wellnigh hopeless and yet was but a great questioning and quietude before action. It was the all-embracing, all-penetrating mystery that she questioned.

When she was at last aroused with the tenderest affection from her state of rigidity by Lolo Smith, she was wont to say: "Were you afraid, my dear Lolo? It was only Saturn looking out of my eyes once more."

For all that it became gradually evident why Laurence in her recent farewell address had advocated with an emotion so much more profound than formerly the ideal of the spiritual mother, and had established anew, at two different places, the cult of the Bona Dea. She, herself, had been visited by the Genius loci of Île des Dames, and chosen to accomplish the miraculous creation. From the moment when she became aware of this she felt the glory of the divine favour at least as keenly as Babette had done, only she gave no account at all of how the mysterious event had occurred. In thought, if not in speech, from that time on she used the word "We" instead of "I," and all her thoughts, words and deeds were designed to serve this "We," and especially the second person in it. The new life within her, both physical and spiritual, had not only to be protected from every disturbance, but to be nourished only on what was choice and pure. So from

-C 160 ϶-

this necessity there arose anew the conception of the sanctified and the unsanctified. Her inward life was all-absorbing. Whatever her infinitely refined senses perceived she bestowed almost completely upon herself with a tender self-love that was yet not self-love. "We know well," she often said to herself, "of what We are deemed worthy and what We owe to each other."

Often she repeated aloud in Lolo's presence the sentence: "We have become a single hope." And yet Lolo was the very one who knew best that the lovely recluse had to overcome hours of melancholy weeping.

"Jesus wept over Jerusalem," she used sometimes to say in conclusion. "Why should not a mother weep, who must bear a life which from its first moment of existence, hour by hour, day by day, week by week, month by month, year by year is threatened in a thousand ways by death, until inevitably at last it falls a victim? But let us love, hope and believe. Above all love, and love again!"

"The bitter knowledge of this," she said, "cannot help us. Only beauty and faith can do that."

IX

ANNI PRÄCHTEL and Rodberte Kalb often took tea together alone as they had first done soon after the landing on Île des Dames.

It was always a peaceful function, for each of the ladies was a match for the other in sarcasm and, when occasion arose, in malice. But for the most part these attributes of their natures were directed by mutual agreement against the social life of Île des Dames.

"What would the world come to," said Anni, on one such occasion, "without social taboos? One has plenty of time here to realise the importance and significance of taboo in the damned old masculine civilisation, God preserve it! What a horrible mess it would be in without taboo: not only would sons defile their mothers and fathers their daughters, not only would every straw rick be set ablaze, and the calls of nature be openly satisfied in every panelled salon and ball-room, but one would also stick bits of glass and coal into one's mouth, as children do. If one felt so disposed, one would kill, roast and eat up other men, yes, one would ride out paper-chasing on a pregnant sow without finding it remarkable. It is conceivable that, without taboo, one could not distinguish the Kaiser from a man with two legs, nor his ministers from grass-hoppers."

After this example of her well-known cutting style the President was silent and shrouded herself in mighty clouds of smoke. Rodberte laughed to herself.

"The taboo," she began after a while, "oh yes, taboo. That means for me not the canonisation of anything, but its inviolability. What sacrifices have I not had to make in my time because of such taboos! With every step that I took, my mother, my governess, and my aunts cried: 'Taboo, taboo!' If I called my ugly grandmother ugly, or my ill-tempered grandmother ill-tempered, or a fetid joint of veal stinking, or an imbecile diplomat imbecile, or an indecent Biblical passage indecent, or denied the truth of a rank lie that masqueraded as a generally accepted truth, and called it what it really was—at once they all screamed 'Taboo, taboo!'

"And yet," said Anni, "our island taboo, as you must admit, Rodberte, is of the utmost importance for our untroubled development, and indeed for our general prosperity."

"You mean the principle: *La recherche de la paternité est interdite.*"

Anni replied: "I mean the whole ramification of the systematic taboo that has grown up around our progenitor."

"My dear Anni," said Rodberte, "let us be prudent. You know that the thing, the object, the author, let us say, whose existence you have touched upon, stands so completely outside all discussion that it might be fatal for us to be overheard."

"What is Phaon doing, by the way? Are you still teaching him, Rodberte? I have not caught sight of him since we visited our newly-installed Mother of God a week ago."

"What brings you so suddenly to Phaon, my friend?" asked Fräulein Kalb, apparently astonished.

"Have you any objection to my enquiries for the boy?" said the artist with a laugh. And she added: "You must be lenient with me if the egg-shell of masculine civilisation, as it were, still sticks unofficially to me and makes me concerned about the welfare of a boy. It is not altogether unimportant, even in spite of the taboo."

Fräulein Kalb answered:

"As far as I know, Phaon is falling more and more into a state of divine barbarity. The good Miss War of course will not admit that. She does not notice that the handsome rascal has completely disentangled himself from her influence. He possesses a perfectly irresistible knack of humbugging people, and especially the worthy War. It is true that they have often a thorough set-to, but Phaon always comes off best when he uses the weapon of his childlike tenderness against her.

"After every such turn-up he usually avoids the Academy, for half a week and longer, and the good War can whistle for him."

The President replied with a laugh; "I declare, as

God is my witness, if I were not Anni Prächtel I would rather be Phaon than anyone else."

"There's many a man and many a woman could well sympathise with you," said Fräulein Kalb. "The wicked young ruffian is in the most fortunate situation perhaps that was ever granted to a young man since the creation. It is remarkable beyond all conception."

Anni wanted to know what was so remarkable.

Fräulein Kalb retorted:

"Everything is remarkable. I shall guard myself against giving you an explanation of what in particular is particularly remarkable. You will not entrap me into taking up or recognising any attitude towards the events on our balmy island other than that officially established and approved."

"I too," cried Prächtel, warmly, "am far from doing so. If truffles are made by thunder, and if a lioness conceives from the roaring of a lion, why should we entertain even the absurd remnant of doubt of the supernatural origin of our merry progeny which sometimes crops up still?"

"When I visited Laurence recently she unfolded to me as the latest result of her mystic researches what I can only describe as an egg-theory. She spoke largely of Leda-Latonia, the Egg-Mother. Apparently it is the egg out of which everything, absolutely everything has emerged."

"If our Popess says so, I agree with it unconditionally," said the artist. "In the circumstances, I even forego the raising of the old problem whether the egg

came before the hen, or the hen before the egg. In
Île des Dames we are so gloriously credulous. And
why should we not be credulous? In this heavenly
river-valley I could easily let it pass if everyone affirmed that my mother laid at least ten dozen eggs
every year, and hatched me out specially under a
broody duck. Let us settle all that entirely as we
please, for our pleasure is the chief thing. And besides
there is no small charm in such capers of the imagination. At least they annihilate ordinary triviality.
And somehow such unnatural ideas have something enticing about them; they seem to express symbolically
something profoundly obscure, a truth which could
not be apprehended in any other way. Symbolic eggs
of this kind, for example, are mostly eggs of air or
wind. They escape from every attempt to touch them,
to grasp them with one's hands, and examine them,
because they are insubstantial. Yet in spite of that
they are real. And surprising as it may sound, the
fate of humanity is mostly and predominantly determined by such realities. An instinctive mystical thirst
of the human soul makes us revel in them: its satisfaction produces every conceivable pleasure, even the
highest; and 'faith is happiness,' as the hackneyed
proverb runs, a sentence which the most completely
of all sentences in the world expresses the truth. But
the power of faith which brings happiness must be well
exercised, like every other organ, if it is not to degenerate."

"Well," said Fräulein Kalb drily of a sudden, taking

the coffee cup from her thin lips. . . . "Well, we shall not venture to doubt that our worthy Laurence will have laid the said egg of wind or air, in four months from now at the latest."

After this remark there was nothing left for the ladies but to give way to an uncontrollable fit of laughter.

When it had subsided Fräulein Kalb said: "All the same! I laugh, but all the same! Satisfied faith, poetic illusion, and holy ignorance, these alone are poetry: and yet poetry, strange to say, is rooted in the purest truth."

Fräulein Prächtel thought the matter over, and agreed with her.

"And in general," continued Rodberte, "although we are so antipathetic, and although I am often forced to slash my way through Laurence's poetic island-obsession to give myself room to breathe, yet I recognise the value of her strange and powerful influence."

"Let us admit," she went on, "that for us the problem of faith presents a real difficulty in one of its aspects, that is to say, where faith absolutely contradicts the inevitable appearance of reality, the obviously true."

"For what other reason has our island-taboo been established with so much obscure Orphic deliberation, or created in such concerted silence?" said the artist. "And it is not only the gods who love mystery: wherever the most dangerous breaches in religious doctrine happen, the love of mystery inherent in mankind will evoke the strongest faith so that mystery and faith together make the gap more impenetrable than the rest of the structure. And besides, in some way or other the famous Mormon spy-glasses Urim and Thummim, which no doctrine of revelation can ever quite dispense with, have fallen into our hands. If we look through them properly we can see what is invisible to the profane, though if we look through the wrong end we see much that is objectionable, but not the sacred truth."

"I admit that I often get a great deal of amusement from looking through the wrong end of Urim and Thummim," said Fräulein Kalb. "For example I was once fishing in the Bay of the Enchanted Fishes. There appeared . . . but we had better leave it there."

"Why?" said the artist. "There is nobody within hearing, Rodberte."

"Well then," began Rodberte, "you know the Bay of the Enchanted Fishes. Let me serve up to you a romantic little fairy tale, which may not be so far from the truth. Well, it was in the Bay of the Enchanted Fishes, where I chanced to be on the day the steamer was sighted, which fortunately, or unfortunately, did not land. I was there, anyhow, and as I have said already, there appeared . . . no, that won't do. I cannot begin in that fashion."

"Bless my soul, who appeared?" cried the artist laughing; "don't make such a fuss about it."

"You must be patient, President. If you break the thread of my story I shall be guilty against my will

-❲ 168 ❳-

of an offence, or a crime, against the inviolability of our supreme mystery. The whole affair is a pure vision, although it would be difficult, even in a mere fabrication, to out-do a thing so marvellous as the Bay of the Enchanted Fishes.

"For I always clamber down to that bay when I am seized by a certain impulse, which has its dangerous side. I might describe it as an irresistible desire for Nirvana, although one cannot prove the existence of Nirvana. Believe me, President, that without being in any way a prey to despair I have often been within an ace of taking a final plunge into the Nirvana of the enchanted bay."

Fräulein Prächtel announced that such things were completely against her fundamental principles, and persisted in enquiring who it was besides Rodberte that appeared on the shore of the bay.

Rodberte however did not let herself be bullied. "Listen to me," she continued: "I lay on a hot tongue of basalt, and considered the exquisitely clear, exquisitely coloured waters of the bay. One is reminded of Sindbad the Sailor and of countless other tales from the Thousand and One Nights when one looks down into those crystalline green depths, in and over which play scaly fishes of every known colour, some of them actually like denizens of another planet. And naturally I looked up also to where, above the mighty enclosing walls of rock and the overgrown crags and cliffs, the sky is dark even at high noon. I beg of you, President, do not be daunted by the slight inconvenience; pay a visit some time to this earthly paradise. I assure you, all your previous impressions will seem stale by comparison, and you will shudder at the thought that you could have been so unlucky as to die without beholding that highest manifestation of earthly beauty, which seems at the same time to be the first glimpse of a super-terrestrial beauty.

"Into the bay, as you know, there pours from an immense height a water-fall to which Phaon has given the ineradicable name of Pisse-vache du Ciel."— Fräulein Prächtel interrupted enthusiastically: "The boy has some wonderful inspirations."—"This cow of heaven, then, sends down continually foaming masses of celestial water. It gives one a gruesome shudder to look at the place whence they are hurled from the bowels of the rock in a ponderous arch down into the precipitous chasm. Cloud upon cloud of water shoots into it and rises in fans of vapour, especially at the point where the majestic sweep of the fall loses the character of a solid stream defying the surrounding free and boundless air, and dissolves into watery veils. But with what refreshing and fragrant clouds of exquisite pearly drops the heavenly water sweeps and waves and ripples on its long descent, till its glorious diamond dust turns the surface of the bay to a blinding glitter of gold and silver!

"I find it impossible to stop. Upon my word, it is no wonder if the recollections of such an intoxicating hour, of such a natural impression, should beguile one from the hundredth to the thousandth repetition.

Think of a perpetual triple rainbow, whose coloured sheen illumines the many ravines, overgrown with lovely verdure. I would take it for granted, Anni, that even you would become a poet in this bay among the magnificent revels of Nature. Imagine, for example, a flock of three to four thousand large milk-white crested cockatoos with flamingo-coloured breasts, which flutter to and fro in this contest between light and water. Think of an enormous bird like a peacock, also white and with an enormous trailing tail which falls in a green plume perpetually bedewed with rainbow drops. A spray of jewels glistens around him. It is as if he scattered from his pulsing wings diamonds, rubies, sapphires and every other kind of jewel, a second rain within the rain. And think—he spreads his tail and shows his semi-circle of metallic blue peacock-eyes behind flying and glittering strands of glass. Such birds, and many other feathered marvels wheel and perch on the rocky walls and enjoy the reviving, ravishing and intoxicating lovers' quarrels of the light, the darkness and the flood, of the rock and the living world, whose children, the colours, appear in an inexhaustible variety.

"And imagine now that you have withdrawn your gaze again from the majesty of this drama which is both sublime and radiant with loveliness, and which is accompanied by the echo and re-echo of a soft and gentle murmuring, composed of whisperings, rustlings and sighings, sometimes near and sometimes far away. You have, then, withdrawn eye and ear, and directed both toward the depths of the enclosed arm of the sea, where in countless colours, duskier than white and brighter than black, these mysterious dumb fishes continually flicker as if in the rhythm of a peaceful dance, these enchanted creatures, representing a form of life perpetually alien and removed from us, which seem to be dyed in the glittering rainbow spanned over the rushing waters of heaven,—and, President, you have had more than a glimpse into the unfathomable empire of Beauty.

"When one has seen and experienced this, as I say, it is easy to believe that the meaning of existence on this side of the grave has been exhausted."

"It is obvious that, like all of us, you are gradually succumbing to the local climate, my dear Kalb. You are far removed from the diabolically sarcastic and overweening super-woman whom I knew you to be in Europe. You are markedly inclining to the extra and super-terrestrial attitude prevailing here, which well-nigh regards life itself as only another myth. I recommend you to give a sermon next Sunday instead of the handsome René. But now tell me at last who appeared in the glorified ravine of the Bay of the Enchanted Fishes. For I am bursting with impatience and curiosity." These were the artist's words.

Rodberte replied: "Do not think that I have no purpose in dwelling so long on the description of my stage setting, which in any case, I am sorry to say, is not yet finished. Absolutely you must gain the impression that here we are dealing with a place outside and beyond this world . . . so that you will not be astonished by the apparition of a real god and a real goddess."

The artist said: "I have guessed it! Eros, my dear Rodberte."

"Whoever guesses Eros," she returned "is nearly always right, for in every way he is life itself. Only Eros is everywhere. He does not need to be brought into the scene." With these words Rodberte set herself to continue her story.

"The god who arrived first from the southern shaft of the brightest of the three rainbows on one of the glittering emerald cliff-terraces might best be compared with one of the twenty incarnations of Vishnu, the all-sustaining, when he appears as a beautiful youth bearing a bow and arrows, and, when asked, does not himself know that he is Vishnu. At any rate, there came out of the perpetual rainbow a young god radiant with more than human beauty, whom, I am convinced, the gods upon their thrones adored, and who seemed to have come to overthrow the thrones of earthly kings. And whether you believe it or not, celestial choirs of welcome suddenly sounded, sang and echoed from all the rocky walls, yes, hundreds of the enchanted fish leaped sheer from the water with joy."

"Did not this youth," asked the artist, "bear a certain resemblance to Phaon?"

"There is a Phaon who was celebrated by the poetess Sappho. He lived on Lesbos and plied his ship as the most beautiful of ferrymen between that island and Chios. Aphrodite in person appeared to him and unveiled herself and proposed that he should be her lover. Therefore he remained cold when not only the divine Sappho but all the other women in Lesbos burned with desperate love for him.—If you mean that Phaon, President, the shining apparition had really a resemblance to Phaon, as you will see presently. For I saw what he did not see, glowing eyes appearing here and there, fixed upon him; let us say, the eyes of the Lesbian nymphs."

"And the poetess Sappho? Where was she?" asked Fräulein Prächtel, looking up with a grimly malicious air.

"Let us leave Phaon, Sappho, and the island of Lesbos out of it. It was an analogy, and nothing more. If you see anything more in it you do so on your own responsibility," said Rodberte. "The place might more easily be some place among the Hyperboreans, and that youth a son of Apollo, newly alighted from his fiery chariot."

"If one were willing to adopt the symbolism of our noble Laurence, the Sappho of Île des Dames," interjected the President, "that might equally well point to Phaon again."

"Well, this way or that," returned Rodberte, "arrange it as you like. I will tell you now quite soberly what befell me, whether waking or dreaming, in connection with this divine boy, doubtless the Genius of our island.

"The blissful youth came leaping—leaping like a god, of course—along a path which was certainly known to him down towards the blue bay of the fishes. I thought to myself: You are the loveliest prey that was ever pursued through the coloured echoing water-spout of Pisse-vache du Ciel. It was literally as if he were being pursued. But scarcely did that become clear to me before this lovely Epiphany disappeared like a deceiving mirage."

"I am very sorry for that," said the artist drily, "for I had really set my heart on something quite different."

"It can't be helped," said Fräulein Kalb, "I sometimes have visions.

"For example, I am always obsessed night and day by one and the same vision. A hunt is proceeding. An extraordinary hunt!—It is not, thank God, a hunt like that described in the Bacchæ of Euripides, where men and beasts are rent in pieces by divinely frenzied mænads; it is much more reminiscent of a hunt with Diana and her huntresses. But even a hunt like that, where hounds are set on the trail of a wild boar or of a sixteen-pointer, is much too bloody and wild and noisy to correspond to the visionary hunt of my dream. That is rather in its essentials bloodless, silent and mysterious, but yet it has a wild fervour of its own. My inner eye sees only a woman taking part in this hunt. It is a never-ceasing hunt. It is followed by the huntresses both day and night the whole year through. Not in close-ranked Bacchic troops, nor yet in hunting-trains like Diana's, as they are painted by Rubens and others, but in hidden isolation. There are many huntresses, perhaps they are aware of each other,

but they dare not recognise and see each other, for
they are taboo to each other!—So there are many of
them, but what they hunt is always one and the same
game.

"I am reminded of a strophe from the Bacchic
chorus:

> O, could I fare to Kypros, island of Aphrodite,
> where the Loves dwell, the hearts of mortals enchanting,
> and to Paphos, where hundred-armed
> fertilizing the rainless fields
> runs the untameable river:
> or where rises in beauty the seat of the muses, Pieria,
> the majestic slope of Olympus.
> Thither carry me, Bromios, Bromios,
> thou that leadest the Bacchæ:
> there are the Graces, and there is passion,
> and there the Bacchæ follow the rout in freedom.

"If we like we have the island of Aphrodite, we have
Loves, we have the seat of the Muses, we have an
Olympus towering in beauty, and certainly smoking!
Here are the Graces, and Passion is here, and the
Bacchæ follow the rout in freedom—of course, all in
my hallucination.

"Well, in my hunt the prey followed is always one
and the same, yes, it is even in a certain sense torn
piecemeal and divided, although bloodlessly.

"'For the goad of desire urges women more in-
sistently than men,' says Pausanias. So it is goaded
women whom I see circling our island Olympus by day

and night in pursuit of the one prey, following the trail of the same precious victim through ravines and gorges, caves and thickets, forest and river-banks, by sea-shores and in desert places, between heaps of slag and fuming craters."

"Well and good," interrupted Fräulein Prächtel again. "I am now completely in the picture. And the prey is none other than your rainbow-genius."

"In the dream-sense, you may be right."

"But, confound it," said the artist, "give me a somewhat more carnal description of your handsome, rascally divinity."

"That I can do, for without having an inkling of my presence, he appeared next quite close to me.

"I was still in that magical pleasure-garden, seductive beyond all conception, which is maintained by Pisse-vache du Ciel in a state of perpetual luxuriance, bearing blossom and fruit together, on the shore of the gulf called La Rade des Poissons ensorcelés.

"Bright yellow and well cared for the ambrosial hair, falling to the shoulders, and there cut short evenly. Shoulders, arms, hips and legs, as if made of copper-golden bronze. The whole body not too large but yet firm, supple and slim. Every muscle defined with youthful symmetry, and yet athletic in development, like batteries or gloriously vital accumulators of fiery and living powers. A countenance full of the highest nobility, and yet alive with an expression of Promethean audacity, betraying the kiss of Aphrodite ecstatically given and received.

"So stood the hunted hunter, the magnificent archer against whose beating heart and heaving chest the arrows of so many quivers were directed, a few paces away from me, quite unexpectedly there, returned to life, and mirroring himself in the blue of the bay.

"He looked over in my direction. I lay hidden under the laurel bushes that grew down to the very edge of my promontory. His eye, absorbed in the pleasure of its own enjoyment, wandered over me without seeing me. So I saw the blue of his eyes, shining like the Bay of the Enchanted Fishes itself. If you would give me time, President, if you were ever disposed to grant me time enough, I should give you a longer description of them; they are worth it, believe me. When you think their fire is blue and true, it flashes suddenly a feline green, and when you think it is all soul, the next moment you would swear that you were looking at the hard brilliance of an emerald. Giordano Bruno said certainly: '*Non est lapis sine anima,*' but this stone is absolutely soulless: when I saw these eyes and their almost burning glitter—they seemed to shoot out tiny phosphorescent sparks—I was quite in agreement with Laurence's idea of her pupil as the son of Hyperios, the youthful Helios, or at least as a descendant of the sun. Pindar too calls the sun's rays the mother of the eyes—"

"Hello," cried Fräulein Prächtel, "I should like to know what your bronze genius has to do with our madcap and Miss War's fosterling, Phaon?"

"Oh, nothing, nothing at all, of course. We are suffering from the heat, President, and I, too, suffered finally on that day from the glare of noonday, for in my retreat by the bay, I imagined the following:

"In the vision I thought I saw our revered Laurence Hobbema appear on the same spot where the island-genius first appeared."

The artist said: "I am not surprised. I was quite definitely expecting that."

"You would not say that if you had experienced yourself the utter convincingness of that astounding vision. It would have thrown you into a state of amazement to see a certain person standing clearly and tangibly before you, and yet to know that it cannot be and is not she.

"Of course, I must to some extent qualify what I have said. Laurence does not always appear in this grand style.

"The rainbow spray through which she came on to the rocky terrace hung like a divine gloriole behind her. And, besides, everything about her was heightened into freedom, wildness and majesty.

"I was sufficiently astonished to see her at all, but I was even more astonished by the fact that a person can remain the same and yet be transfigured.

"Without doubt she had arrived in great haste and precipitation at the spot where she stood and eagerly spied around her, and after a terrific chase. It seemed to me that her beautiful limbs quivered from the exertion like those of a race-horse. Her hair was loose. It fluttered snakily around her, fanned by the wind from the waterfall, and moistened by its pearly dew. I thought I saw that she was hot and blown with running, and that she inhaled with satisfaction the draughts of ozone and the reviving freshness and moisture of Pisse-vache du Ciel.

"I thought that I must infer from the slow movement of her bronzen breasts that she was drawing breaths of almost superhuman ecstasy. It seemed to me that she was drinking in beauty, health, and divine life in a transport of rapture.

"Beneath her the spray was rising in vapour from the warm moss; so that she seemed to be standing with her feet in a small white cloud. And suddenly I heard the cry of a bird of prey. To call it the cry of a bird of prey is to describe only the first momentary impression. If an eagle had uttered it, he would have had to be as big as a griffin. It was the basalt walls of the ravine that gave it such resonance. They tossed it to and fro, this distinctly bird-like cry, which brought a dithyrambic note into the holy choral music of the ravine and the Bay of the Enchanted Fishes, wonderfully thrilling it.

"A second and a third cry rang out, such cries as I would not credit Laurence, or any of our island-mothers, with uttering, and were answered on all sides as if by divinely-frenzied Bacchantes awakening within the basalt walls. My dear President, I assure you on my oath that I am not in the least capable of describing exhaustively the nature and the effect of this penetrating cry.

"About its nature I can only say this: it bore a certain resemblance to the cry of a bird, and to the halloo of an Alpine herdsman, but its most characteristic attribute was a tone absolutely new and to me unheard upon the earth. And yet it aroused a strangely exciting, primeval, cosmic memory. The effect of this unearthly yell of triumph, of hate, of love, of yearning, of pain and pleasure, of life and death, this scream of terror, of desperation, and of eternal bliss—the effect of this trenchant alarum was manifold.

"As far as I was concerned, it seemed to me that immediately, throughout the whole of Nature, the coming of an invisible god was heralded. The same feeling made my heart palpitate. I had the feeling that a spirit had entered into the cliffs, the plants, the stream, the air and the light, and that the rich music sounding in the great bell of the ravine was heightened into the festal solemnity of a wedding hymn, amorous and captivating. The heat can cause curious states of intoxication.

"In spite of the heat, however, an icy chill crept down my spine, so that in the end I was as numb as a block of wood.

"The cry had a similar effect upon my Genius. His mouth opened; he breathed deeply and quickly, after forgetting to breathe at all for some minutes; his head was wrenched round towards the sound until he saw the Bacchante, who was now recognisable as Laurence, flying rather than leaping down from terrace to terrace, as from one cloud to another, with the flame of her black hair streaming behind her; I heard sounds of anguish wrung from his bursting heart."

"You have a great talent for roasting people before a slow fire, my good Rodberte," said the artist.

"That may well be," retorted Rodberte, "for when without any fault of mine I had to look on, not daring to cry out or betray my presence, I was myself roasted at a slow fire."

She fell silent, then continued: "I was stretched on the spit then, as I have said, and had next to overhear a discourse of the gods. It was not at all pleasant for me to be a witness of such a delicate encounter. I have never taken pleasure in eavesdropping and spying, nor can I reconcile either of them with honour. But what is to be done when an ardent goddess is on the track of a coy young god, and corners him in the heat of noon in the pleasantest and most secluded of all ravines? And I could never have forgiven myself if I had interrupted an irretrievably divine hour. So for the moment the only thing I could do was to keep myself more deeply hidden than ever. It was as much as my life was worth to betray myself.

"I endured it. And to-day I would give up for nothing in the world the remembrance of my delight in that drama."

"So it was not a mere vision after all!"

Rodberte cried: "President, it was a vision! But it was of such a kind that it sent a flame of astonishment, a flame of devotion, a shudder of wonder, through all my limbs. Only think, President, only think, I was present at the consummation of the highest and most secret mystery of our island."

X

THANKS to the mystic connection which a God, a demon, or a Genius had formed with the colony, it had gradually bloomed as has been said, into a flourishing state.

In the House of Good Hope the artist still presided, while the lovely Laurence exercised, of course, as the chief priestess, a much greater influence.

A kind of spiritual inventory, one of Rodberte's ideas, was carried out in due time. Each of the colonists had to undergo an oral examination by the committee, whose subtle questions were framed for the purpose of discovering any existing abilities, accomplishments, knowledge and experience. This interview marked only the beginning of the whole procedure, which continued with interruptions for a year, or longer if required, and in some cases never came to an end.

Each person thus interviewed had a special record opened for her, and some of the records grew to gigantic proportions, and often where results were least to be expected. Results, however, were above all desired. The idea was to rescue and make available for the present and future life of the colony every resource of civilisation which it had brought with it into exile.

The whole of this harvest was accommodated in a room of the so-called Academy, which was entitled the Record Office. Rodberte was in charge of it. The whole harvest was here set down on evenly cut square tablets of slate. One part of the island consisted of shale, and a spot had been discovered which yielded any number of fine slates.

This Record Office was a model of organisation. The slate tablets were arranged and housed in strong cases. From what the mothers could remember of the trades, professions and occupations of their parents, grandparents, brothers, sisters, and other relations there resulted a store of practical information that could be utilised to train potters, carpenters, wheelwrights, and many other kinds of artisans.

Fräulein Auguste, an elderly hump-backed woman, had offered her services as secretary to Rodberte, and it was thanks chiefly to her unwearying zeal, her regular and loving labour among the records, that the whole establishment had achieved a high importance. Since there were no illiteracies among the mothers of Île des Dames each of them was enjoined after the first oral examination, the results of which formed the nucleus of each record, to write down a circumstantial account of her life. It was added to the nucleus. From that time on the record was kept open year in, year out for supplementary information. If the colonist wished to add something (only experiences, subjective or objective, dating back to the time before the landing were required) she had merely to write it down and give in the slate to the hump-back Auguste, or report it verbally in the record office.

Every slightest addition was then scientifically classified in the record.

Thus they succeeded in assembling from A to Z a thoroughly valuable and useful encyclopædia, which gave tolerably good information on every branch of science and art, and on a number of practical matters.

Needless to say, the best of them, such as Anni Prächtel, Tyson Page, Fräulein von Warniko, Rodberte Kalb, Miss War, the lovely Laurence, and Doctor Egli took their own records in hand, and carried them through with a high moral seriousness. They knew very well what they owed to themselves, and still more what they owed to posterity. For example, if Doctor Egli had not tabulated little by little her still fresh medicinal knowledge, the science of medicine would have disappeared from Île des Dames on the day of her death. And if timely measures had not been taken to avert the danger, all memory of the old masculine civilisation and its cultural elements, together with the whole history of the world and of humanity outside Île des Dames would eventually have been lost. In the opinion of the leading ladies that would have meant the death of all spiritual life on the island, which was now usually called the Island of the Great Mother, and with the death of its spiritual life, of its world-redeeming idea.

The influence of the Academy, and especially of its Record Office, its library, and its continuously vital

currents of information, was unexpectedly rich in blessing. If one counted the manifestation of the procreative god, genius, or demon as the first great gift, truly
a gift from heaven to the poor outcasts, this would
have to rank as the second, proceeding from a more
earthly and rational source: it could not thus have the
same value as the divine gift, but it took the highest
possible place next to it. Because of it, the colony began really to take root, to establish itself, to enter upon
a final, rounded, full and rich growth.

The spiritual honey was, as it were, unweariedly
carried into the hive of the Academy, and there ex-
changed for information which could be carried away
and disseminated. It became a social centre, inspired
by what must have been in Rodberte an eminently social idea. It was like a spiritual beehive, but in one
respect infinitely superior to a real hive, since in its
cells the stored honey could only accumulate, and not
diminish, however much was taken away. This ever-
increasing, inexhaustible wealth of the community, in
the creation of which even the least of the colonists
could boast that she had shared, constituted already a
body of knowledge too great for individuals to survey,
a second great world, fearlessly to be explored even to
its most remote regions, where the boundaries of Île
des Dames were non-existent.

It was a pleasure to see with what foresight and pre-
caution, with what genuine, maternal joy and industry
the island mothers, lovely and warm as mellow fruits,
brought in spiritual nourishment for their children.

All they did in this way sprang from an inner joy of creation. As they had continued with patience to bear children, and had held them to those blessed founts of milk, their bosoms, with a passionately creative joy and love of life, so now, moved by the same instinct, they gave, as it were, the life-blood of their souls to shield from future spiritual death those whom they had once carried under their hearts. They did it, however, as, in spite of their ardour, they did nearly everything, with a feeling of solemn exaltation; for they were deeply aware that they were building a world anew from the very foundations and in the most enigmatical circumstances.

The mystic procreation, the canonized mystery of Île des Dames, had produced a new system of morality, in accordance with which, for example, the miracle of creative love was restricted, for each of the mothers, to a certain day, or at most, to a few days, the period of the mystic marriage. In connection with this there prevailed certain customs, which had been established, strangely enough, in almost silent unanimity, and the observance of which was enforced with jealous severity by the community. In every other respect both severity and jealousy were almost completely eliminated from their social relations, partly because there were no men, and partly because the heavenly climate and this natural simplicity of life were highly conducive to a pleasant and harmonious existence. Their common need, their common rescue, their common election, their rise to a new form of society, passing from the patri-

-C 188 }-

archate to the matriarchate, bound all of them together as if by a family tie.

Unfortunately, with the increase in children the matriarchate ceased to be a matter of course. The leading women, the women of intelligence, saw the continuance of their Paradise vaguely threatened by the birth of each boy. In this Eden at all events Woman had appeared first, and then after her, as if made from her rib by the invisible Demiurge, Bihari Lâl, the Man. But here too the serpent, the Tempter, seemed to be hidden somewhere, and to be lifting his menacing head in places.

They wanted to prevent the mischief in time, since this time, quite reasonably, they had no desire to be cheated by Adam of their garden of Eden, as they had been once by Eve and the serpent. So secret councils were held by Laurence, the President, Rodberte and Doctor Egli, in which these resourceful women discussed every possible method of countering the danger.

It was natural that Doctor Egli should tackle the question with that cold-bloodedness and readiness to help which characterises the surgeon, and that she should make the most radical proposals.

The advice of Malthus could not be considered in this case, since no one could give orders to the invisible and divine procreative power. Of course, the life-giving genius, whether he was Zeus or some other Olympian, ought to have known what he owed, excuse the expression, to his harem, and should have arranged for the birth of one boy at most to every hundred girls.

Either this did not lie within his power, since perhaps the gods as little as modern medical science could solve the problem of how to produce male or female infants at will, or he had no further interest in this Women's State than his deeds evinced: and so the Mothers in Council also passed lightly over the matter.

It must be interpolated that the President, Rodberte and Fräulein Auguste had all received the honorary title of Mother.

The method of Lycurgus, who exposed sick or otherwise superfluous children on Mount Taygetus, and still another method which left the patient alive, endowing him only for life with a somewhat high and often valuable singing voice, were both suggested by Doctor Egli. But that clever and determined woman could not prevail. Laurence, Rodberte, as well as Fräulein Prächtel, opposed her successfully, knowing that a similar defeat would be her lot in the full assembly of mothers.

They thought rightly, though the influence of Doctor Amanda Egli on the island mothers was naturally very great. For though the difficult business of bearing children was easier here than elsewhere, the doctor was indispensable. This serious business, moreover, was the most widespread and the most important on Île des Dames. Amanda Egli had already trained a staff of assistants, and educated each of the mothers to a certain extent in medical knowledge, but still she remained the highest authority and did all the essential work. Her round of work and duties was so large, especially as she herself bore children, that perhaps she was the only one who was not bemused by the trance of bliss on Île des Dames.

As was remarked, her influence was great, but yet she could not have dared to put her proposal to the hazard. Even though she was necessary to all the mothers and had bound each one to her by obligations, still her cold-blooded intentions would, in the general awakening of maternal feeling, have aroused a storm of indignation.

In this phase of the colony's development, when the oldest children were not yet more than five years old, there still prevailed everywhere the still and ardent passion of maternity. It blossomed in these women as a completely new experience. Unhampered by the presence of men everything that was purely feminine could intensify and express itself freely. Suckling their children openly at the breast, these mothers felt themselves curiously changed and renewed, and at one with the meaning of their existence. Their sensuality glutted itself almost completely in this way. In this world and at this time they would have felt men to be alien creatures, unpleasant intruders. Along with this maternal warmth, there developed a concomitant sexual coldness. The complete naturalness of their condition had made prevalent a morality akin to that of the purely animal world, where, as is well known, the female's need for the male is restricted to a narrowly defined period of time.

Laurence's influence and will towards the ideal were

chiefly responsible for the noble orderliness which distinguished the whole of Motherland. Ville des Dames was by this time only a historic city. On high-lying healthy places, on grassy hillocks and in lovely thickets, by streams and fountains, lightly-timbered shelters, pleasant and airy, had been constructed, proportionately disposed so as to be sufficiently far from or near each other. They rang with joyful life. It would be a fascinating task to expound how easy was work here, and how manifold the interests of the day, with the increasing swarm of children. Along with the increase of population, the growth of a new generation which knew no other world but Île des Dames, the feeling of desolation that the mothers had became more and more evanescent. And how delightful, how bursting with vitality were the beings whom one saw growing up! Thanks to God knows what secret principle of selection they all had an air of breeding. The races of Europe seemed to be fused in a new and higher type. But in spite of their differences, all these demoniacally exuberant creatures were bound by a common and unmistakable resemblance in the colour of the eyes and hair.

It must here be mentioned and admitted that the coloured ball of existence and growth on Île des Dames was not without a few dark spots. The pretty mulatto, Alma, had hanged herself about the year one after the birth of Bihari Lâl. Three or four of the other castaways had come in the course of time to sad ends in different ways, because in spite of all their efforts they had not been touched by the procreative power. A few went mad for that same reason. Rumours which could not be laid hinted that Mother Amanda Egli had something to do with these occurrences.

It must also be ascribed to Mother Amanda that eventually, in spite of everything, energetic steps were one day taken against the danger which the matriarchate ran from the constant accumulation of boys. Now again, as before, there were bitter contests, which, fortunately, however, made only a temporary disturbance in the fruitful peace of the empire of mothers, and were suppressed by general consent. As a result of this unanimity the five-year-old boys were deported to a certain far-off district. This measure certainly dispensed with any cruelty, but yet it bore witness to the fact that it is impossible to carry out an idea beyond a certain point without great harshness. Naturally this excursion was attended by many tears, shed not by the departing ones, but by the mothers who were left behind; sighs were heard, and even shrieks. But at last the mothers pulled themselves together and overcame this weakness.

These urchins, who had brought with them into the world a wanton strength and demoniacal wildness, had become a plague, indeed. Every admonition, every attempt to rear them in gentleness, was fruitless. The rascals were at the bottom of all the confusion, breaches of the peace, and mischief that ever annoyed the mothers They often asked themselves how it was possible that they had come to have such offspring, such semi-brutes, who seemed to have tiger-teeth and claws, with which they fell not only upon each other, but not seldom upon their mothers too. Sometimes they beat those holy women regardlessly with their fists, and it happened sometimes that even the most majestic mother was unable to settle one of these youngsters.

The geographical formation of Île des Dames provided excellent means for a separation of the sexes. The island curved round the wide Golfe des Dames, which, on the west, had only one small rock-bound outlet to the sea. On the east of this lovely land-locked sea the two embracing arms of the island were joined by a small and rocky isthmus. The boys were conveyed over it from the southern to the northern part, and established on the northern shore of the gulf in a settlement which, for the time, certainly required the help and supervision of women specially selected for the task.

It was a touching scene when the first batch of boys took farewell of their respective mothers, and were conducted over the isthmus by the hump-backed Fräulein Auguste, who rode on a zebu-cow. After the way in which they had been taught, the youngsters could only look upon the expedition as a kind of school excursion. They did not understand the cries and tears of their mothers. Indeed, all of these had to catch their offspring for the last farewell, here with a kind of lasso, there by the collar or by the hair. Many, however, did not succeed even by offering a banana, or an enticing piece of sausage or the like, in luring their wild monkeys down from a peak or a palm-tree.

In this newly-created Manland, besides the humpback Fräulein Auguste, Mucci Smith and Phaon more particularly took charge of the outcasts.

The whole measure was criticised as inadequate by Mother Egli and a certain Mother Philomela Schwab. They declared that an opportunity had been definitely let slip which could be only imperfectly retrieved. A small boy called Bianor proved to them quite superfluously that they were right by spitting almost continuously at them and at the other mothers as they took their leave.

From now on in Motherland everything went its quiet and orderly way. For nearly a decade there was no disturbance that mattered, and on the other hand there was a remarkable general development. Automatically year by year the five-year-old boys were expelled, youngsters with wild eyes, white teeth, powerful chests, magnificent biceps, with arm and leg muscles rippling in bronze beauty, with calves like bronze balusters, and buttocks like the halves of white pumpkins. And as the lovely daughters of Heaven, growing like flowers, saw only boys of five years old, they had no conception of how these creatures would look in an adult state.

In an open hall thatched with thick palm-straw the appointed teachers instructed the coming generation. Like the mothers, each of these was addressed as Holy Mother by the girls of ten years old and upwards, and

by all who wanted to be considered grown-up. School
was also held here and there outside the Academy.
The syllabus of instruction was drawn up in essentials
by Laurence, Rodberte, and the President. The Council of Three had agreed that knowledge brought from
the Dark Continent should be but sparingly imparted,
and should be derived from a carefully compiled selection. The Dark Continent had been adopted on Île
des Dames as a name for Europe and its civilisation.
All instruction had to further the idea of the matriarchate and of supernatural procreation. It had also
to refrain from encumbering the minds of the girls,
and influencing their natural development. In itself
this luxuriant ripening of body and spirit in Île des
Dames was a surprisingly glorious manifestation of
power which was nevertheless everywhere apparent.
It could not be helped, Laurence had said; here one
must put back the clock of civilisation to an earlier
hour. This artificially induced primitive state had a
better right to consideration than anything in the older
civilisation of the Dark Continent. Education was
adapted to these principles.

In the teaching of Doctor Egli man did not appear,
far less the fact that man and mankind were once one
and the same. Humanity for Doctor Egli was Woman,
and this was true also of the other teachers. In the
Dark Continent Man was mankind, and Woman
at most only a human being; a point which was never
raised here at all in connection with man, that is to
say, whether he was to be described as a human

being. The doctor was a party to this physiological suppression not because she was in sympathy with the Zeus or Mukalinda cult, which she regarded as an inevitable evil at the best, but because she was not in sympathy with man. This feeling of her had secretly developed into a physiological hatred.

Rodberte, the most learned woman and the most comprehensive mind in the colony, along with the President and Laurence, took no part in the teaching. They felt that they would be the least capable of holding by the prescribed limitations. They unloaded all their knowledge upon each other in conversation, and above all upon Phaon, who, now a mature man, sought every opportunity for enlightenment.

A strange devotion still bound him to Dagmar-Diodata, who had now become a tapestry weaver. He seemed to adore this maiden, but at a respectful distance. Miss War was dead. She had followed his mother. In her stead Laurence was his counsellor in all his sorrows and struggles. The madcap, humorous, and often cynical side of his character he was in the habit of showing to Anni Prächtel, the artist. After he had, as it were, imbibed Rodberte's learning Rodberte often declared in wonder, after she had been disputing with him for hours, that she saw in him a rare mind, much superior to her own. But Phaon also visited the curious Babette, who still had her hermitage by the Lake of the Serpents near the peak of Mont des Dames. He was accustomed to listen for hours while, like a sibyl, she brought up legends, wise sayings, dreams and mystic experiences of every kind from the depths of her soul, which was drunken with eternity. But for her the centre of all things was her firstborn son, Bihari Lâl, in whom she saw nothing less than an incarnation of the god Krishna.

From Babette's hermitage and Laurence's temple issued a perpetually woven web of myth and mysticism, which, together with the natural incense-breathing airs of the tropical island, kindled and enraptured its inhabitants, and was met more than half-way by those natural, unruffled and but indifferently learned people. Rodberte's soberly enquiring mind was able to confirm the existence on Île des Dames of a world of spirits and of a matter-of-fact belief in miracles and superstitions. Out of the sea surrounding the island, out of the crater of Mont des Dames, appearing always in the self-same form whether seen in waking or in dreaming, there arose spirits which knew neither time nor space, and which, besides, did much to remove the feeling of desolation among the exiles.

To mention only a few of these, the wandering soul of Rita in its phantom shape lived upon the island; Miss War, although dead, came to visit the Holy Mothers; and the dead mulatto terrified some one or other of the mothers by a vivid apparition almost every night. Many of the boys in Manland could not distinguish between waking and dreaming, so much were their dreams peopled by shapes of reality, and their reality with dream figures.

The religion of supernatural procreation had its

temple in Laurence's grounds, which were dedicated to Mukalinda. The vestibule or prytaneum was divided from the holy of holies in the background by one of the pieces of tapestry which Dagmar-Diodata had woven. In the prytaneum a perpetual fire had to be kept burning. On the tapestry was shown how this sacred fire was brought every midsummer day from the lip of the crater on Mont des Dames. Twelve chosen boys carried it on twelve flaming coconut torches, with which they leapt in mighty bounds down the mountain-side. These twelve light-bringers and their torch-race, Dagmar, who was the Arachne of Île des Dames, had woven into her pattern.

The maintenance of this fire was finally entrusted to these light-bringers, after weeks of discussion. Bihari Lâl was their leader. Next to him in rank stood Alexander, Answalt, and Ariel. The beautiful chosen boys, already youths, were thus domiciled in the temple precincts, and had their quarters in the Hall of the Lightbringers near the temple. There must have been weighty reasons for this apparent breach of the matriarchate. It was, however, promulgated as a decree of the Council of Three, backed up by Doctor Egli. Moreover a carefully .thought out plan of education was devised for these twelve exceptions from the rule. The inhabitants of Manland sank more and more into the class of Sudras, while the Twelve were expressly raised to the rank of Sons of Heaven. They knew it, and were radiant with divinity. Owing to the spread of Babette's apparently definite information, Bihari Lâl was regarded as something still more.

A certain powerful taboo defending the temple precincts could only be broken by an express invitation of the Council of Three to one of the Holy Mothers. The general assembly was allowed in the temple precincts only once a year, on Bihari Lâl's birthday. What the individual mothers found to do there when they were invited is easy to tell. But it is impossible to explain how the miracle happened, thanks to which they usually brought a tiny islander into the world nine months after the visit.

The individual Holy Mothers were invited to what was called the temple-sleep. Laurence had borrowed this sacred observance from the ancients. In many temples of Greece the temple-sleep was customary. Barren mothers achieved by its means the desired conception, and the sick learned in dreams how to cure themselves.

The linga-cult is known not only to the Hindus. In the Christian Catholic Church today women make pilgrimages to certain shrines and practise customs which differ little from those of primitive times. Generally speaking, anyone who made it his business to discover whether Polynesia or Europe possessed the greater number of superstitious ideas would probably find that civilised Europe is far ahead of the Polynesian and Micronesian islands in this respect also.

We do not know what happened to the Holy Mothers in their temple-sleep, and certainly not what happened during the nights they passed in the House of Mukalinda. Did they practise a kind of linga-cult? Did they adore a linga of light, as the Hindus do in Benares, as an emblem of Vishveshara, the Lord of the Universe? There was nothing shocking in Mukalinda's temple, and there was no object to be seen which resembled the linga. In Cidambara, however, in Southern India, an invisible linga of ether was reverenced; and although the linga in the temple of Mukalinda was invisible, it could none the less be reverenced. Let us decide that we are ignorant of the precise state of affairs.

At any rate the temple of Mukalinda was a symbol of the holy revelation, the highest mystery of the island. It was regarded with general awe, even with holy dread, and yet the miracle of Île des Dames was always renewed in it.

"We have now everything that we need," was a frequent remark made by the President in the Council of Three: "the kindling spark of the supernatural reality, an idea as closely as possible bound up with it, the idea of the matriarchate, and, thirdly, a mission, to extend the matriarchate, the domination of the Mother, over the whole world. If one only has a faith, an idea, and a mission one can hang on for a long time by the skin of one's teeth. A heavenly faith, an earthly idea, and a mission, can do good service for a long time even without any prospect of their realisation."

We know that such an attitude could not be approved by Laurence. Her faith was strong, her idea possessed her, and she had no doubt at all of the eventual success of the mission. Both in the shrine of the Bona Dea and in the temple of Mukalinda she officiated as High Priestess with an unimpeachable seriousness. She had passionately identified herself with the conception, the idea of the matriarchate. Since the address which she had given on her farewell to Notre-Dame des Dames, that first tiny bamboo church, she had remained firmly attached to this idea. "Daughters of Earth and of Heaven," she had then called the island-women for the first time. She had said: "We wish to be spiritual mothers." She had criticised the old civilisation, and declared that the Roman Catholic Church had foundered on its contempt for woman. That meant contempt for the basis of life, on which everything depended. "Whatever the paradise we hope to enter in the future," she had said, "it must always be entered through the gate of life." And she had gone further in asserting that in a civilisation supported by mothers the noise of flails threshing empty straw and the deafening clatter of talking mills grinding chaff could never prevail as they do in a masculine civilisation. That Christ himself was born of woman. That his teaching of love for one's neighbour would long ago have been completely realised in an empire of mothers. That Love too was born of woman, not only because she gives birth to everything and thus implants love in the boy, but because she carries and shields the developing human being within herself for nine months, and because during this period,

-< 202 >-

in this relationship, human love is for the first time effective.

This, as we know, was at that time the case with Laurence. She carried Rukminî under her heart, whom she bore six or seven months later, and who had grown up into a lovely flower of maidenhood.

The name Rukminî had been communicated to her by Babette, who saw in her the future chief consort of Bihari Lâl, and thus the incarnate spouse of the incarnate god Krishna.

Laurence, as we know, was both poet and philosopher. She had duly rescued some fountain pens, a bundle of pencils and several thousand sheets of paper. A dye discovered on the island served as a substitute for ink. Her Sylvan Book contained the philosophic part of her writings. The poetic part was embodied in an epic, which was about half finished, a kind of feminine Æneid. In the place of Æneas, the saviour, leader and founder of the Roman state, stood a woman.

It is easy to conjecture what supplied the groundwork of this epic. The state founded was the mother-state of Île des Dames, the empire to arise was the empire of the Mothers.

So for a long and happy period life on Île des Dames pursued the even tenor of its way. Children and mothers, like plants, became more and more an expression of the magical climate of their tropic island. A daily time-table of work was generally observed, but to carry it out was as easy as a game. The herds of zebu grew fat and multiplied without attention. They were milked in the pastures by the mothers and the daughters of Heaven, and it was as if, in fulfilment of Laurence's anticipation, the cattle of the Sun-god were being milked by Hesperian nymphs. When one saw these nymphs going home with beautiful red earthenware jars they reminded one of the loveliest of all caryatids. Bucolic innocence had here allied itself to an extraordinary dignity and majesty, which were both childlike and divine. Human beings and animals seemed to be here united in peaceful harmony both on the animal and on the divine level.

And when the young Iphis, daughter of the onetime Miss Tyson Page, rode on her zebu-steer through the herd, a spear in her hand, she made one believe that one had fallen among celestial beings.

Every time that Laurence was by chance admitted to such a spectacle she trembled with amazement, and could not suppress a sudden sparkle in her eye at the sight of so much beauty.

The zebu had been first caught and tamed in the boys' half of the island. They had turned it into a useful draught and saddle beast. Motherland heard of this when one day the saucy Bianor, in defiance of rules, appeared in Ville des Dames on a zebu cow. Soon after that the zebu was domesticated also in Motherland.

Beside the lovely inland sea called Golfe des Dames there was a favourite bathing-place where the Holy Mothers sometimes resorted in a body, especially to-

were mingled in him with the most blissful throbbings of corporeal existence. He knew well that, in spite of his favourable horoscope, such a fortunate destiny had not been intended for him in his cradle. Although he had known the world of European civilisation only as a happy child, still he was aware that it could never have developed his sense of life to anything approaching the same intensity. It was a system far too gigantic and communistic, much more communistic than the average man or the community was conscious of. The individual was a parasite upon the community, but the community was much more a parasite on him. Any movement anywhere in this net spun over the world made the whole net quiver, and with it the individual who was entangled in it like an insect. No, he was rather like a tiny living knot in the net which was woven through him with countless threads in every direction. So he was painfully stretched on the rack, and, to be sure, also kept safely in his place. If this living knot were to be cut out of the net he would be useless, senseless, superfluous and dead. But he could make no independent movement in the net either.

But even here, in the freedom of Île des Dames, one must take care to preserve one's independence. One lived without being taken up into the net of civilisation. But it was a net that stretched its myriad tentacles like an octopus greedily after every living thing, to draw it into itself. "I have possibly," he thought, "conceded far too much to it already in being so eager for Rodberte's learning. Am I not already bothered by

superfluous European problems of every kind?   Is not
my happy freedom, my blessed irresponsibility, my
divine innocence, already threatened daily by the laws,
the morality, the knowledge, of the Dark Continent?
And is there not besides a certain fascination about
them?   Do not millions of severed threads, like scarred
wounds, itch with yearning for the old net again?"

Such thoughts and many others occupied Phaon in
his solitude.   "I stand," he went on to think, "so to
speak, alone in the world, outside the confines of the
great civilisations, and also outside the Mother-state
of Île des Dames.   My connection with wild Manland
is also only a superficial one.   My strength rests on
this isolation.   Therefore I must maintain it."

Phaon acted on this principle.   However numerous
the contacts he had in a day he finished by re-instating
his independence, his isolation, his solitude.

XI

THE atmosphere of Île des Dames was steeped in magic, which was communicated through the channels already mentioned. But it was Eros, the greatest of magicians, he and no other, who above all was its primal cause.

Invisibly caressed, and glowing through with soft increase, the island women felt themselves daily and nightly renewed, while beauty bloomed around and within them. And for most of them, a beauty of such a kind that it was its own enjoyment.

To give a notion of that atmosphere one would have to conjure up the being, the soul, the life of Île des Dames. Keen intellects like Rodberte and the President felt eventually its vague intoxication in their blood, and often did not know whether they were not already dead, bodilessly incorporated with the spaces and perfumes of paradise.

And Phaon, too, often said to himself: "The one reality which I know is the spirit and its brood of images, sensations, and thoughts."

While still a boy he had distinguished three different kinds of dreams: his waking life as dream, his voluntarily evoked day-dreams, and his involuntary dreams when he slept. His father Erasmus had early pointed out to him in jest how hazardous and difficult external reality is to grasp. Often, in the early morning, when Phaon lay in bed, he had gone silently into the bedroom, had gone out again as silently, and then had returned suddenly with a simulated cheerfulness and wished his son good morning as if he were seeing him for the first time. When Phaon told him then that he saw through the jest perfectly, and that he was only pretending to see his son for the first time, and in reality had been there only a moment before, his father demanded that he should prove it.

"I saw you," said Phaon.

"Even if you had heard me as well, I might still believe you and not believe you."

"I both saw and heard you, and that perfectly clearly," said Phaon. But his father replied: "Prove it to me. Compel me to recognise that I have been here. Compel all the world to recognise it. It must believe you, even should you not believe yourself."

"Why should I lie?" asked Phaon. "There is such a thing as illusion," said his father, "and why indeed should you not lie, seeing that you have often lied before?"

Really Phaon at that time knew already of the mind's strange incapacity to go outside itself. When he was five he was looking at himself one day in the mirror. "That is you," said he to himself. "Therefore you are!" Let us suppose that this was on Monday. On Tuesday he did it again. "That is you," he said to himself in the mirror, "therefore you are." "Did I not do the same thing yesterday?" he then asked himself. "It may be so. I believe I did," was the answer. But he was not able to prove it to himself.

So undemonstrable seemed to him also the all-embracing yesterday, yes, sometimes even the to-day of Île des Dames. To him it seemed that he was bound in the closest unity with the whole creation. Only, he could not prove it to himself. As soon as the caprice seized him to prove it, and he strove to grasp Île des Dames as naked reality, he attained only the opposite of what he sought. He saw the island as a phantasmagoria, an insubstantial mirage. But as soon as, credulous and without thought, he submitted to its magic, it became immediately a reality.

Who dare not think of their yesterdays, will not dare to think of their to-morrows.

"My dear good Laurence," said Phaon once, in conversation with the High Priestess, "what endures and originates here I can regard only as an end in itself. As such, it is either justified or not justified. If in this place an elevation of life to harmonious beauty has taken place, if the vales and heights of the island re-echo with joy and pleasure, we have in that every justification. But instead of joy and pleasure I would rather set pain and pleasure in that variously mingled but indissoluble union which is able to mount to all the highest and sublimest gratifications of sense. I have nothing to do with your matriarchate, if it is to spread over the morning of the whole world.

To stand still on one step of organic development is absolutely impossible. Is a thing perfected, then comes its fall; and that would be the fate of a matriarchal world civilisation."

But Phaon could also speak in a different fashion. Sometimes, from over the ocean, the tentacles of the net which encloses that world, so often the object of his thoughts, would seize upon him. The ambition of the Dark Continent, which Laurence more than any one else had nourished, drew him on. Then he desired to be a warrior, to be that great world-reformer who would realise the ideas of the exalted High Priestess and raise the Great Mother of Île des Dames to be chief ruler over the Dark Continent.

Rodberte, too, had often said to him: "What have there been but petty reformations and revolutions? The Lutheran reformation was nothing more than an outward and inward commotion of images, the French revolution, as people say, was the emancipation of the Third Estate, and the latest revolution that of the Fourth. Through all this absolutely nothing was attained, because the objects of revolution were themselves so insignificant. The relations between the two chief parties of mankind, the world of women and that of men, were never affected. And what is meant by the women's movement in Europe to-day is, alas, only a bagatelle. This ocean of life, love, self-abnegation and creative power which animates women in the present world of oppression, must sometimes be moved from its very foundations. And then, by another and more primitive and fundamental natural phenomenon than these little reformations and revolutions quite a different mass of rubbish and refuse will be cleared out of the world."

On that morning Phaon felt the full influence of Île des Dames. Credulous and without serious afterthought, he saw the idea of a world matriarchate becoming a reality in his mind; his ambition burst into flame, and he felt himself called to a long and passionate flight ending in death. Yet the more he tried to demonstrate to himself its reasonableness, importance, necessity and reality the more it seemed to become mere phantasmagoria.

FIFTEEN years had flown, and the lovely Iphis was just fifteen when, riding on her Zebu bull, she crossed Phaon's lonely path in the mountains. She had been educated in the fear of Mukalinda. It had been related to her, too, how this island demon or divine genius at times was used to assume the form of a powerful and savage man. When, enterprising and adventurous as she was, she went for long rides into the remotest parts of the island, it happened that once she came to believe that she had encountered the mysterious power.

Iphis was the pride and joy of the colony. For his part Phaon could not believe that he beheld merely one of the Daughters of Heaven when, undaunted, the zebu-rider came up to him, sitting in goddess-like nudity on her bull. Her saffron coloured hair, fastened loosely in a great knot, fell down nevertheless to the silvery back of the bull, behind whose hump pressed the strong thighs of the rider. She and the noble animal seemed to have grown into one. Immovable, as if rooted to the ground, Phaon gazed at the girl and she at him, her eyes full of fear and curiosity as she rode past.

After a few weeks Phaon again encountered the lovely Iphis and her bull. In this high and remote part of Mont des Dames he had met once before one of the Holy Mothers, but never till now any of the Daughters of Heaven, to whom, indeed, this upper range of Mont des Dames was strictly interdicted. When that radiantly harmonious spectacle, when the delicate rose of the bull's nostrils, the palpitating silver of his shining fell, the rich copper of the girl's body, her sea-green eyes, her saffron hair like a skein of light, —when all these burst through the darkness of the forest, Phaon involuntarily made a movement with his hand as if his eyes were blinded.

Since Phaon, as one is compelled to assume, led the ascetic life of a monk, it can be imagined into what temptation he was led. All the more because the eyes of the proud and disdainful Iphis fearlessly met his for the second time with that half-impish scorn which in reality said, Conquer me! but appeared to say, You will never conquer me!

A third encounter took place. Phaon had gone one day very deep into the green forest which covered a great part of the volcano, to drink his fill of wonder at the interlacing branches of the rhizophores and the gigantic fig-trees with their meshes of stems and aerial roots, when down the palm-pillared aisles, over ferns in whose emerald green the zebu ambled up to his belly, Iphis again came riding. She had followed the bed of a stream to penetrate into this hidden world, for the waters hissed and gurgled round her and among the bamboo canes. The bull stood still, when he saw Phaon, and Iphis drew her brows together.

Tangled in liana chains and priceless orchids, perfumed with the scents of the waters and of countless aromatic flowers and leaves, the girl might have been taken for a wood nymph, were it not for the spear she carried and for her cold and proud Penthesilean glance, which struck Phaon now as it had once Achilles. That glance was challenge.

What happened next was never made completely clear. This time Phaon was not quite able to keep himself in check. Infected by the morality of the Dark Continent, he had set an insurmountable barrier between himself and the Daughters of Heaven. Rightly or no, with it the carelessness, freedom, frankness and happiness, the very innocence of his actions, were lost. From that moment a process of disintegration had set in which was to spoil Phaon little by little for life on Île des Dames and for its happiness. But now, seeing that he had already overleapt these barriers in himself, little more than a disobedience of his own will was needed to entangle him in what was guilt for the Dark Continent, but what would have saved him for Île des Dames.

Phaon caught the spear which Iphis had cast at him. He held it as if in a dream in his right hand. Then he seated himself on the zebu behind the rider, embracing her with his left arm as with a band of iron. At first the bull collapsed; then he felt a mighty stimulus and rushed with his double burden through the tree trunks. Suddenly it became light just as Phaon, now scarcely master of himself, thought of bringing the beast to a halt. He did so, yet he did not drag his prize down with him, as he had intended, to cool in her his burning fire, but, relinquishing the girl and the beast, stalked with indifference, as it seemed, from the edge of the forest, where he was, along the shore of the foaming Lake of the Serpents.

A fourth encounter was still more extraordinary both for Iphis and Phaon. In relating this mystery many will believe that we draw nigh the province of fable. Yet, if there is any truth in the world, here too it will certainly be found. For Phaon it was the highest truth, guarded in the deepest mystery of his being, the holiest possession of his heart.

One day Iphis had come, as many a day before, to a certain island plain, wild and overgrown, whose aspect had each time excited first a feeling of strangeness, then of awe, for something unutterable seemed to look out of it. From bastions of vertically mounting rock issued a stream, now almost sunk to its bed, whose waters had made a delta in the barren plain, covered only with bushes. Iphis was tempted to follow that stream flowing between two gigantic rocky walls which almost met and which the torrent seemed to have parted like a saw. The bull snorted and trembled as she guided him through the dreadful gate into the gloomy, faintly whispering ravine, and let him walk farther and farther with his cloven hooves over the boulders of the shallow river bed.

Iphis, too, had to master terror after terror in her advance into the bowels of the earth. When she looked above her between the higher edges of the ravine she could divine rather than see the open sky, which there was only a white twisting line. A bird of prey had strayed into the ravine. It struck with head and wings against the walls, and often fell for a long distance. Whatever stage Iphis had reached now on that road of horror the zebu divined her wishes and of himself turned back. He returned with all possible speed, but that did not prevent the journey from seeming far too long to the rider.

It was not merely a panic fear which overcame the girl; she had heard coming out of the bowels of the rocks, as she often declared later, great chorales such as ear had never heard before; cries, too, and echoes of all kinds, which crowded down from above. Courage returned to the fair rider as soon as she reached the open.

But now she had a sudden presentiment that there was something of the most marvellous nature yet to be discovered there. Her hunger for such food was not appeased by the wonders, to her obvious and natural, of Île des Dames. The common life of the island could not give her the nimbus of a marvel such as she would like to experience. So she rode exploring along the outer walls of rock, and with keen and wide-ranging gaze examined their upper reaches. Only after she had repeatedly broken off and again taken up her topographical task, and had encircled the mountain, did she return to the delta and realise that the mysterious plateau held up to the heavens was on all sides impassable. This plateau gave her a strong sense of mystery, for it seemed to her that on its edge wonders and marvels of all kinds occurred.

For example she saw flocks of birds which made precious stones look dim. Never had the like happened before in her wanderings, although she had discovered beautiful things in plenty, not to mention the wide, swampy desert round the foot of the island of rock. In their circling flight these feathered flying jewels never went far over the edge of that upper world. Like doves, they seemed to have their cote there. But, what surpassed these strange yet natural phenomena, the birds sang in unison as they flew, reminding Iphis of a choir, and, indeed, according to her, the music somewhat resembled that which might be evoked from the harps of the Dark Continent.

Now on this impregnable plateau lay Phaon's Lake of the Birds of Paradise. The story of his discovery as he relates it becomes too a record of bewitchments, hesitations, fears and enigmatical happenings. At the same age as Iphis was now—he had reached, as if enticed by the gloom, first the dreadful ravine, and afterwards the plateau, which seemed to be filled with the magical effulgence of all mysteries. After more than a year devoted to attempts to scale the rock he one day gave it up as impossible. The scene, the mass of impassable rock, and everything, fell at last for him into oblivion. This was a time when he was busied with countless lovely adventures of another kind. One evening when he was returning from one of these he was overcome by a strange melancholy. It seemed to him that there was something from which he was shut out forever and without hope. In this state he became unconscious of time and place. He watched the southern stars come out in the darkening cope of heaven. He wandered through the night, aimless, silent, and lost in abstraction. Sometimes it seemed to him that he was descending, often he seemed to be climbing upwards, indifferent to his goal. Fire-flies and glow-worms glimmered in clouds around him. At last he became weary and lay down.

When he awoke in the early morning he was lying by the Lake of the Birds of Paradise. After he had caught one of those miracles of colour he set out without further thought on his return journey.

Rejoicing in his extraordinary prize and absorbed in wandering, he recoiled all at once in terror from the sheer verge of a precipice. With the idea of finding a way down he walked then along the edge of the rock, but after walking until the sun, which seemed foreign to him, stood at noon, he found himself still on that plateau devoid of island flora or fauna, on that other island which seemed to waver in space and which could only be left, it seemed, by a leap from its verge into the void. Late in the afternoon he had walked round this island of the air and had returned to the point at which he had entered it.

At this his mood suffered a strange transformation. Now and then he was sure that he was dreaming, although every glance at the magical scene before him and every step he took seemed to refute him. Out of a brook which ended in a sheer leap over the edge of the rock and which sent up a veil of vapour, a great indigo-blue fish arose and, as if the air were its element, swam rustling round Phaon's head. Then Phaon knew at once that he would present the bird of paradise to little Dagmar-Diodata.

And now he had to give up the thought of returning that day, for to descend the path in darkness was not to be contemplated. Moreover there was nothing that could tempt him back to the soil of Île des Dames but Dagmar-Diodata, and her he would rather have had up there. And then, after the magic of the scene and the multitudes of other enchantments around him, after the bird of paradise and the blue fish, he experienced a third marvel, by far the most profound of all.

Between an avenue of dark trees like cypresses, which might have been planted by the hands either of gods or of men, and which swarmed with thousands of sparrow-like, tiny purple birds like drops of blood, walked calmly a woman of noble mien, who here and there lifted up a flower between her slim fingers. She lived here, as it seemed, in holy peace, given over to still meditation, whose elevated and divine object was betrayed in the gentle sweetness of her smile.

Phaon divined that he might not address, save at the risk of death, that lovely, noble form, around whom the dark branches of the trees rustled continually. Nay, thereby he might be guilty of a crime which never could be expiated. For not only would that supernal harmony be shattered, dishonoured, defiled, blasphemed, but the very soul of his own mother would be annihilated.

But great as the crime was, greater still was for Phaon the task of abstaining from speech with that lady. Like wild gusts of an inner tempest his speech pressed against the barrier of his lips. And although this was indeed Rita, his mother, even that name he did not dare to pronounce aloud. Phaon felt that it was not permitted to her even to see him. And, his unending love transformed into self-abnegation, bathed in tears, while a thousand times the word, Mother! Mother! was born and died within him, he crept after her from tree to tree. Until once she turned round and gently shook her head.

From that moment a transformation came over Phaon and signs of maturity decisively appeared in him.

For forty days and forty nights Phaon had been

seen by no one, when, pale and with a deeply altered aspect, he returned and resigned the bird of paradise to Dagmar-Diodata.

It happened with Iphis as it had with Phaon. As she became accustomed to the mysterious impulse to scale the upper reaches of the rock and had at last given up all hope of the ascent, she saw one evening, whether in reality or in dream she could not say, while she was standing once more in the vicinity of the ravine, a mighty form resembling a man vanish into it. Fleeting as this glimpse was she had felt through her whole body a stroke as of lightning, along with a compulsion to follow the shape.

Strangely enough the zebu bull, which lay beside her chewing the cud, appeared to have the same impulse and sprang up ready for the chase. In the next moment he felt the weight of his mistress and the pressure of her legs on his flanks. Her heels beat on his flanks like hammers. But curiously, this time he needed no incentive. Without use of bridle or whip the bull continued to rush through the ravine, even when the twilight thickened into black night, even when the lovely Iphis with wildly beating heart recognised the dreadful peril of a rash ascent in the darkness, even when, shuddering with apprehension, she saw the hope of return to be dubious if not impossible. At last anxiety and exertion rendered the rider almost unconscious. Now she heard only the sound of rocks clattering into the abyss and the snorting of the animal, which seemed to scent something in front of it.

When she awoke, as Phaon had done, by the Lake of the Birds of Paradise, with the zebu grazing near by, it was not a bird of paradise that she saw first. No, she saw a sight which at once excited her greatest astonishment and in some way cut into her soul. She saw an animal taller and slimmer than the grazing zebu at her side, which had on its brow a spiral horn, as long and straight as a spear. On this animal which it is said only a virgin can subdue, sat, not astride but sideways in perfect ease as on a chair, a young woman who seemed to Iphis curiously rather than excessively beautiful, and alongside, almost naked and with long, waving hair, went that man or god by following whom she had succeeded in reaching the crest of the rock.

Iphis kept this encounter secret for a long time, as well as all the rest of her marvellous adventure, indeed, the whole experience, which, as sometimes happens in dreams, had released in her an inexpressible effusion of feeling. In peoples' dreams such effusions are not unlike spiritual eruptions, which release, nay, shoot forth amid tears and cries, a confusion of sensations. She saw the man and the fabulous animal with its golden cloven hooves; she saw it twofold, as it were, in the air and in pictured reflection on the water. She saw its living burden, and she ran into the Lake of the Birds of Paradise up to the knee, up to the breast, weeping and crying, stretching out her arms over the water towards that trinity. It seemed to her in that instant that an opportunity long missed was found and again forever lost.

Phaon, Iphis and Diodata did not remember these dreamlike adventures long after they occurred. They returned vividly to the minds of all three alike one day when Iphis first visited the hall in the temple grounds where Dagmar-Diodata-Arachne weaved, and found Phaon contemplating the work. From the weaver's hands there was even then issuing a carpet of such opulent beauty that it seemed rather the work of Pallas Athene herself than of a mortal. It represented in a medley of colours and yet in the purest harmony a wealth of imagery which the eye could scarcely take in. Blue fishes floated round the trunks of cypresses and round the figure of the son of Anak, which perpetually recurred. There were clouds of purple-hued sparrows whose notes, imaging their song, issued from their beaks. There was another ever recurring motif —that of the lady who walked, too, between rows of cypresses. But everywhere birds of paradise.

All these dominated an indescribably lovely landscape which breathed an unutterable magic. There was a lake whose waters reflected all the colours of the birds of paradise which flew above it, and on its marge stalked the rare beast of fable, the unicorn, in appearance not unlike a horse, or a stag, or a gigantic goat with shaggy fell; and on its back sat a singing lady. Everywhere went the strange animal, the singing lady, and by her side the silent son of Anak.

Among these strange enigmas the strangest was the figure of a huntress, a Diana, a slender virgin, who was woven into the picture as she dashed into the lake with bow bent and pointed arrow, so that one had to assume that either the unicorn or the man or the singing rider was the mark at which she aimed. Iphis, who was almost untameable, and as shy in society as she was rash out-of-doors, and who was now for the first time in the temple grounds, had come by chance on Diodata's workshop—or what, indeed, had drawn her thither? She gazed at the carpet, glanced at Phaon, stared at the weaver, and in the same instant divined what the picture, the man and the woman, typified in her soul, what each of the three was to her. And as she saw it so did the others. The huntress had stepped bodily out of the carpet.

In this description of a sort of Cloud Cuckoo Land one is conscious of making considerable demands on credulity, and even of passing beyond it and into the extraordinary, though what is extraordinary here, it is true, will appear to the majority trivial. On this marvellous island a second marvellous island has been superimposed, what may appear perhaps to be an excess of the marvellous. The noble Laurence would deny that. She would say: "Every human being lives in double reality. Reality is dual, or there is no reality. Countless gods swarm round a single human head." She would have affirmed this opinion as out-spokenly as Cicero did, even if she had never read him. And one heard her often saying in conversation with Rodberte and Anni Prächtel, who, in spite of their keen intellects and dry wit, were yet essentially artists, that people who at every turn complained of the improbable

-: 225 :-

would do better to complain of their own spiritual narrowness. That the whole universe, our solar system, our earth, ourselves, were obvious improbabilities. More, that among all the great men born there had not been up to then one capable of grasping, even remotely, the total improbability of existence as such. The utilitarian thinker, Herbert Spencer, had said: "With the mere interpretation of all the phenomena of the cosmos as expressions of matter and motion, and therefore of energy, nothing more is attained than a resolution of an agglomeration of thought-products into their simplest symbols." And about the nature of the universe nothing could be said but that subject and object are only symbols for an unknown, unknowable reality.

The fact remains that the unicorn was apparently present on Île des Dames; and this fact was not one of those which could be interpreted as peculiarly auspicious for the fortunes of the colony. And soon, too, the pious Laurence came under its spell.

It once happened that Phaon, as indeed not seldom occurred, paid a visit to the High Priestess. He found her busied with her papers. A quick glance and a gentle smile were her greeting to him.

"I knew you would come, my dear Phaon," she said. "I felt sure of it in my mind."

Phaon replied. "And I may say, too, that suddenly, as I was going in another direction, I turned round, as if I had heard a voice telling me to seek you out at once."

-¢ 226 ꝑ-

"Well, and what have we to speak of to each other, my friend?"

"I think," Phaon replied, "that the conversation can only consist of such words and thoughts as lie outside or perhaps above Île des Dames."

"Maybe on a metacosmion?"

"For my part, on a metacosmion," said Phaon.

"Where the unicorn is and the lake and the Birds of Paradise and. . . ?"

Phaon said: "There, too, my holy, beloved Mother Laurence."

For a long time Laurence looked at her former Helios, son of Hyperion, silent and serious.

"Why should we conceal any longer, my beautiful Phaon, that in us both there has happened something like a farewell. Farewell . . . farewell," repeated Laurence in a sighing tone, when Phaon did not reply. "Or do you find it otherwise? Are we not inwardly a little disloyal already to this radiant world, which we have helped to build?"

"We dare not both leave the ship together," said Phaon.

"Nor both go into the boat together?"

"Nor that either, beloved Laurence."

Thereupon the Anglo-Dutchwoman said: "And yet I have hoped for something like that, dear Phaon. I do not conceal it, for I have decided that I shall not be honourable but frank, when it comes to the drawing up of my account."

She continued, seeing that Phaon did not reply: "I have spoken with Iphis, Phaon. The stubborn child, who is so close to you, as indeed the others are, has told me rather a confused story. Can you inform me who it was who sat on the back of the unicorn?"

"Dagmar-Diodata sat on the back of the unicorn."

"At least I am glad to know," said Laurence, "that I rescued your destiny for you in the shape of a puling suckling from the cold breast of its dead mother."

"I will be grateful to you for that till death."

"Your gratitude," said Laurence, "is like a knife turning in a wound. Let us talk of other things."

The earnestness, the agitation in the very being of the noble Laurence, drew nearer and nearer to a climax. Finally she lifted herself from her chair, which was made of light cane, and went up to Phaon, with her peculiar expression of pain and sweetness in which, as in a melody of Beethoven, melancholy and cheerfulness were mingled.

"Come here, Phaon," said she, "I want to whisper something in your ear."

Phaon was accustomed to do whatever the beloved Holy Mother desired of him. He saw that her mouth, eloquent even in silence, was twitching convulsively. Like a mother she took him on her breast.

And though she whispered a long time in his ear she had often to control herself and swallow down what rose in her breast. But it would not be stifled. Her voice escaped now and then into audible speech, and when it did it betrayed that it had been bathed in tears. Her voice grew louder, in tone and word lay something not to be resisted, and all ended suddenly in a strange sobbing and a long and wordless stream of tears.

In these short minutes the proud woman had laid bare her heart to Phaon. A hundred times, perhaps, she whispered to Phaon the one universally known word by which love is accustomed to betray itself. Phaon learned, as he had to learn, that all that this woman had planned and accomplished had been for his sake. A great and sanctified love, supported by an inexhaustible strength of renunciation, had been in her work. She had finally found satiation in meditation. In the contemplation of a beautiful and growing life and value she had been satisfied. To that end the possession of Rukminî, that one divine fruit of love, had been granted her. She had kept her from feeling that her affections were famished. On the other side the growth and development of Dagmar-Diodata had presented new and painful problems. Confronted with her, Laurence felt the agonies of jealousy. She had recognised and marked the power which already as a small child Diodata had exercised over Phaon. From a hundred little signs she had learned that the youth felt for Diodata the same passion which she herself felt for him. She knew that to gain the love of Dagmar-Diodata or even only to please her, Phaon would if necessary give her Motherland no less than Manland, the whole Île des Dames, to be her footstool. Laurence would have done the same for Phaon. So she said to him: "For your own sake, my love, I have often, often been a traitor to the Mother-state."

Still another rival to Laurence had appeared in Rukminî, and a third in Iphis. But she had come to an understanding with these two, since they were doomed to the same renunciation. The time came when the shy Iphis at midday and the soft Rukminî at evening wept out on her bosom their tears of sad confession.

This brief conversation lightened the long and suffering road of her passion. And headstrong passion it was which not only in Iphis, in Phaon and Laurence, and in the silent weaver Diodata, but over the whole Île des Dames was already secretly announcing or manifesting itself. The immense resignation into which the noble Laurence had sunk on her arrival at Île des Dames, and against which she had fought for more than sixteen years, lay now again upon her with its full weight. Except for Phaon there was no one to whom she allowed the truth to appear. Her refuge was the almost inaccessible hut among the rocks, near the Cooking Pot of the Anchorites, where she withdrew, appearing now very seldom in the Temple grounds.

It was strange that a great and universal festivity which was planned, cast less of light than of shadow before it, and kindled into flame the smouldering passions. Dissension broke out over the same apple of discord, which had once in former years released it. After it had found its solution at that time in the sending away of the five-year-old boys, it had slept, until now once more the question of the supremacy of Motherland, and with it the whole Manland question, became acute.

Several hundred island virgins had reached the extreme boundary beyond which nature would not or could not let them rest content with the state of virginity. A step was now to be taken which must initiate a decisively new era on Île des Dames. Already an unruly spirit was beginning to prevail, which found expression most vociferously on the coast of Golfe des Dames, naturally on the Motherland side, but in full view of the opposite shore, where the Manland youths were working mischief, and sending a cry across which in Motherland was notorious as the Manland cry. The youths sought to imitate Mukalinda's lion roar, but at best they only succeeded in copying it as a wretched, hoarse dung-hill cockerel caricatures a splendid, mighty-voiced cock of the walk. Nevertheless the Daughters of Heaven heard these cries in their dreams and found no rest from them even in sleep.

To prevent scandal, therefore, it was now full time to convey this harvest of ripe flesh and blood to Mukalinda, and marry them to him. The great festival, the great sacred ceremony, in which this should happen, was prepared. Not only the Council of Three, not only Doctor Egli, and a circle which had gathered round her, but Phaon also racked his brains, and suffered many a headache, over the approaching solemnities.

In the last year and a half Mukalinda had exercised

his privilege over the island no longer with the old fiery zeal. Whether the fault lay in the aging Mothers, whose beauty could no longer ensnare the pampered god in the old way, or whether someone had angered him, no one knew. Now there remained, at any rate, his twelve sons, the Flame Bringers and Flame Slingers. But one hesitated still to take the step which would compel the Serpent King of the island to abdicate and delegate his rulership to his twelve sons. Religions have their esoteric and their exoteric aspects, even if to most the esoteric is only an augur's jest or the lumber behind the scenes of a puppet theatre. The esoterically minded on Île des Dames could not decide whether it was expedient to fling the torches of these Lightbringers, still only to be subdued with great pains, among the peaceful huts of Motherland. They were not sure what the chances were that the streaming brand might leave one roof uninjured.

The nearer the festival approached, the more exclusively Phaon attached himself to Dagmar-Diodata. It was evident to Laurence that by these two some enterprise was being secretly prepared. It was connected in some way with the coming festival. This knowledge nourished in Laurence's soul a mood of seriousness, nay, of grief. But in the soul of her daughter too, the lovely Rukminî, sorrow grew, often to be sobbed out on the breast of the mother. And in the lord and prince of Lightbringers, in the first gift of God, Bihari Lâl, sorrow grew also, for he saw that Rukminî was sad, and knew why. In the silence many

-〔 232 〕-

sighs must have been heard by Phaon, but of all of them those of the noble Laurence pierced most deeply into his soul, and after hers those of Iphis and Rukminî.

Outwardly, however, they took from him none of his security, his cheerfulness.

The question round which the dispute developed was brought to a head through a deputation from Manland which, led by the youth Bianor, presented itself one day in the Temple grounds before the Council of Three. Bianor expressed the desire—it was almost a claim—of the Manlanders to take part in the festival of the dedication of the brides. He was merely told that the wishes of Manland would be brought to the attention of the Holy Mothers.

By these they were then rejected in a storm of indignation.

For Phaon this verdict and the demeanour of the Holy Mothers were a spring of endless amusement. It soon appeared that the most orthodox doctrine of the matriarchate, advocated by Amanda Egli, the Holy Mother Philomela Schwab and their party, had been responsible for this hard decision. Through it, both in Manland and Motherland, a popular excitement was called forth such as had never been seen on the island.

Even the Holy Mother Babette by her Lake of the Serpents was drawn from her seclusion. She appeared one day in the Temple grounds and summoned the noble Laurence, the President and Rodberte, as well as the twelve Lightbringers, to receive in the prytaneum of Mukalinda's Temple a revelation which had come to her. Seeing that everyone did her will it was not long before not only the summoned, but also a few chosen people, among them Phaon, Diodata, Lolo Smith and the Holy Mother Egli, were gathered in the appointed place.

The first mother, Babette, always strange and self-absorbed, and with the years grown more strange, had for her prophetic purposes constructed a tripod. She had laid within it some innocent but pleasant-scented herbs which, kindled, sent up smoke around her while she sat on it. Her aspect was not really absurd. Grown old early, bleached alike in skin and hair, she had shrivelled into a little, old woman commanding reverence, so that she might well pass for a magician, a sybil, or a norn. Behind the curtain the Lightbringers at her command had set a few drums of zebu hide, which made a subdued but solemn accompaniment to her speech. All the same, there was a slight twitching round the satirical mouth of the old artist, and Rodberte had to keep herself in countenance by a remarkable coldness of expression. The poor, meagre body of the prophetess was visible through a thin, grey veil, and one could see her extraordinary breasts, which by everyone, even by the Lightbringers, were regarded with reverence.

"I am visited several times weekly, as everyone knows," she began very faintly, "by the pious vulture Jatayus. His nest is the crater of Mont des Dames.

Who on our island has not seen his white form shooting from the crater and winging down to the Lake of the Serpents where my dwelling is? Then all the hosts of flamingoes rise from the smoking shores of the lake to greet him, and circle round him until he reaches me.

"Who does not know that I have been the most richly blessed of all the Holy Mothers of this most blessed island? I have always had the belief that he to whom I gave birth is a redeemer. But who it was I bore I know now through the pious vulture Jatayus."

Bihari Lâl, the leader of the Lightbringers, became uneasy.

Babette continued.

"It was Krishna himself whom I bore under the name of Bihari Lâl."

Here Bihari Lâl, that marvel of beauty, blushing scarlet like a girl, interrupted his mother. He said mildly but firmly:

"I am nothing more, and would be nothing more, than an ordinary young man, dear mother."

"That may be," was the answer. "But Krishna too, did not know in many of his incarnations that he was Krishna. You are Krishna, though it is not needful that you should know it. You are Krishna, the only Lightbringer. The other eleven do not matter. As Krishna you have descended to dally with the shepherdesses of this happy island. Out of the husk of Mukalinda Krishna has now become fully incarnate

in you. Before, he lived in you, in Mukalinda, and in
many other forms at the same time.

> Every shepherdess is trilling:
> For me alone is he so sweet.
> I hear the sighs his bosom filling,
> And his echoing silver feet."

And she continued:

"In Bihari Lâl, which being interpreted means the
Playing Lover, Krishna manifests himself as the lord
of shepherdesses. Among his everlasting divine games
he loves this also. Frolic! Frolic, Holy Mothers!

> Krishna has arrived, your king,
> And taken you beneath his wing.
> Your children he will bless with love
> And rain down manna from above."

"Dear mother," Bihari Lâl once more interrupted
her, his voice trembling a little, "I must protest that
I am nothing more than the twelfth of twelve dear
comrades." He added: "If I did not love and respect you so much, my dear and holy mother, the
words which you speak would be very painful to me."

Babette did not allow herself to be drawn aside:
"You are speaking now only as the husk of Krishna,"
she said. "The god in you will soon refute you. As
Krishna you will yet possess sixteen thousand women
besides Rukminî, and have by them one hundred and
eighty thousand children."

Rukminî, the daughter of Laurence, made a movement of horror when she heard this, and departed in haste.

The President whispered: "Poor boy, that will be a hard task for you."

"Informed by the pious vulture Jatayus, I announce another divine incarnation on Île des Dames. In the daughter of the pious Laurence, Rukminî, is incarnated Rukminî, the wife of Krishna. Thus there rule over us

> Spouses eternal,
> Rukminî and Bihari Lâl."

As the good Mother Babette was greatly loved and honoured, the uneasiness caused by her words was tacitly concealed, and was not even suspected by her as she sat there. So the seeress could continue in perfect good faith: "Scarce twenty years will Bihari Lâl and Rukminî have ruled in unbroken happiness on Île des Dames, scarcely a third of the one hundred and eighty thousand children will be born, when the great earthquake will come and soon after that the frightful eruption of Mont des Dames. What purpose Krishna may have this time on the earth the pious vulture Jatayus has left me in no doubt. His children will not on this occasion be chiefly sons as heretofore; they will be daughters. These he will again make mothers, and after he has pursued and conquered all the demons of the Dark Continent, he will renew through these mothers the human race, the whole world of the Dark Continent."

Anni whispered to Rodberte that he had always done so.

But now Babette laid claim to their attention by a grandiose myth. She spoke much of an ape king and his minister Hanumân. "Before the disappearance of Île des Dames (for the island must vanish through the operation of the volcano, and with it, go under) this ape minister from the Empire of the Apes, which lies somewhere between the twentieth western and fourteenth eastern longitudes, and the seventeenth and fourteenth northern latitudes, will with one mighty leap traverse Asia and the Pacific Ocean, set foot on Île des Dames, and put himself at Bihari Lâl's disposal. Then the Shepherdess Kingdom will be over, Bihari Lâl will wholly renounce his incognito, throw over him the purple robe of Krishna, take Krishna's sword in his hand, forsake Île des Dames, and advance against the demon hordes of the Dark Continent.

"This will happen in the following way. At a sign from Hanumân and by command of Bihari Lâl, an immense host of apes, in numbers surpassing all mankind, will throw in two or three days a bridge from beyond the Pacific to Île des Dames. When Krishna with his Holy Mothers and children have marched over the bridge, the god will set himself at the head of the ape host and deliver the demon hordes of the Dark Continent to that slaughter whose issue, through his agency a complete victory, shall establish the dominion of the Mothers for millennia, yea, until the end of time."

Naturally poor Babette's pronouncement did not elucidate the situation; it could only confuse it still more. Motherland and Manland alike showed themselves enraged that Bihari Lâl should supplant the eleven other Lightbringers, indeed all the other men in Manland; and Motherland in particular was indignant that he should be designated ruler and king, and Rukminî queen and empress, over Île des Dames. And, moreover, the prophecy of Babette raised an unrelenting enemy to her son in that Bianor who had led the deputation from Wildmanland.

Among the Twelve the evil effects of the manifesto were soon eradicated as much by the straightforward and friendly amiability of Bihari Lâl as by Phaon's diplomacy. There remained nothing for these well-born and well-bred youths, who were equals in beauty, strength, and nobility of feeling and thought, and were bound together by mutual love, but to be united among themselves. Their blood pulsed far too easily and happily, the heavenly fire of inexpressible anticipation, that impatient anticipation of youth, which guesses at infinite happiness and with youth is lost, was too mighty in them. This radiant band comprised in itself all the strength, splendour and intoxication of youth. One must see the warm patina of their flesh, the superb play of their muscles, when in their playgrounds and wrestling theatres in the temple, the Lightbringers exhausted themselves with spear and discus throwing, running, jumping, wrestling and all manner of sport. There occurred miracles of strength, sureness, and dexterity. And when the steely elasticity of these young limbs was freed in the full intoxication of healthy play, in the communal dance, one might believe that the laws of gravity were repealed.

It was a remarkable sight when Phaon now and then entered into these games. The impression must have been similar when Odysseus did the same thing on the island of Phæacia. Even among those magnificent youths who called him father (in the sense of step-father, or the father of all their arts) his superiority was always evident.

Moreover in his exuberance and lightheartedness he seemed to be one of them. This lightheartedness and exuberance, however, extended not only to physical things. Not only must discus, arrow, spear and ball be there for every mood of the youths, but there were countless things on Île des Dames which could not elude their healthy mockery. That fate overtook the whole ape host and above all the ape minister Hanumân. Nothing could be done without Hanumân. It was one of his duties, sometimes for days, often for hours, to evoke spasms of disrespectful laughter.

The festival of the dedication of the brides drew near. It had been postponed to Midsummer's Day. But the signs that its course might be stormy became more threatening. One day Phaon had to inform the Council of Three that it became daily more difficult for him to keep Wildmanland under control. At one of the assemblies where the Lightbringers had to be present, so that they might not lose their feeling of solidarity with Manland, the decision had been reached that should they be excluded from the festival, they would break in force into Motherland. Phaon himself, whom they called father up there, had not been able to prevent the decision.

Mother Egli, Philomela Schwab and other illustrious Holy Mothers, with whom the newly created situation had to be discussed, had at last to agree with the proposal of the Council of Three, that a Mother's Commission should be sent into Manland to investigate the state of mind and, so to speak, the qualifications of the Manlanders to attend the holy festival, before finally and by a definite decision they should be confined within their own frontiers.

XII

NATURALLY, Anni Prächtel was the leader of the
Wildmanland Commission. With her, as ever, went
Rodberte, who was now over fifty, while Anni herself
had reached the age of seventy-five. But the paradisaical climate of Île des Dames had had more effect
upon them than oncoming age.

As Anni and Rodberte were being mounted upon their
zebu cows—for it was easiest to ride over the Défilé des
Dames—the President expressed her joy that now at
last she could examine at first hand what Phaon had
accomplished.

"How is that? Accomplished?" asked Rodberte,
and cried to the other Holy Mothers who, mounted and
on foot, awaited the moment of departure.

"Created," answered Anni.

"How accomplished? How created?" they asked
again among themselves in a tone which showed only
too clearly that they did not wish to admit or to hear
that Phaon had accomplished or created anything.
The President only answered with a hearty burst of
malicious laughter.

The early morning was lovely, as it always was on
Île des Dames.

"Do you still realise, ladies," began the President once more, "how lovely it was when that first sad and beautiful morning dawned on Île des Dames, and you wakened me out of my sleep with your cries of delight before the White House? That was the first great sound of hope on Île des Dames, and was only to be followed by a greater in the lion roar of the island demon, rich in blessing. And think, ladies, what we have become!

"You came back led by our Holy Mother Page, from the first expedition on the island, with magnificent fruits and still better news. Yet, Mother Page, you have only become more beautiful in spite of the lapse of twenty-odd years. Mother Warniko too, is, thank God, still of our party. I always recommend the younger mothers to think of what was accomplished by these ladies at that time. Our dear Rosenbaum is no more; otherwise we should not have so many formalities in the settlement of many a burning question. She was a true Berliner and always hit the nail on the head. Our able Mother Egli was often at variance with her; and it is true that Rosenbaum was scarcely a savant. Many things she refused to understand. She would say, 'I rely upon my sound common sense.' Whatever did not agree with it and whatever was beyond it, she promptly cast to the winds."

It could be seen already that the twelve mothers composing the Wildmanland Commission were divided into two parties. The Holy Mother Philomela Schwab, a magnificent woman with a mass of auburn hair, who was unsparing in great words and gestures, apparently led the greater one. Although Doctor Egli avoided taking sides overtly, she belonged to this group, who were determined rigidly to maintain the pure principles of feminine sovereignty, cost what it might. She and Philomela Schwab did not see and feel this as did the great loving soul of Laurence; they were animated rather by an emotion which partly at any rate might best be designated as subconscious hatred of men.

Both women felt little affection for the members of the Council of Three. Laurence and Anni Prächtel as well as Rodberte were women of the world. Their demeanour, their taste, their culture, presupposed all this. Their qualities were felt as an oppression by many of the Holy Mothers, especially by Philomela Schwab, who, when the shipwreck overtook her, had been for two years the wife of a prosperous brewer. But to the doctor also, who, supported by the sense of her remarkable efficiency in her profession, had scarcely any sense for art, philosophy or religion, nor a developed taste, the members of the Council of Three could not be acceptable; she did not comprehend their refined culture, and she could not recognise the value of their civilisation.

The cavalcade at last was set in motion: twelve Holy Mothers, and a guard of ten mounted Daughters of Heaven armed with spears, led by the rider Iphis. By evening they hoped to cross the Wildmanland pass, the Défilé des Dames. Here according to programme the band of girls was to be relieved by a band of ten youths.

Rodberte remarked to the President, who rode next to her:

"Just hark how the women gabble. I am never bored and hardly ever irritated when I am with our young girls, for so much lovely life and growth bring me joy of themselves. But to the company of my old comrades in fortune I really prefer solitude. All this is not new to you, Anni, yet what can even we say to each other that we have not said a hundred times already? You know that I am a selfish woman; I have always been for myself alone, in social matters an anarchist. It is never a triumphant established system—moreover that does not exist—that brings me joy, but rather the play of nature. And our whole human development is nothing but the play of nature.

" 'For in very deed primal matter was not disposed by wise deliberation in fit order, and it passes and re-passes through itself by no plan.'

"So said Lucretius, and so the truth remains finally in every way.

"Here we have our women's state. Very good; it is all a game. As that I am content to appreciate it. It does not put a stop to the irresistible creative power of nature. But when I regard the solemnity of Mother Egli in handling the question of Matriarchate versus Patriarchate, I am struck by the comedy of it. She takes herself so seriously, like an infant builder of card houses.

"Truly all is fleeting, all is perishable. And that does not justify shiftlessness in the least. But whoever thinks he has found the absolute, and is persuaded he has built a structure for eternity, has only achieved the betrayal of himself and others."

"In spite of that," said Anni, "we will have to find now whether Wildmanland can be allowed to take part in the festival of the dedication of the brides or not. And, Rodberte," she continued, "let us not forget our beginnings. A stroke of fate made of us, *nolens volens,* an avowed woman's state. Why should we not carry on our experiment a little farther to see how far it can go?"

"I am convinced it cannot be carried much further now," said Rodberte. "In that connection I am bracing myself to see what we shall find on the other side of the pass. On this side, too, certain presages of dissolution already show themselves: for instance, Babette's speech. Above all, this absurdity of the temple has often gone sore against my grain."

Anni said: "I am not sufficiently implicated to enjoy the temple except artistically. From that aspect it pleases me and I hold it as not an unreasonable affair, for it is grounded on the universal poetical tendency of humanity, on its natural aspirations. And if man makes himself dependent on, yes, a slave to, his own poetic creations, that is no fault of Île des Dames. In all the five continents you cannot take three steps without coming across a host of proofs of this truth. Not only the Vedas, not only Buddha,

Spinoza, Kant, Schopenhauer, proclaim the attempt to find the absolute to be hopeless. Even a realistic thinker like Herbert Spencer, if I remember rightly, called the subjective consciousness a raw and inadequate measure of objective existence. There could, he said, be no essential similarity between the appearances created by our consciousness and their external causes. External causes, external things remain, by their nature, unknowable and unknown. Then why should we not poetise in that province as we like? Why should we not enthrone phantasmagoria there? Why should we not people and equip our island according to our pleasure with purely subjective realities? Even if the spirit is nourished only from the spirit, yet is it, that eternally unreal element, the real content and epitome of all our joys and griefs. For myself I can only demand of subjective realities (like Mukalinda and others) which are transmitted through suggestion, that they should arise out of the aspiration towards beauty and that the faith of their believers should be artistic, a yea and a nay, and not a stupid, priestly infatuation."

At a moderate distance behind the President and Rodberte rode the Holy Mothers Schwab and Egli, zebu cow by zebu cow.

"But just mark, dear Mother Egli," said Schwab, "how these two celebrities there (she meant Prächtel and Kalb) take care to distinguish themselves from the rest of us. One could more easily believe that they read the 'Arizona Kicker' than that anyone could come to the point of calling them Holy Mothers."

The Holy Mother Egli responded: "If there is smoking and drinking of alcohol on the island to-day these two ladies are certainly not the least to blame." Further than that she did not care to go.

"I have the impression that a plot is being hatched behind us," said Anni once more to Rodberte. "Truly they would do anything to keep the mass of the youths away from the festival of the dedication of the brides. And it must be confessed that the question, yes or no, is very ticklish. What one can see and hear from our side of Golfe des Dames of the opposite side seems to show that the youths are a little insolent. If we drew their attention too directly to the banquet reserved for Mukalinda, I would not like to guarantee that with their sound stomachs they would restrain their appetites. But," she concluded, "all that is immaterial. What should we be to-day had not a real god seen our wretchedness and graciously stretched his creating hand over us? Let us congratulate ourselves on all this growing and becoming, and on what has been accomplished." She concluded: "To the deuce with it all, that is my view!"—and let fall from her high-raised hand an enthusiastic slap on the haunches of the zebu cow, which thereupon obediently began to trot.

"Look! Look!" said Schwab. "I bet the old girl has considerably depleted her travel flask already."

By the Lake of the Serpents, in a thicket of date palms, whose branches interlaced in green vaults, they took their mid-day rest. The water of the Lake of the Serpents was warm. It warmed all the boggy soil round about, and made it a suitable place for spawning life. It was alive with flocks of flamingoes.

Here one could see, beyond the Portail des Dames and Golfe des Dames, the twin peak, the extinct volcano in Manland, to which Babette had given the name of Hemakuta.

"Magnificent!" said the President. "So the Portail des Dames is guarded and flanked by two mighty giants! But I will not have these linked with any symbolical associations. It would not be to the advantage of humanity if the virtue of women were guarded by such fearful sentinels!"

It was not only the lake, nor only the wide and extensive view, which gave the place its incomparable charm. That was given by the handiwork of nature, which here had constructed through the silences of ages terraces of colossal dimensions, which stage by stage fell like a marble stairway to the lake. Truly it would not have been hard to believe that a god had planned this glorious stairway going down to the bath of that boiling lake shrouded in vapour. The stairway was itself overflowed by water. The water made its way, rushing, splashing, running, constantly dropping, trickling, oozing, bubbling, sputtering, hissing, from a higher basin to the lake below, at boiling point when it escaped from its source, and, losing heat from step to step, still hot when it entered the lake. Countless cavities and natural baths held the hot turquoise element, as if to proffer it to the light, to the heavens, to genii or to gods, in superb frames, in lovely vessels, which in eternal silence, eternal fullness, it overflowed.

"Near here," said Rodberte, "lies Mother Babette's hermitage, and we will certainly have to visit it."

"One must admit," commented the President, "that she has known how to choose her place of residence, as it were in a watering-place of heaven. Baden-Baden is nothing to this. Here in a few weeks all the gouty and rheumatic sufferers in Europe could be freed completely of their itches, twinges and pains. A pity that on this island one cannot have the smallest touch of gout for love or money. I itch as it were, to wander like a credulous Lazarus from one bath to another in this wonderful Bethesda, and then ascend from terrace to terrace, from the luke-warm to the warm, from the warm to the hot, and at last enter into the boiling spring itself."

Thereupon the two ladies took a neatly kept path which led to the now visible hut of Babette, which had a thick funnel-shaped roof of palm straw.

"It is good to be here," said Babette who, when they found her, was roasting bananas over a little glimmer of fire. She wore a yellowish robe without armlets, which reached to her knees, with, round the hips, a kind of Brahminical girdle. Her uncovered hair, already a little grey and of extraordinary length, heightened the peculiar impression which she made.

"It is good to be here, beloved Mothers," she said. "You have your feet on the hill of the gods, the fire-spitting Olympus of the noble and dedicated Laurence, and you have Hemakuta before you, my hill, the other hill of the gods, beyond Golfe des Dames and the Portail des Dames, which morning and evening shows his peak of gold, and on it that crystalline palace in which my gods assemble.

"And I have here my Lake of the Serpents and the magnificent flint bath terraces of Mont des Dames, beloved by the gods of both mountains as a bathing place. They come almost every night to bathe. Besides a host of flamingoes a few chatakus have settled in the neighbourhood, although they do not drink terrestrial water, as you know, but quench their thirst only at the clouds of heaven."

While she spoke Babette was surrounded by a flock of small, grey, noisy parrots, which not only quarrelled for places on her head, shoulders and arms, but stole something from every bite she took. Her arm seemed to be a favourite switchback for the birds, and the holy woman seemed to be quite indifferent to the fact that she was continually being flecked with a kind of guano.

"Ay, ay," she continued, "the gods love me. When they bathe I must be present. How magnificent they are as they flit up and down the terraces in white raiment in the moonlight!"

"One might give you," said the President, "the title of bath attendant to the everlasting gods."

She retorted: "You might well give me that title. But you could also give me quite other and higher titles. If you only knew how the pious vulture Jatayus speaks to me, he who flies to and fro between Mont des Dames and Hemakuta with tidings, and also when the gods bathe! The Greek gods of the noble Laurence and those of Hemakuta love one another. But those of Hemakuta are spiritually mightier than these. They pierce deeper into infinity."

When Rodberte related to Babette that with other Mothers she was on a journey to Wildmanland to see how all went there, Babette said: "Oh, my dears, all is well. Do not forget that our boys have powerful guardian lords over them. Hemakuta, remember, stands on the soil of Wildmanland. Now and then one of his sixty thousand little spies, no bigger than my thumb, finds his way here when he has been out to bathe in the holy waters of the terraces. Then sometimes a little of his mysterious knowledge falls into my lap. The sixty thousand guard the chariot of the sun. But I believe there are more of them, and the holy books are in error. The sun gives them seercraft. My little Tom Thumb has said to me that the gods have great things in view for Wildmanland.

"Yes, Manu Vaivasvata bathes sometimes here. Who does not know that he is a son of the sungod, and lawgiver to mankind? He has confirmed to me the promise of little Valakhilya, and says that a new Buddha shortly will come out of Wildmanland."

"But you prophesied only lately to us the triumph of the Great Mothers to all eternity," said Prächtel.

"Yes, but their protectors, their shield," continued

Babette, "shall be heroes mighty with the sword. Absaras, too, bathe here among the rest. I know through them that as son of my son Bihari Lâl and Rukminî, Purûravas will be re-born. He will once more take Urvasî, an Absara, as his wife: Urvasî who even now is to be seen amid the assemblies of the gods on Hemakuta.

"Manu Vaivasvata, the son of the sungod, had a daughter. The son of this daughter is Purûravas. In him, too, rolls the sun-blood. But his father was Chandra, the moon."

In such ways the speech of Babette flowed on without a stop, without intermission, like a stream, and she scarcely marked when Rodberte and Anni departed.

When the ladies were alone Prächtel said: "It is all very well, and I am fairly understanding when I encounter hallucinations and illusions. Perhaps it is immaterial whether one clothes the breath of the divine in a nothing or in a something. Nevertheless I am concerned for dear Babette. I do not know whether she is already quite insane, but it is impossible that her brain should withstand for long this crowding swarm of gods, demons, messengers and I know not what of the impossible."

Not long before sunset the zebu cows with their riders had reached the Défilé des Dames, that high-lying, narrow pass, which was the only practicable means of communication between Motherland and Manland. Here Phaon with ten of the youths took in hand the transport of the twelve-times holy and precious load, while the ten girls led by Iphis, together with their steeds, turned back with defiant glances.

The Mothers, mounted on fresh zebus, were scarcely ten minutes in motion, ascending through a narrow, rocky ravine rich in caves, ere Rodherte began to realise that all the circumstances were in keeping, that the atmosphere was in some way quite different and told quite a different tale.

Whether Phaon wished to have a joke, what he was indeed quite capable of, or whether it was simply the custom of Wildmanland, they began now to gallop in swift time up the mountain, so that the mothers had to hold on desperately. It did not avail the alarmed cows, urged on with whips and shouts, that they lashed round them with their tails, bellowing savagely. As if on winged feet, by each of them went a naked, athletic genius, who scarcely heeded the cow, but yet forced it to unbroken, furious motion. Like the lovely Iphis, Phaon had broken in a zebu bull to be his steed. But the skill of the lovely Iphis was left far behind by this horseman, who, knit to his steed, seemed to become a new kind of centaurish creature. This bull, bigger and more fearful than any which the Holy Mothers had yet seen, recognised no obstacle when his possessor was on his back. He had learned to know and to make use of his strength. Even when a terrible rage was visible in his eyes, it but heightened his strength, which broke out almost in portents of rage.

Helter skelter they went zig-zag over bridle-track

and bridle-track, through rocky streams; and tree-
trunks were no obstacle. Without hesitation they slid
down a slope covered with boulders, without the slightest wavering they urged the cows up over a confusion
of sharp-edged blocks, so that the bravest among the
Mothers felt themselves going hot and cold. All this
seemed to be designed to impress the Mothers from the
start with the superiority of masculine strength and
dexterity, and it certainly did not fail to do so.

The fatigue as well as the peril of the ride, and
naturally the anxiety of the Mothers, too, increased
when they reached the highest point of the pass, and
began to descend. Suddenly, however, they were without accident on a lovely green terrace, from which
they saw, not very far beneath them, the level stretch
of the lagoon in its full length from east to west, and
the gigantic rocky gap of the Portail des Dames.

On this terrace, in a tidily kept, airy hall roofed
with palm straw, the Mothers found the night quarters
prepared for them. With all that the Mothers found
in and under their beds (which were separated from
each other by beautifully painted mats), they had
reason to be content. Oil wicks to light the compartments were not needed. The ten youths who were
commissioned to receive and attend the Holy Mothers
had been commanded to keep twelve great fires going
all night in their honour. Moreover, the full moon
was now mirrored in the gulf, and shed a light as of
day, by which one might easily read. And at last
appeared also the smoky torch of Mont des Dames,

which threw its blood-red glow on the waters of the gulf, and among the glistening silver of the moonlight.

In Motherland the idea had prevailed that mankind was like the orang-outangs, graminivorous, and should avoid flesh. Here—it was certainly a failure in tact—no notice was taken of this truth. True, all manner of fruits, and of fruit and vegetable salad, had been made ready as a night meal, but appetising smells stole in, from the twelve fires, which announced that on every side good roast was being cooked on spits.

Doctor Egli was not a strict vegetarian. She had, however, submitted to the inclinations of the majority of the women and especially those of Philomela Schwab, and she was not against the principle of vegetarianism. Moreover, she could now confirm that a fleshless regimen suited the mothers admirably. But when Philomela Schwab, not meaning ill, went forward to one of the fires and at once turned away with a pretended shudder, it was she whom Phaon, still less meaning ill, took as the object of his powers of persuasion.

It was surprising how different Phaon was here on the soil of Wildmanland, and how he sunned himself in the eyes of the Mothers; strange was this transformation, stranger still, almost, his increase of light. He moved here with the serene freedom and strength of a man who knows of no human power higher than himself, and who, when he is prudent, is so only out of consideration for the weak. Up there in Motherland, and especially in the Temple, such had not been his bearing. There he took on a habitual appearance of obedience, sometimes, indeed, of diffidence, like a well-born child, who, troubled, recognises the superior wisdom of his father and mother.

Rodberte said to Prächtel: "In God's name, look well at that man. I ask myself if I have ever in all my life seen such a man before, a man of such noble and powerful proportions. The only one whom I can think of who might have been like him is Leone Battista Alberti. But he was before my time; he must have lighted this world round about 1442. What strength of limb, what a fire in his glance, what securely established serenity! Yes, by Heaven, we make a woman's state sure enough, but he can wind us like a thread round his finger."

Phaon's laugh boomed out, and all around the birds flew away. He had just held on a spit a roasted bird, at least as big as three geese, under Philomela's nose. Her screams were heard, but they could be savoured again in echo.

"You must give it a trial, Philomela," said the strong, fearless man. "Otherwise it is impossible for you to take home a proper conception of the frightfulness of Wildmanland."

When among the fires, under the lamp of the moon, they sat down to table, everything on it and about it had been set out by the ten youths in the most superb fashion.

"Splendid," said the President, almost involuntarily, "to be once more among such eaters! I find that in Motherland we make far too little of these things."

The Mothers had never been served on Île des Dames as they were served by these ten youths. Phaon presided over the table, and none of the youths was allowed to take part. A beautiful lad, still half boy, introduced the meal with a clearly recited, trifling little verse:

> Seek, ye mothers, now repose,
> While the moon in heaven glows.
> Food and drink is set before ye,
> Eye and palate to delight.
> From life's journey and its glory
> Turn aside and rest to-night.
> Think that what the present brings
> Goes the way of mortal things.

"Bravo! Splendid!" cried Phaon and in unison with him all twelve members of the Commission. "Come here, you poet," he cried, and, taking the blushing boy by the ear, said: "Now go round the table, give each of the Mothers a kiss, and say to her: 'Much good may it do you, Holy Mother!'"

No sooner said than done; at that moment no headway could be made against Phaon's patriarchal-imperial style. Kissing, the youth went about the Table Round, a new John the Second.

"John the Second, the mighty kisser," said Rodberte to him, as she granted him the ordained smack.

Phaon shouted: "What do you say to this sprig of Mukalinda? Take hold of the rascal and give me your opinion: is not everything about him iron if he wishes it? And if he does not wish it, is not a handful of eider-down hard compared with him?"

Sprig of Mukalinda was a phrase which would have given Mother Philomela Schwab more vexation and exasperation if the impression which Phaon made had not in some strange way disarmed her. She ate, she drank, she refreshed herself with the moist warm air and the palm spirit, and decided on no account to sleep that night, but to wander alone through that moon-irradiated land of magic. She even thought of letting the splendid usurping patriarch know her decision. Only she did not know in what way this could be done without involuntarily betraying the fact to the Mothers. Even as she was busied with these thoughts she heard Mother Page, Mother Page who in voluptuous beauty was so far superior to her, say: "I simply shall not be able to go to sleep to-night. I shall have to go wandering the whole time."

Rodberte cried: "May I accompany you, Mother Page?"

"No one, no one may accompany me," she received for answer. "I would like for this one night to be as alone as a gnat who has been closed for hundreds of thousands of years in a piece of yellow amber."

Throughout this night-meal high on the ledge of the inland sea all the guests, with or without the aid of palm spirit, were thrown into an ecstasy, an intoxication, of beauty. There went out from the moon, from Mont des Dames, from Hemakuta, from all the great, sublime, brooding, transfigured landscape, a

mighty magic. Was it the soft, ardent wind, pregnant
with scents of narcotic spices, that the magic resided
in, and with which it covered as with a cloud its
victims? In any case these had fallen, as it were, into
a sensual-supersensual state which made their limbs
like air, and let their souls breathe themselves out into
the All, the One. It might well be, too, that the immediate presence of the youths, who silently brought
forward delicious food and drink, and above all that
the presence of Phaon himself helped to produce this
state, although Phaon, even for the taste of Anni and
Rodberte, let himself go far too far in his speech, and
indeed enjoyed it.

In a little address which he made Phaon finally welcomed the Mothers to Manland. In it he said a number of things at which the Mothers laughed, because
they took them to be deliberately humorous.

"There is no yesterday," said he, "no to-day, no to-
morrow: there is no reality. But what is, is, and real
being," said he, "everybody who encounters it must
take by the forelock." In such ways he spoke.

Although they laughed, and believed that Phaon
intended them to laugh, it seemed to them sometimes
as though he spoke seriously. Everything around them
was phantasmal. Were they actually on Île des
Dames? What had been and what was—was that
truly a reality? Had not all that been blotted out in
one strange moment, remaining now only in the imagination, like the sunken ship, the *Cormorant?* Did not

this serene, laughing, tyrannical man who entertained them make them completely thoughtless? And had he not blown away the whole woman's state, as it were, like a feather from his hand? And these youths, these outcasts, these sudras around them—were they not like darlings of the gods sent down from Olympus or Hemakuta for the entertainment of the Holy Mothers, as the Absaras are ordained for the entertainment of the masculine gods, sweethearts and mothers at once? What could be sinful or impossible in the kingdom of heaven? Did they not see that these masculine genii were confused, indeed, struck dumb, by the strange physical presence of those they served?

The meal came to an end; morning arrived; reality was again with them. Had Mother Philomela Schwab carried through her decision to remain awake all night? Or had she slept badly, or honoured the palm spirit too well? In any case when once more she sat on the haunches of the zebu cow her expression had become foreboding and gloomy.

"I declare I am quite decided," said she to Mother Egli, so that only she could hear, "I declare I am quite decided against these untamed, raw Manland powers being allowed even once, even on the day of the festival, over the Défilé des Dames. It would simply mean the dissolution of the woman's state. I say that," she concluded, "although as yet I have seen only a small sample of the unbridled Manland spirit."

She was still to see other things, as surprising as

miracles, but which were to show her even more significantly the danger which had grown, without its knowledge, against the Mother-state.

The Mothers were at once conducted by Phaon *in medias res*. By noon they had reached a place of whose existence no one in Motherland, except Dagmar-Diodata, knew anything; namely, the so-named Capitol. Its pillared façade rose in a wide, gravelly square surrounded by arcades, in whose centre was a statue hewn from stone, a hand pointing to the heavens. From the Capitol buildings ran paths in all directions; among bushes and trees spaces had been left for meadows, the centre of each being occupied by a little wooden temple. These were in reality little workshops in which indefatigable artists occupied themselves with all sorts of handwork, such as stone-cutting, pottery, carpentry, instrument making, and so on.

The Holy Commission found in the Capitol a very comfortable and clean lodging, and a suitable starting point for their studies. Their arrival marked the beginning of a festival for Manland.

The Mothers were astounded to see how much Phaon changed now once more. He showed to the eye a calm and dignity to mount to whose difficult heights was no light task even for them. The Manlanders, great and small, who all obviously regarded Phaon with the greatest love and respect, were without exception greeted by him with: "My son, my dear son," as it is the custom with generals to greet their soldiers.

The inspection began with a tiny and tidy colony of

seven-year-old boys, who were entrusted to the care of lads of twelve. The latter received the Mothers with a strict reverence, such as is due to superiors, while the little ones, amazed, stared at them with open mouths, as if they were fabulous animals.

"In as far as the supernatural impression which they wish to make goes," observed the President to Rodberte not entirely without irony, "the Holy Mothers, I think, may be quite satisfied here."

Riding, swimming, nesting and date gathering from the loftiest trees, shooting parrots in flight, leaping, walking on the hands, and still more useless sports, were exhibited before the Mothers, who remarked only the zeal displayed in everything. It seemed to them as if all these sports were designed to meet some definite purpose in the future.

All these lads were distinguished by a distinct and kindred beauty. With exceptions, most of them seemed as if their lovely and supple yet hardened bodies had come out of the same mint. Verus, a pretty defiant rogue, was called by Phaon; whereupon at once, as dexterous as a little ape, he was hanging round the strong man's neck. He made the child let go, and set him before the Holy Mothers.

When the still wonderfully beautiful Mother Page reached him her hand, affably indicating that he should do the same, quick as lightning he hid his hands. But at Rodberte who spoke kindly to him he stuck out his tongue as quickly, and with the greatest vivacity. Philomela Schwab, who became severe and thereby perhaps came too near him with her noble countenance, received, seeing that she was spat upon, a new proof of masculine incorrigibility. At this performance Anni could not restrain a heart-easing laugh, a laugh taken badly by her entourage; and this also gave Verus a chance to box the ears of his inoffensive neighbours vigorously right and left. No one knew whether it was in this instant or immediately when she saw him first that Philomela Schwab recognised her offspring. At any rate she rushed on him with the intention of inflicting chastisement, an attempt which Phaon checked, shielding the child. "This lad," said he, "will perhaps discover the south pole some day."

The Holy Mothers had the first, the second, the third colony behind them, when Anni Prächtel asked Rodberte what struck her most here, in contrast with Motherland.

Rodberte said: "Here one is hardly any longer on Île des Dames."

"But that is obvious," said Prächtel.

"I do not mean," Rodberte completed her impression, "because we see everywhere these youths, these men, but because everything goes with such verve and freedom that we hardly feel any more our captivity on Île des Dames."

The boys of twelve on Île des Dames surpassed those of eighteen in European civilizations, the youths of fifteen surpassed European adults. One of these was asked by the President: "What is your aim in life?"

"I shall go to sea," he answered, "for I have decided to look thoroughly at the world."

After these words the naked, reddish-brown youth continued to free a pine of some branches which he wanted, whose crashing fall was soon heard.

Thereupon he sang in a beautiful voice, which echoed and re-echoed in the valley, as follows:

> Iphis, thou Daughter of Heaven!
> Iphis!
> Thou didst appear
> High above us
> On thy golden-hooved zebu,
> On thy zebu with golden horns.
> High over us didst thou appear
> On the morning cliffs
> In splendour.
> Round thee was splendour;
> The hide of thy silvery bull quivered.
> He snorted silvery mist
> Out of his nostrils,
> Clouds of silver
> Out of his rosy-coloured jaws.
> Bless us, Iphis,
> Daughter of Heaven!

Among her comrades, Iphis, it was known, had made herself particularly prominent by her agitation against the participation by Wildmanland in the festival of the dedication of the brides. She had once soundly cudgelled a boy who, ignoring the frontiers of Motherland, had come upon the huntress. On that account the song which they heard impressed the Holy Mothers only the more curiously.

"She has acted most inexpediently, our quick-handed Iphis, to insult her brothers with outbreaks of violence. Here with great and small she occupies a position of grace, and takes on, as she herself knows, almost the rank of a deity."

As Phaon said this, they rounded a cliff, after having pursued a mountain path, and had beneath them a bay hitherto unknown to the women. But what they saw on its blue and tossing surface drew from them cries of amazement. For a number of boats with brown sails were cruising there.

One knows what an impression of animation can be evoked by a little flotilla of fishing boats on the swell of a bay. The seven sailing boats which cruised here lifted from the souls of the Holy Mothers an oppression to which they had been accustomed for decades. The barriers of the ocean seemed to have fallen, the word of banishment seemed lifted, the return to human society, in sight.

What wonder that they were thrown into transports!

"They have gone far beyond us," said Prächtel. "The most good-for-nothing of them have been pulling our legs while we have been making mythology."

There was a lively cross-fire of questions from every side, which Phaon finally quieted by a brief explanation of the origin of this fleet.

"The boats," said he, "are of the double-keeled type.

It is the simplest type of sailing boat, and I have seen it on cruises with my parents on the North Sea, off the coast of Portugal, on the Atlantic, as well as round the Italian coast. But it was especially in the small port where I stayed as a boy with my parents that I came to know it better. Often and often have I sailed in such a two-keeler with the fishers when they put out for a catch. On those occasions my parents were naturally anxious about me, our tutor would give notice, the governess would not know where to turn. They argued that the cruises were dangerous and led to nothing, for I should never become a fisherman. How this prank was to be later of use to me they did not guess. We simply did not rest until, with the help of one of our historical ship's-boats, as text for the hull, we had afloat one, two, three ramshackle two-keelers, of which the second was better than the first, the third better than the second. So it has gone on; now we have achieved our seventh."

"Children," said the President, and—it could not be concealed—she broke into sobs, "if at any time you set off on an expedition to discover the Dark Continent among the seas, and you do not take your President, you will all be drowned as a punishment."

Then she controlled herself and continued: "Why have you kept all this a secret from us, my good Phaon? Neither I, nor Rodberte, nor Fräulein Auguste has had the least knowledge of this bay and your sailing boats. Not even we three, who have surely deserved it from you. With the thought of these sails and a half-suspicion of this bay I might have got more easily over the dead period of my life."

She said then, seizing Phaon's hand: "In sight of this bay you will build me a hut, my dear son. I shall dwell in sight of this bay. For it makes me young, stimulates me to phantasies. That should not make you marvel, Holy Mothers. I am simply too bad for Paradise; an old, hardened sinner. Matriarchate, patriarchate; if matriarchate were heaven I would quite certainly sit at the gate so that occasionally, when it was opened, I might take a peep at the patriarchate. If Peter should let me sometimes enter the most holy patriarchate of the heavenly paradise, then I would beg the sublime apostolic door-keeper by some means to give me a place beside him, so that I might look often through a crack or through the key-hole at the diabolical matriarchate. And perhaps, if he slept . . . we Holy Mothers know well how occasionally of nights, I am thinking of the Dark Continent, what free and happy uses a latchkey can be put to.

"Children, children, what refreshing, strengthening air streams in here, as if through an open door. You do not live on the western peak of the island in vain. Truly the west rather than the east is the orient of mankind. God knows I do not long for China, Japan or India. I long for Europe, for a landing at Hamburg, for Berlin. I would like to hear steamers blowing their horns, locomotives whistling. I would like to see an art exhibition, enjoy the Ninth Symphony, look through a gigantic telescope, see a performance at the Burg Theatre in Vienna, and after that have supper at Sacher's, with Cliquot Ponsardin. Malicious, impudent, mad things should be tossed from one to the other across the table. Gypsies should play. A kingdom for a Parisian cocotte, a beautiful, audacious, rouged woman, hung with pearls, swathed in furs and silk, *décolletée* to the very navel, perfumed, consummate!"

"Hold on, President," cried Rodberte. Universal embarrassment reigned. The Mothers almost believed that an attack of senile imbecility, a sort of apoplexy, had overtaken the President. But they had also a feeling as if a sacred taboo had been blasphemously violated. There was also something, which all knew of, but which yet was ignored. This convention had grown quite inevitably to be one of their many necessities for self-preservation, as happens customarily in the Dark Continent. In short, the old lady had touched ungently the wound of homesickness which in none of the original mothers was quite closed; and she marked it first when it was no longer to be altered.

Yet the Holy Mothers of the Commission did not break out in reproaches; that their pride would not permit them to do. Instead, they excelled each other in rejoinders deprecating, even contemning, all that Anni seemed to long for.

Nor was it difficult to stifle the pain they felt in a general head-shaking over the senile decay of the President. At last, apparently, their depreciation fell even on the two-keelers.

Anni had the feeling now that she must speak further and more to the point, if she was to cover up her aberration.

She said: "Where you are, dear Phaon, is the land of youth. But where we are . . ."

But no one listened more to her, for the zebus were already in motion again.

Alexander, Answalt and Ariel were associated with their mentor, Phaon, and thus with the commission. In addition to them it was attended by busy, capable little boys, who had to obey the wishes of the .Holy Mothers.

"The handicraft which we chiefly follow," said Phaon, "is that which the problem of wood presents us. Its chief sub-divisions are: tree-felling, carpentry, the art of the cart-wright, the cooper, the joiner, the turner. It cannot be denied that through the general discipline this has involved, amazingly good results have been obtained."

As Phaon said this they came upon a group of young carpenters, overflowing with vitality, who amid cheerful shouts were working away at tree trunks in a sunny pine forest. The interest of the Commission had already been claimed for a long time by this spectacle. The noises, the crashing and whizzing of the splinters, which flew fast and thick, the power of the swinging arms, all held them fast. Here work was done at a rate which seemed to say: "We would rather finish it to-day than to-morrow." An unrest, a creative haste, as it were, which was not to be explained entirely by insular necessity, lay over the joiner's theatre high above the sea. This was remarked not only by Anni Prächtel, Rodberte and the hump-backed Fräulein Auguste, but by all the members of the commission, and the more forcibly, the more they saw.

"How did you come by so many and such good tools?" asked Mother Titania, formerly Page.

"As the men of the stone age," answered Phaon, "came by theirs. We searched the shore again and again for suitable material and suitable chance formations, and set specialists to carry on without intermission an investigation of this province. The material found was then, I can say it now, re-touched in the most expert fashion."

By the light and athletic Alexander, Answalt and Ariel, the ladies were shown stone hammers, axes, knives, wedges, rasps, in short, all manner of tools.

"Happy Phaon!" said the President. "Divine youths!"

With outstretched left hands raised in greeting, the radiant sons of Anak appeared, holding tools in their right for the inspection of the women.

The origin of all the customs had to be told, and, not least, that of this odd but in no way ignoble greeting.

Phaon said: "It could not remain always a mystery to you, even if I were to keep it secret now: in addition to Mukalinda and the Bona Dea we worship other gods, or, say at least, one other god. You will say we have sunk to the stage of semi-animal savages if I tell you that besides this third god whom we honour we follow after idols. Perhaps you have not observed that the tree-feller who sang the undeserved hymn to Iphis was making use of one of the saws which was left us from the equipment of the ship's-boats. And you noticed as little how, after his work was done, he reverently pressed the saw-blade against his brow. Well, that is what he did, for every bit of our old irreplaceable equipment of tools is counted holy among us. Our peculiar Manland god, however—do not be too horrified, noble ladies—is the Hand. I repeat: the sacred Hand. I hope you will not sin against us as the holy Boniface did against the Saxons, overthrowing our divine image of the Holy Hand as he did the pillars of Irma. It glitters, as you know, in the Agora. But the greeting, noble ladies, whose origin and meaning you wish to know, springs from our reverence towards the Hand, and confirms us as guild-brothers in the service of the Holy Hand."

To this the Mothers had little to reply. They did not grasp yet the range of this idea, this symbol. True, Prächtel and Rodberte remembered that in a drawing of Rembrandt van Rijn the hand of Jesus Christ when he was scourging the money-changers from the Temple, was irradiated by a blaze of glory. When they mentioned this fact, Phaon declared in confirmation that this blaze of glory is merited not only by the hand of the Saviour, but as well by the human hand.

One day in the course of his solitary meditations

the whole mystery, the complete miracle of the human hand, had been independently revealed to him.

He did not know what support his original intuition had received from the great scientists of the Dark Continent, for instance from Charles Darwin; Darwin, who in his "Descent of Man" made his own the view of C. Bell, which was, in effect: The hand supplants all instruments and through its correspondence with the intellect endows the intellect with universal empire. By this new Sun of thought the social structure of Europe and its particular ethic should be elucidated, illuminated, should like the Phœnix bird be burned to ashes and then renewed in its spring.

Phaon thought it advisable to say still more of the nature of the human hand, as he conceived it. Till his twelfth year he had lived in the Dark Continent, an intelligent boy, in the brilliant circle of his parents, and had brought hither from it his models and examples.

"The concept of progress," said he, "is taken from the foot. The concept of creation, from the hand. Name me anything material or spiritual in the monstrous totality of the Dark Continent's civilisation or its European off-shoots, whose origin would be conceivable without the human hand. It is immaterial here whether you regard the written or printed letters of a poem by Goethe, the paper or the format of a book; a curb-stone, or the whole of Strassburg Cathedral. And now enter the cathedral. Regard the crucifix over the altar, the rich pictures, their canvas, their wood; or look at the stained glass windows on which the sun brings to life an Olympus of saints, a Valhalla of German emperors, kings and princes; all is the work of the human, which means the thinking, hand. Plato and Kant, of whom my tutor spoke often, while I listened, alas, only with one ear, Plato and Kant wrote. But even if they had dictated they could not have completed their work without the mediation of a hand. And take the most immaterial of all things, music. Leaving aside the fact that one score of music is the result of countless thinking hands; what would music be without instruments! And now imagine the countless swarm of thinking hands which must be employed to bring to completion even Mother Gerte Bergmann's violin. Murder and violent death—that the cat-gut tells us—must have come into it. For the whole monstrous province of action which thinking humanity rules, from the lowest to the highest, from the most disgusting to the most enticing, from the frightfullest to the most auspicious, from the roughest to the finest, from the noblest to the meanest, from the most hateful to the loveliest, from the most gruesome to self-sacrificing *Caritas,* is the work of the human hand. But if you would understand how inseparably the human intellect is bound in unison with the human hand, then look at the hand of the violinist. Or look at the hand of the pianist. Swiftly, quicker than thought, countless, inconceivably countless movements of the human soul and the human intellect up to the most ethereal, unrecordable tremor, are brought to expression through the hand of the violinist and of the pianist. Here this apparently dumb organ has shaped a language which is able to express even that which to the language of words is inaccessible. I beg you, dear Mothers, to pursue the matter in thought still farther. Think of the tiniest nail, the tiniest needle, in the Dark Continent; think of the simple brick out of which perhaps is constructed your parents' house, even as the great city of Paris, the great city of London, the great city of Berlin is constructed; and then you will see hands and hands and once more hands, yes, a deluge of hands stretching to the horizon, and, thus regarded, the sun will seem obscured and the earth buried by them. But no, what am I saying? May still as many, many endless clouds of such hands, may hands as countless as the sands of the waste come to us up from the horizons of our spirit; to our spirit, it would only be a new manifestation, endlessly enriching instead of overwhelming and stifling it. It is not to be estimated what would happen in the Dark Continent if the hand were lifted from its state of contempt to one of honour. Then for the first time humanity would be guided no more by fools and mystifiers, but by a firmly established consciousness. From the creation of this consciousness onwards, mankind will feel and experience the growth of a noble humanity, a growth which little by little will make us worthy of the marvellous works of the thinking hand now apparent in the Dark Continent."

When Phaon was finished there fell again an apparently embarrassed silence. Only Rodberte forced herself to say: "I wish the pious Laurence had been here!" whereupon Prächtel nodded agreement.

Phaon enquired distantly: "Why do you say that?" "You have," retorted Rodberte, "it seems to me, developed in many ways into what the noble Laurence long ago expected of you."

In the Holy Mothers' demeanour towards Phaon there was betrayed from now on a curious reserve. It was as if he had become a complete stranger. Was it because he paraded with so much freedom and energy views which were strange, if not subversive of society, or because the Mothers were unaccustomed to the sight of men, and were disturbed, even fascinated, by it? After all, it was monstrously strange that besides the feminine there was another human division, whose nature and habit allowed them to forget for whole periods their helpless birth out of their mothers' bodies.

In these circumstances the situation of one of the Holy Mothers must be marked out as peculiarly painful. She was a beautiful, voluptuous woman, whose tiny foot had to carry a noble burden of feminine charm. Her hair was black, her neck almost always bowed, she spoke little, but sang on and on, and plucked strange flowers by the way. Sometimes she opened wide her very dark, dewily shining eyes, until then, as it were, directed inwards. She did this when Rodberte finished: and then as if she were quite alone, without the smallest embarrassment, she fixed Phaon with the glance of those moist dark eyes, walked calmly up to him, and threw two superb arms round his neck. Then she pressed a kiss on his mouth.

"Mother Erdödy! Mother Erdödy," cried the Mothers, horrified, dismayed, as with one voice.

It would be hard to say to what should finally be referred the shock which each of the Mothers felt at seeing this very natural proceeding; nevertheless no act of immorality, of shamelessness, of treachery, not even the defilement of their sacred words and mysteries, could have been more offensive. The Holy Mothers became mute and dumb, they grew sickly pale, their rigid lips pressed together, their mouths twitching with wordless anger.

Phaon at once knelt down on one knee, and, full of respect, kissed the hand of the Holy Mother Erdödy.

"Mother Erdödy," said Rodberte, "only desires to bestow her blessing on our Phaon in his great and difficult mission to the Dark Continent." Mother Erdödy was a Hungarian, and beloved by all on account of her simple goodness and innocent sensuality.

Going uphill the mothers had now once more reached broad, green meadows. Before they had time to look, to their renewed astonishment a sound which they had not heard for decades fell upon their ears. They would have been compelled to think it the sound of cow-bells, if the small variety of available metals in the island had not been known to them. But now they saw in truth the herds of zebus, and beheld bells hanging on broad thongs round the animals' necks.

"We play many idle tricks too," said Phaon. "One day I remembered the cow-bells of the Dark Continent and a longing to hear them fell on me. Yes, I had often cooked potatoes over the camp-fires with the young herds. But I wished ardently to have a jest ready for my dear island boys, to make live for them something of the sad music of our Swiss mountains, yes, to give them finally in connection with the cows, Friedrich Schiller's Wilhelm Tell himself. I wanted to see and enjoy their astonishment when they saw even the unreasonable zebu cow making music. Then I called to mind a certain wooden instrument of the gypsies, which they strike with hammers. So musical tones could be coaxed from wood. So I decided to entrust to our clever joiners the task of forming a bell out of wood. I am always as glad as my children whenever a new task offers itself. Ambition, which is a devastating thing among us, is then for a while busily employed, a state which in every way brings us up to the scratch, and lets us forget that, originally accustomed to the ocean, we are to-day, alas, carp in a pond. It was not long until the first wooden bell was ready, after my design, and then we soon had a second tone, a third, and finally a complete octave."

"One must give you your due; you have magnificently and beyond all expectation fulfilled the task handed over to you by the Council of Mothers. Perhaps it is as well that we did not think you at that time capable of it."

"The development of Manland," said Phaon with great deliberation, "would not have been hampered even by the fact of your not desiring it."

At that moment a song arose. It was not particularly melodious, for it was shouted rather than sung by a naked boy rapt in meditation as he sat on a grazing zebu cow. He sang his song in English, which according to Phaon was due to his having learned it from his mother, an American, before he was five, and having brought it with him to Manland.

> Lady-Cow, Lady-Cow,
> Fly away home.
> Thy house is on fire,
> Thy children are flown.
>
> All but a Little One,
> Under a stone:
> Fly thee home, Lady-Cow,
> Ere it be gone.

As this pretty pattern of a young herd-boy began the second verse of his ditty, the Holy Mother Titania, formerly Page, broke into violent sobbing.

And now befell another scene somewhat painful to the dignity of the high Matriarchal Commission. With magnificent spacious movements of her Dian limbs the Holy Mother Page bore down on the zebu cow, which suddenly shied and unseated the singer. The boy was still roaring when Titania Page, kneeling on the ground, enveloped and seemed to be smothering him. Fräulein Prächtel said, blowing her nose: "Thank God, I have at least one salvaged old handkerchief still."

This proceeding was taken in quite another way by a certain group of the Mothers on the Commission Moreover, the Holy Mother Doctor Egli associated herself with it. But Philomela Schwab seemed to be its centre and *spiritus rector*. She said, turning to Doctor Egli, "I do not think that such behaviour shows us up well before these outcasts!" And Mother Egli's brief rejoinder "Doting idiot!" in iciness left nothing to be desired.

None of the Mothers could tell on which side Mother Egli actually stood; even Laurence was uncertain on this point. In reality the doctor was the only one who was wholly in earnest about the idea of the Mother-state, and intrigued secretly and fanatically for its realisation. The pious Laurence and her transcendentalism she did not rate very high. Her nature was inaccessible to it. She only felt that it furthered her secret purposes. Her mentality was of necessity very different, since her attention was fixed so preponderatingly on physical incidents both bloody and distressing; and to her the violation of living and quivering flesh by sharp instruments was an everyday matter. With her entry into the medical profession her ethics were subsumed in the ethics of her guild. She was ruled by the cold, rational morality of the medical profession, which simply because nothing resembling a soul had ever come under the scalpel in any post-mortem examination or dissection, doubted the existence of the human soul.

Phaon knew well, even if the aspersion "doting idiot" had escaped him, what he had to expect from Mother Egli. Her scientific automatism could at best only be broken, never bent. Phaon was willing to learn where there was anything to be learned. So, like a young assimilative animal, he had in part made his own her Darwinism and her ways of regarding humanity. For the human animal, as he felt in himself, was the greatest wonder of nature, and as such worthy of reverence. Therefore one must build on this animality, and if one looked back upon the astounding emergence of the human animal through millennia, and thought of the millions of years which the fact of his development might still postulate, then one had to admit that the grandeur of this creature, this animal who from the other end of that dispensation of time sent his greeting down to us, far surpassed even our powers of imagination. But Phaon combated Mother Egli in every possible way, inasmuch as her secret hatred of men and glorification of women might lead her to sacrifice Manland, that is, man himself. He let her know privately and explicitly and also by the way in which he crossed her intrigues that he was her deadly enemy. At the moment, however, when Titania Page after a three-years' separation once more recognised and embraced her son, and Mother Egli uttered her phrase about doting idiocy, his deadly enmity shot from Phaon's eyes in one glance before which Mother Egli's eye wavered.

"These zebu cows," he said then with a hearty laugh, turning to the orthodox group, "these zebu cows can certainly not be called holy mothers, seeing that they are incapable of such a true and heartfelt expression of mother-love."

All that the Mothers observed, in general and in particular, for the next three or four hours drew from Anni Prächtel the admission that the horizon of Manland was wider than that on the opposite side. Rodberte said this happened because a mother is synonymous with a family. For the attribute of a family is stability, and the less nomadic its life the more favourable is its development. Therefore the spirit of a mother is turned more inwards, being absorbed in the tiny circle of the family, children, house, farm, hearth, garden. The boy, the youth, the man, is a creature for himself alone. He dare say *"Omnia mea mecum porto,"* and so he can travel free and untrammelled into the infinite. The feminine life-function imposes intensity, in the physical as well as in the spiritual. The masculine is expansive, and with it is associated the danger of excess in the physical as in the spiritual. That at evening he may not feel that a wasted day lies behind him the true man must have penetrated into the unknown to the very limits of his bodily strength, while the woman must weary herself out in the sacred precincts of the eternally familiar. Where the foot of man because of exhaustion or because of an obstacle can go no further, both exhaustion and obstacle are overleapt by his spirit, which unwearied, inconquerable, proceeds further into the infinite. She concluded by saying that the nature of women is, as it were, centripetal, and the masculine nature centrifugal.

Here the doctor could not resist opening her mouth and maintaining the superiority of women precisely on the basis of this conclusion, since the centrifugal can never have the power of constructing states.

The President gave a jesting turn to the discussion. "I will not let myself be drawn into deep questions," she said. "I have simply enjoyed the rich abundance of healthy boyish and youthful beauty, and the many curious characters which we have found. That we have had to hunt many of them, as it were, out of their isolated hiding-places, and that such a circumstance, together with the solitary occupations it denotes, scarcely betrays a remarkably strong social sense, I readily admit. Also that most of them do not find our paradise all-sufficing. Still, it is a delicious pleasure to breathe once more the aura of masculine foolishness with its high-flying plans. I myself incline to variety. A fourteen-year-old rascal broods over the problem of flying. The problem of flying will never be solved. But that does not trouble him. The birds can fly, why should he not fly too? He is happy, he is none the worse for it, he looks like an Adonis, but he would prefer to-day rather than to-morrow to cast himself headlong into the unknown on the wings of the morning.

"Another has got the idea of imitating an Alexander the Great, a Cæsar, a Napoleon. It even makes him a nuisance to his comrades. But it never occurs to him to become king over our wretched little hamlets, whether in the women's or the men's paradise. No, he will some day be the Dictator of the Dark Continent, and that great, siren world will be reduced to reason and delivered, by the blows of his wooden sword apparently—for he has no other. And I wager his will is so strong that somehow or other he will land one day in Cape Town or somewhere else, even if he has to swim there like a frog."

Phaon said, "Time is too short. And besides, the Holy Mothers through a dignity and nobility, which is now once and for all attributed to them by the Manlanders, have deserved our small confidence. It would take a long time to understand the motive force of the spirit in Manland. It comprises infinite mirth and folly, which a mildly humorous and certainly not exhaustive generalisation might well put down to masculine foolishness. We have pixies which have peopled every tree on the island with so many gods and demons that even our pious Laurence would be seized with astonishment. They call up every half hour another spirit, another phantom. The Bollandists, of whom Aunt Rodberte used to tell me many things, did not gather together so many Christian legends, and could not have gathered so many, as one of these tiny, active brains phantasies in his spare time about the relations of Mukalinda and the Bona Dea. In the heads of our youths and boys there are constructed already temples, churches, cathedrals, bridges over rivers and seas in such incalculable abundance and of such monstrous dimensions, that even the ruins of Baalbec, and St. Peter's in Rome, and Strassburg Cathedral, would appear petty and wretched beside them."

"That is pure nonsense," said Doctor Egli. "That is not even bubble-blowing. What is the use of it? If I had my way, I would make a clean sweep of every kind of fantasy, and perhaps on Île des Dames most particularly."

This was farther than Mother Egli had ever ventured before.

The Holy Mother Schwab struck in bitingly. "Why, even the unicorn has been sighted on Île des Dames! This nonsense is already more than can be borne."

"Well, why not?" answered Phaon. "Why should not the unicorn eventually appear on Île des Dames? I can assure you, Holy Mothers, that he appears here."

"And perhaps," Philomela Schwab enquired further, "the fabulous garden hanging in the air, with its queer zoology and botany, a Cloud Cuckoo Land of which our Daughters of Heaven have already related all manner of ghost-stories, also appears?"

"Certainly, Holy Mother, that appears too."

Prächtel said: "I marvel over nothing more, dear Doctor Egli, over absolutely nothing more. For a long time now I have been seeing not only unicorns but God knows what mad and fabulous creatures wandering about on our dear, absurd island. It is a red-letter day for me when I chance to see a real brown European flea."

In the neighbourhood of the Capitol the Commission were shown a small workshop occupied by three hand-workers. Here, to the renewed astonishment of the ladies, violins, beyond all question, were being made after the pattern of Gerte Bergmann's instrument. The fifteen-year-old violin-maker, whose appearance must have set the heart of any rightly constituted damsel on fire, was made to set forth circumstantially after how much trouble and abortive attempts the task was in the end painfully mastered. It transpired that Gerte Bergmann without the knowledge of the Mothers had often penetrated as far as this workshop, and had helped by word and deed in the mastering of the great task. The completed violins, a quartette, a quintette, nay, a small orchestra, whose rehearsals were directed by Gerte, was to have been on the first available big occasion a great surprise for the Holy Mothers.

"Since we are applying for admission to the festival of the dedication of the brides, I have persuaded myself to let you into the secret of one of our most beautiful mysteries. But what would not one do to show oneself worthy of such an honour as being permitted to participate in that festival? I told you before that we have devoted all our strength and intelligence to the handling and exploitation of wood. And that is the sole reason why we have had the happiness of piercing in some measure to this, its most subtle mystery, its musical soul."

As the ladies walked across the square a reception was being prepared for them on the steps of the Capitol. Garland-crowned boys and youths stood there in ranks, and all of them suddenly broke into a storm of hymn-like melody.

> Holy Mothers!
> Mothers of Bihari Lâl, Son of Heaven,
> Known by God, and bearing gods!
> Mothers of the Daughters of Heaven,
> Ye who wander
> Over the chalices of flowers,
> With the touch of your soles
> Strewing colours.
> If you give your lips to the tree
> It waxes and blooms.
> Soon will the falling of the fruit,
> Like the sound of drums,
> Shake the ground.
> Let your kiss awaken the rock,
> So that the crystalline rill breaks out,
> Rill of Heaven, to nourish your children,
> Divine,
> As the milk of your breasts is divine.

If this hymn went on and on, and even, as is the way of such things, lasted far longer than was seemly, yet the Holy Mothers could not but be pleased by the spirit in which it was composed.

The historic tour of inspection by the maternal delegation ended with a ceremonial banquet in the Capitol, at which roast meat was again eaten and, to the exasperation of Doctor Egli, palm wine liberally enjoyed. In a welcoming address Phaon said that no one in Manland doubted woman was a creature of a higher type. Except for a few muddleheads no one on their side thought of upsetting that axiom. Man must ever hold something in reverence and wonder, and there was nothing which could present itself to boys as well as youths, and to youths as well as men, more worthy of wonder and reverence than the Holy Mothers and the Daughters of Heaven. Of all living creatures woman was incontestably the most perfect. For what was the unrest, the thirst for knowledge, the necessity in man to seek, find and experience, but the admission of his painfully realised imperfection? The circumstance that women mostly remained at a stage of development where their voices still retained a boyish shrillness, and that their way of life never entered the sphere of men's coarseness, rudeness and brutality —that in itself spoke for them. Their true power was not the less on that account. Woman was also superior to man in courage, seeing that at the time of her greatest happiness every woman had to face a pain which men were spared, and seeing that passive courage is the highest. That arrest of development, as it were at a stage of holy childishness, enabled women to conserve the dæmonic genius of youth, which they so seldom displayed only because the brutality of man found it easy to suppress the passive and unambitious genius of woman. For that reason, said Phaon, one simply dared not call to mind the crippled forms of womanhood in the Dark Continent. Phaon called women angelic, but men quasi-possessed by the devil. In short, if after-dinner or parliamentary speeches ever have an effect, this one would surely have melted the doctrinaire ice round the hearts of the Philomela Schwab party.

"Our eyes," continued the broad-shouldered, long-haired orator, "our eyes, the eyes of Manland, are fixed with pious devotion, with devout love and reverence on the Temple of the Gods on Mont des Dames, on the Temples of the Gods and their mysteries. We are aware, proudly and reverently aware, that we likewise have to thank the miracle of Île des Dames partly for the kind of existence we lead and partly for that very existence itself, even if at the same time we have not, and never can have, the claim to be known to the Godhead immediately like the Holy Mothers. Nevertheless we say to Him 'Father,' and to the Bona Dea 'Mother.'

"Should you not, noble Mothers, admit us to the festival of the brides, then we shall celebrate here another festival, that of the birth of Bihari Lâl. We shall postpone it to the day of the winter solstice, the twenty-first of December, which, it is true, is hardly distinguishable here. Yet we shall do this because on the day of Bihari Lâl's birth the fate of Île des Dames took its turn towards the heights, towards light and splendour, away from darkness and oppression."

What happened now was the climax of the surprises which the Holy Mothers experienced in Manland. A strange whispering sound, a marvellous vibration, caught the ear, which resolved itself into tones, into the most delicate harmonies. Sounds such as these Prächtel, Rodberte, and the others had not heard for so long that at first they did not know what meaning to ascribe to them. Yes, it was quite a long time before each of the ladies knew clearly whether she alone was sharing in this airy vibration which was like a singing in her ear, or whether it came from a common source and was heard by all. Gradually, however, this Ariel, continuing to make music, revealed himself, and when a curtain rolled back at a sign from Phaon they could no more doubt; for before them were two violins, a viola and a violincello, in fact a quartette, played by youths. The young artists developed their Haydn with divine sweetness, freshness and serenity, and sensitive souls felt that despite Mukalinda and the Bona Dea, the divine had never come so near to them as in hearing these heavenly harmonies and rhythms.

At this moment the Schwab-Egli party had become very, very small. The dice would certainly have fallen luckily for Manland if at the end, as unfortunately often happens, an incident had not occurred which put the Commission into a decided and easily explicable bad humour. By Phaon's command and with the assent of the Lightbringers a young man called Bianor had been excluded from the reception given to the Holy Mothers. He was known as an unsociable, quarrelsome spirit who had from his childhood nourished hatred against Motherland. It was noteworthy, and only to be explained by the sweetness and happiness of life on Île des Dames, that this bitterness, the bitterness of the outcast, did not appear in all of them. Next to the climate and the favourable conditions of life, Phaon had the most credit for this. This Bianor was not to be diverted from his hatred of women, which went as far as contempt. He had marked all too well certain occurrences of a slighting nature of his infancy, while he was still in the keeping of his mother; and certain words which the Mothers at that time thought were far above his comprehension had painfully burned themselves into his soul. These had caused wounds which could never be healed.

Thus the proscribed Bianor, who, at the time of his removal to Wildmanland, had spat round about him, was suddenly in the festival hall, and unfortunately began at once with biting interruptions to accompany a very friendly address by Mother Rodberte. Neither the unanimous voices of the boys and youths nor Phaon himself could do anything against the mischief, for they dared not provide the Holy Mothers with an exhibition of rudeness and violence by expelling Bianor. They knew that roughness and violence were strictly forbidden. Rodberte and the other mothers marked, as a dentist might mark when he touches the nerve of a tooth, that here the nerve of Manland had been touched. And they all thought at once: "It is neither killed, nor has it lost any of its sensitiveness." In truth, the Mothers' thoughts had hitherto been too comfortable to take any account of this aching nerve of Manland. So they had overlooked it. Their alarm was great when they recognised at one and the same moment the existence of the nerve and the danger which it implied for them.

Never had any one before hurled such a violent indictment at the Mothers as Bianor did now, striking in with great eloquence after further speech had been made impossible for Rodberte. He overwhelmed the Mothers with reproaches, and said that they had no right to the sacred name of mother since they had deprived themselves of it by their conduct towards their male children. He did not conceal the fact that at night he had crept into their settlements. He had overheard certain conversations which Mother Egli and Mother Schwab had held with their fine accomplices. There they had planned things against Manland which he would be ashamed to make public. "Your maternity," he said, "is the meanest and coldest cruelty. Gainsay it, Mother Egli, gainsay it, Mother Schwab, that in your eyes, of any nine hundred men, at least eight hundred and ninety are superfluous! All Manland seems superfluous to you. What you would like best would be to murder us all, only you do not know how you are to set about it. Do you not point to the bee-community, and remark how the male bees are killed off after the mating of the queen-bee? Know that you have erased us from your souls and from your hearts. You execrated us already when we leapt under your hearts. Should we perhaps be grateful to you for that? We live, we work. We go about on great projects, and you do not even wish us to exist. But we exist, and we will pay you back your nihilism. For what are you with your puny spirit, your puny strength, your barnyard life, your schoolgirl accomplishments compared with man?"

The scandal was extreme, and not to be made good. Helter skelter the Mothers decamped, and the doctor said to Schwab as they rode back: "A smart turn of the wrist at the right time, and all this would have been impossible."

XIII

THE festival of the dedication of the brides had now been delayed for about a year, for no common decision could be come to over the participation or exclusion of Manland. Additional grounds were always being discovered. Finally the Egli party, which concealed itself behind Philomela Schwab, had carried the original festival programme. According to it Phaon, Bihari Lâl and the twelve divine Lightbringers might take part in the festival, seeing that their inclusion in the life economy of the Mother-state was indispensable.

The solemnities in the Temple grounds were designed as a kind of mystical marriage. Three hundred nubile young girls were to be present in the Temple of Mukalinda. Led by the Mothers and the younger girls down to the age of eight years, they appeared in an inexpressibly lovely procession at the gate of the temple grounds. A wave of loveliness, a wave of youth, a wave of divine beauty, seemed to break there. The noble Laurence, surrounded by all her entourage, by the reverend Mother President, the reverend Mother Rodberte, Lolo Smith and several others, was deeply touched and gripped by the spectacle.

Hundreds of flower-crowned cars with spokeless

wheels, of a classically primitive appearance, were drawn in part by zebu cows, in part by emus (great ostrich-like birds), in part by girls under ten years. The cars moved on, each bearing a woman, a star of heaven, through the gate of the Temple precincts. In festal order they were led by a thousand girls bearing palms and singing a hymn in praise of the Bona Dea, whose separate verses, taken up by different groups, answered each other in liturgical fashion.

In these women no one would have recognised the survivors of the shipwreck. Their increase in years was only to be seen in their growth in feminine charm and beauty. It would be quite immaterial to designate which of the former derelicts it was who stood on the first car. Firstly, none of them bore the old names, and then, they had become new creatures. Who could that Holy Mother be, sitting on her throne, voluptuous and fair, sunk in sweet revery, whose red hair fell like a mantle to her heel, and who pressed a suckling babe to her breast? Such a free, such a blossoming Madonna, full of Pagan abundance, was truly never essayed by any painter. It was an Aphrodite who stood in the second car, and so on. The chaste nudity of all these strangely sensuous nuns was nearly complete.

Now that all this thronging life, this riot of blossoms beyond price, which the strangeness of the climate combined with the character of the old and beautiful races of Europe had brought to expression, were within the temple grounds, they were given freedom for the first time to move where they wished; and it would not be easy to give an exaggerated notion of the joy, the delight, the wantonness, the beauty, which at once unfolded and grew in all the paths and alleys. Up here the air was of that unutterable, living sweetness and paradisaical lightness, which one enjoys in Europe perhaps only in a place like Amalfi in April, where one almost fears to dissolve into the ecstasy of universal life.

All those innocent Bacchantes, from whose eyes broke a world of living joy, whether those eyes were brown or blue, black or grey, whether their hair was red-brown, golden yellow, saffron or blue-black, as it fluttered under the palm-fronds, showed in their appearance in some curious way a common kinship. No one who had seen them would have doubted their divine origin.

There lay in their movements a natural grace and power; and they had no artificiality, even although the noble Laurence had led an attempt in Motherland to revive the Greek dance, and the attempt had been successful. Out of art had come forth a second, higher nature.

Himself unobserved, Phaon regarded these lovely children moving over the gravel walks and the grass lawns, and his soul was profoundly moved.

"How hopeless it is for us," thought he to himself, "born as we are into the midst of all these marvels so meaningless, and so opulent. We see operations and we see effects which in their intoxicating abundance in

㆓ 296 ㆔

form and life have somehow and sometime been called
forth through us, and yet we dare not let ourselves feel
that we are their creators. Perhaps we are a necessary,
though we remain a contemptible, an undeserving part
of life which stands in no relation to the kingdom which
it procreated and those eternal and divine forms of life.
Who but a god would claim to have created this Garden
of Eden with all its Houris whose voluptuousness en-
snares and maddens, whose beauty is almost a pain to
the wounded eye and soul? Was I indeed alive yesterday? And how should I persuade myself, if I am not
a god, that this or that small adventure, this or that
little intoxication or enjoyment which has passed without a trace, was real and not dreamt? Yet all this is
here before me, it laughs, gambols, shouts, springs
around me, and blinds and almost maddens me with its
power of life—or is that too, only phantasmagoria once
more? It is the only reality, it has this power of life,
and again it is only phantasmagoria. How do I reconcile these two realities? They have at any rate one
thing in common; they are both transitory. And what
a bitter shame—" Phaon ended his train of thought—
"that this spectacle, whether it be reality or phantasmagoria, will not be enjoyed by all among men who
hunger and thirst after beauty."

About the eleventh hour and towards noon the procession, preceded by Rukminî, had reached the cave of
the Bona Dea, and it cannot be gainsaid that this marvellous tail behind that earthly comet now first made
her divine radiance shine out with its full light. Ruk-

minî, it was clear to all the Holy Mothers, could not have had a human mother, far less a human father. The ceremonies in the cave took their course, whereupon the train proceeded to the Temple, dancing, singing, clashing tambourines, and looking now not unlike a disciplined train of Bacchantes. The girls' hair, like a sea of flame, flashed above them.

In the entry hall, the prytaneum, of Mukalinda's Temple, richly decorated by Dagmar-Diodata's chief masterpiece, and reserved from the Holy of Holies, the twelve divine Lightbringers, led by Bihari Lâl, were, in the presence of the reverently waiting assembly, presented to the dedicated brides. For the Holy Mothers this was an almost overpowering moment. Now it had to be admitted that, as Rukminî left the girls far behind in beauty, so Bihari Lâl far surpassed the twelve Lightbringers. A stillness of prolonged expectation set in, only broken by the muffled sobbing of the Mothers and the crackling of the perpetual fire upon the altar. It was not only the President who showed a lively interest in the cross-fire of glances which would now be expected to commence between the brides and the Lightbringers. In this respect everyone was disappointed. The youths were inconquerably slow. One could not but think, and the President was not long in drawing the conclusion, that behind this there must be hidden some cunning design. The President, throned on a dais with other persons of rank, whispered to Rodberte:

"An eight groschen piece, my good Rodberte, if it

can be proved to me that a single one of these Firebrands feels himself obliged to direct even one glance at his willing partner."

She was interrupted by the entry of the pious Laurence in her priestly regalia from the Holy of Holies.

It cannot be said that the ceremony in Mukalinda's Temple passed off in complete harmony, since the orthodox party in the teeth even of Laurence's objections had appointed Philomela Schwab as second speaker.

The speech of the noble Laurence was noteworthy, and had, in brief, this import:

At the beginning of things stand two powers. One power cannot exist by itself. In order to know itself as power, a power stands in need of a second one. God however, is one power, and therefore he cannot be almighty. But he is the victor over the other power. And so he is the artist of all, the subduer of all. To the subdued powers belongs fire. But fire is only subdued so long as the hand of the Subduer rests on it, and only a part of fire is subdued. Fire is within all things, and yet it is outside, too. Our world stands and we ourselves stand, by a compromise of the Most High, between this Within and this Without. But God, the Subduer, has smelted this omnipotent power in the bonds of matter, and that is the true sense of the Promethean Word. The gods of Olympus would not have been immoderately disturbed if Prometheus had given men only a little fire, and the art to enslave it. No, Prometheus was fire itself, before which all the gods save Helios tremble.—The thought of the existence of the Fire-world is not only fearful, but also incomprehensibly great. Fire is perhaps one thing and yet all things, bringing forth from itself all things, drawing all things back into itself, spiritual things, great things, last things, all things.

And as a pastor reads passages out of the Bible, so she read out of a book:

"By means of fire we can lay our hands on established things, divide, pulverise, melt, refine them, dissolve them into ever finer and less sensuous fabrics, while we burn their invisible molecules and imponderable electrons until they become clouds, mists, gas; transforming what can be felt into what can be heard, the audible into the visible, the visible into a perfume, a perfume into nothing, into absolutely nothing and not merely the final blue of heaven. These are the mighty operations of fire, the crucible in which we might throw all the worlds and find that in their final transformation they do not become something so palpable even as smoke."

And Laurence referred to the altar flame. She likened the heat to a plant and the flame to a dancing flower. "But," she said, "all speech is at last insufficient to grasp, even approximately, the mystery of fire. Regard this flame, Children of Heaven, Daughters of Heaven. Why should not I dare call you so, who in the world-embracing Dark Continent would submit to be called children of earth, daughters of earth? Fundamentally earth and heaven are one, a great mystery, and only arrant shallow-pates could fall into the error of thinking their earthly half the less noble, the less mysterious. This flame, this holy fire, which is outside you, is also re-born within you, its glow as well as its light; and you go now to meet one of its supreme emanations, where the living kernel of being, the sense of being, the sensuality of being, the sensuality of the senses, will break open for you like a glowing and radiant blossom."

She continued to speak in this strain, until the platform was resigned to Philomela Schwab.

It would be hard to say whether the girls, or indeed one among them, comprehended the lecture of the High Priestess. From outward signs one would have said that they did not.

On the other hand they listened with lively attention when the Holy Mother Philomela Schwab brought another tone into the assembly, and once more illustrated the view that politics in the church creates the worst discord imaginable, and spreads the most injurious reputation.

In her speech Philomela Schwab played on the wearisome theme of Manland and its exclusion from the day's festival. There was no new aspect to be discovered in this theme, already flogged to death. But the speaker did not allow herself to be daunted. What they had seen in Manland was mostly unprofitable nonsense, and this nonsense was not animated by a desire for the elevation of the life of the divine island, but rather by a desire to escape from its frontiers. In that direction Manland should certainly be given a free hand, for it could be only to the advantage of Motherland if the greatest possible number of men, enticed out into the world by the daring spirit of adventure, were to seek their happiness elsewhere. That there were dangerous elements, who would not shrink from the destruction of all peaceful relations, had been admitted by the leader and protector of Manland himself. Man is not an element of stability in the state, but one rather of destruction. For the empire of woman and of the Mothers, that is, for Motherland, the neighbouring colony was at all times a grave danger. But they would know how to meet it.

"You!" Thereupon she turned to the dozen divine Lightbringers. She pronounced this speech with great vehemence. "You have become participants in our grace, which the Holy Mothers hope you know how to value. Although to us you are alien beings, differently constituted, yet we have in our grace lifted you up to us out of your state of misery. We have at any rate lifted you as high as is humanly possible. But mark this well; past a certain limit it is not possible. But, as I have said, so far as it was possible it was possible only through us, your mothers. And mark this further, that you are absolutely and wholly our creation, from head to sole. You are absolutely and wholly our work, from head to sole, with your skin and hair, your outward members, your five senses as well as your inward parts—heart, lungs, kidneys, spleen, liver, bladder, great intestine, small intestine, vertebral column, spinal marrow, nervous system, grey and white brain matter, cerebellum and cerebrum. We formed you within ourselves. We sent you forth, finished, made, to the last finger nail set on your little fingers. Had we not built you up so, knit you together so, given you life of our life, filled your veins with our blood, to-day you would be nothing. Remember this, you Light-bringers! Let it never happen that you should be tempted to regard us except reverently, with humility and lowliness, as your creators. Otherwise, know this: we shall fling you back into your nothingness."

"In God's name, what is wrong?" said Anni Prächtel to her entourage. "Has anyone a desire for the strait jacket?"

According to programme the hymn to Mukalinda written by Bihari Lâl was now struck up. In the canon throughout almost the only words repeated and mingled were: "Mukalinda, O Mukalinda, my father, my father." By the end of the song the bad impression which Philomela's speech had created was so far dissipated that the pious Laurence was able to bring the holy festival to a successful conclusion.

While the High Priestess laid both hands on each of the bowed, beautiful heads of the youths, one after another, she declared herself authorised by the god to name all of them his sons, what in Bihari Lâl's case was in any case universally acknowledged. And thus the twelve Lightbringers were recognised as the twelve sons of Mukalinda, and with that the festival was ended.

Now followed months which brought nothing extraordinary for the colony on Île des Dames. The days in Motherland glided past in uniform happiness. The orthodox party were pleased and congratulated themselves on having overcome the weak complaisance of the temple authorities in the Manland question, and on having upheld and expressed the strict matriarchal tradition. As before, the newly dedicated Brides of Heaven and Earth occupied themselves with unconsecrated and ever more popular dances and diversions of all kinds, after they had discharged a few hours in this or that occupation. Even labour was a kind of play, for every necessity could be obtained with but little trouble; one had only to pluck the fruit with which tree and bush were richly loaded.

One day the Holy Mothers, Egli and Schwab, were sitting together. Their conversation evinced a common dissatisfaction. The machine of state of Île des Dames was fallen into disrepair. Something or other had for a time been working loose, and now the smash had come.

From Manland a rumour had come through that the men had celebrated there with great magnificence in ceremony, dance and song the birthday festival of Bihari Lâl. Doubtless this was done in mockery, but it was also a sort of premeditated revenge for the exclusion of the men from the festival of the dedication of the brides.

"Perhaps it was a mistake, my good Schwab," said the doctor, who was in a bad mood, "to preach down at the twelve chosen boys as you did, in the Temple and in presence of the girls."

"If I did that," said Mother Schwab, "it was by your advice."

"But I did not advise you to do that. I only said in general that something must be done in time to prevent these trees from growing into the very heavens."

"What trees?" asked Frau Schwab.

"Naturally I mean those trees which we must eventually transplant to Motherland if we are to count upon progress, a future and increase. The blow to our fortunes is directly traceable to your speech, and followed on its heels. Our situation is so absurd that it has become shameful."

"Pooh!" exclaimed Frau Schwab vehemently. "Why, then, does not the all-wise, all-knowing, all-powerful, high, higher, highest Laurence do something in the matter?"

"Quite simply because she has been put in a bad temper by your violent step. It makes me ill whenever I have to meet that old vulture Prächtel, or that pen-and-ink microbe Kalb. They can hardly conceal their laughter. Why do not such superfluous, absolutely useless females die? From the start they have been good-for-nothings. In these frivolous old maids not one serious, practical, useful thought has ever yet seen the light of day. Have you spoken with Babette?"

"Babette says that Mukalinda has been insulted. Of course that is patently absurd, even if he has fallen

-⟨ 305 ⟩-

upon us like a bolt from the blue. Nothing else is discussed except how we may appease the Lord Mukalinda."

Egli exclaimed: "I will go to Phaon and speak my mind plainly to him."

"You will scarcely find him," said Schwab. "He has withdrawn himself with the Twelve and Bihari Lâl, no one knows whither, into invisibility."

What had in reality occurred?

Already last year during the dispute with Manland regarding co-operation in the festival the birth-rate in Motherland had fallen. For two months there had not been a single birth. Moreover no sign had come to assure them that this state would be a transitory one. As everybody knows, among human beings too there must be seed-time and harvest. This is a truth, of course, which people very rarely dare to hint at or mention, for to do so a taboo has to be broken through. But here it had to be broken through, for a society of human beings saw themselves in the deadly state of having both their seed-time and their harvest denied them.

Babette had given out that the procreative and life-giving power was insulted. In fact there were grounds for her opinion.

All the recently initiated novices of the Mukalinda cult had naturally been acquainted with the prevailing ritual, and in turn enjoined the practice of the temple sleep. These charming, gay children, as innocent as they were modest, had had the most entrancing dreams and had never become weary of relating them. But that was all they brought home from their excursion. Their simple chattering about it was scarcely listened to any longer.

In the temple grounds of the Bona Dea especially a remarkable quiet had fallen. One might almost say, if it did not sound absurd, that the gods seemed to be deserted by mankind. At any rate the high-minded Laurence had not been there for several weeks. Lolo Smith, Rukminî and the silent Dagmar-Diodata were there still: apart from them, however, only inferior servants of the higher powers.

According to rumour the noble Laurence had withdrawn still deeper into the solitude of the island and of her soul. There was a path not too dangerous once it was found, but hard to find and easy to miss, which led down to Laurence's new hermitage. It was said that Mucci Smith, the practical gardener, alone visited the hermit regularly and provided her with the vegetables on which she lived. Barefoot or in bast shoes she had to clamber down the sheer cliff to Laurence's cave. The day-star looked into that cave when it arose and still lighted it at the moment of sunset. From a terrace which hung like a balcony over the surf, a lovely, slender coco-palm rose into space. A natural basin in the rock was replenished year in, year out, with fresh, clear water out of a cleft in the crag.

Besides Mucci only Phaon, Dagmar-Diodata, Rukminî and Lolo Smith knew of this abode. For the others the beautiful Laurence had vanished, leaving no trace behind. So they could not expect anything from her if the propitiation of Mukalinda came into question.

By now three, four, five months had passed over the island. It glittered as before in paradisaical beauty. But although no vestige of a cloud stood in that fortunate heaven, and, thanks to the ideal climate of the isle, only softly refreshing and life-awakening showers passed over it, the islanders yet felt as if the shadow of a cloud lay on them.

A third embassy had already been sent by the Mothers across the Défilé des Dames. The Manlanders had retreated from all accessible places into a certain mountain district, where the rider Iphis had discovered them. Even the Capitol with the image of the thinking hand had been deserted, and the approach of the commission found it a wilderness. The women had prudently not troubled to include in this commission the Mothers Egli and Schwab. Nevertheless it had no results to show. Led by Iphis to the very last entrenchments, one might say, of the men folks, they could not even catch a glimpse of Phaon, nor of Bihari Lâl, nor of any of the Twelve.

Instead of these Bianor was sent to meet them. It was with him they had now to negotiate.

And what in truth was there left to negotiate? That grim and dreadful man who puffed himself up with a reckless and mocking dialectic scared the intended message of the women back into the impenetrable fastnesses of their souls, as the lion scares the rabbit.

And so they had to return home with their purpose unfulfilled.

In Motherland there prevailed a state of uneasiness, anxiety and perplexity whose full scope could not yet be comprehended. Fits of mental depression set in such as had been known only in the early times just after the shipwreck. Genuine nervous crises had not yet become universal, but they were there, and they could not be ignored. The idea of despatching a message in a bottle was once more brought forward, for by now there had arisen a painful longing to get back to the great world of civilisation. Round the neck of a tiny sea swallow, *sterna stolida,* of which they had caught several specimens, they bound little tightly rolled messages which told of the shipwreck, the rescue, and the forlorn state of the rescued, and implored the future reader to send out ships to deliver the long-lost party. It was only natural that the mental depression of the Mothers should be transmitted to the island-born Daughters of Heaven. For they, too, felt that something beyond their thought must happen if the wall was to give way which closed up every step and prospect into the future. One day Terror suddenly arose in all its fearful majesty. The ordinary human being can only overcome terror when he is firmly implanted as a part of the complete life of a human society. It is indifferent whether he is conscious of this or not. He must be able to persuade himself that there have always been men, that they do not exist merely at this moment, but that they also perpetuate themselves, that they will exist to-morrow, the day after to-morrow, yea, in a thousand years hence. In two words, he must be a living limb drawing his blood from a body of humanity which is apparently immortal. But real terror comes when the opening blossom, or the leaf unsuspectingly waxing on the twig, realises that the branch has been severed from the tree and that its life is only part of a false growth, an unreal blossoming. We know not in how far flowers and leaves are sentient. At any rate, here in Motherland there existed for the first time an analogous feeling, out of which this terror suddenly arose. Even though day in, day out, Motherland rang still with song and laughter, the old song and the old laughter (after which they had called certain fields the Fields of Laughter), yet the women could not banish any more an ever-returning, dreadful vision, the giant skeleton of Death, which had set its foot on the island.

So one day there arrived a general psychosis, an outbreak of senseless frenzy. The women, with wildly flying hair, ran up the heights of Mont des Dames intending to break into the temple grounds and into the Temples of the Bona Dea and of Mukalinda. Those who begged and implored them to desist were themselves soon in the grip of despair which in its turn passed into insatiable fury ere their more prudent words could have effect. It was not the Temple of the Bona Dea which was violated first; the women seemed to prefer the Mukalinda Temple, where with threatening words and fists they demanded the aid of

the god. In vain the Mothers Lolo and Mucci sought
to intervene. They exhorted the women to self-control.
Dagmar-Diodata walked through the raging and insen-
sate crowd reminding them with tears and pleading
words of the silence due to the place where they were.
She did so in vain. With a universal and resounding
shriek of madness they broke into the Temple; the carpet of the Lightbringer was torn in a thousand shreds,
the altar of Mukalinda was overthrown. Hardly ten
minutes were gone ere the whole edifice went up in
flames.

Behind the rocky bastions of Manland, whither
the men had withdrawn, could be seen as the night
descended the flare of the fire from the Temple mirrored in the waters of Golfe des Dames. But over the
Temple itself it stood like a gloriole. It was not known
at first what to make of the phenomenon. Anything
resembling it had never been seen, for hitherto the
island had been preserved from great and disastrous
fires. Only when the fire from the Mukalinda Temple,
which lay outside the range of vision, was cast against
Laurence's dwelling, could the flames be clearly recognised, and there was no longer any doubt that a mishap
must have occurred.

Soon after that the rumour went round that the
Mukalinda Temple was reduced to ashes. To the astonishment of Phaon, who with Bihari Lâl and the
twelve Lightbringers held the government of Manland
in his hands, the news was received by the great part of
the camp with almost savage jubilation. At that time

Phaon had not yet apprehended how far the sedition of the so-called Rebel had gone.

The existence of the Rebel and his waxing power had above all influenced Phaon in his decision upon the conflict between Motherland and Manland. The idea of the election of twelve new procreative gods to be of the company of Mukalinda seemed to him expedient in the interests of the matriarchate and as tending to the good of future generations. With this intention he had used his influence with the men and tried to enlist their support that thus he might leave to a future hour the solution of the gigantic difficulties in prospect. Unfortunately the fatuity of the fanatical Philomela Schwab had stirred up the Twelve themselves to fury, so that, perhaps overhastily, they had flung up their prerogatives and gone over to the crowd. They were received with small thanks.

The frenetic tumult which had satiated itself in the destruction of the Mukalinda Temple affected Phaon in complex and contradictory ways. The shuttle of his thoughts worked upon such strange and heterogeneous material, that the absurdity of his existence could not but be clear to him. It became still more clear when immediately after the rejoicing over Mukalinda's downfall that was seen to be in some strange way linked with a rebellion against himself. And naturally enough against the Lightbringers also, although Bihari Lâl was not yet implicated.

Incited by the Rebel the sons of Mukalinda pressed on until they reached Phaon's tent, which like all the others was a hastily constructed edifice of palm straw. Phaon should withdraw his decree, whereby Manlanders were not permitted to trespass on the grounds of Motherland. Phaon himself should lead them there.

"No action of mine will give you the signal to destroy our sacred statutes. The main pillars of our state must remain unimpaired by us, even if the other side has failed in that respect. And never will I give you a signal to commit violence. Violence, which comes apt to man, is his worst part. In you I desire that not your evil but rather your good should come to fruition. And the good, that is your spirit. You will say, We desire to act also. But I say to you: violence is not a thing worthy of man, or of any human being. It is fitted rather to animals; or, better still, it is the inanimate reaction of inanimate nature. Through violence the handiwork of the sacred hand is desecrated. I admit, the symbol of the sacred hand has also its dreadful side, but its preponderating operation is marvellous and rich in blessing. This great power equally mighty in destruction and in creation will yet remould itself in thousandfold living forms working good, until in its last elevation and refinement it attain the expression of eternal, godlike beauty. Once more be it said—if on so much violence still more violence were piled, after it all the true manifestation of the human spirit would not be even begun.

"And what, moreover, would you do in the holy land of your birth, in the holy land of your mothers? Insult and dishonour your mothers? Bring disgrace and shame upon them, lift your hands against them, or what, then?

"I who have guided your steps hitherto will do so still for a while. I will find ways and means, when the time comes, to procure for you every satisfaction you have earned and make your peace with the Holy Mothers."

The Rebel Bianor cried: "You have spoken. Before you opened your mouth we knew what you would say. You have spoken, but your words have not flown from your mouth like parrots or birds of paradise, flamingoes or eagles: their wings are broken. Think of that. Your words lie on the ground and do not move. They are as if they were dead. And this is our conclusion: your words were liars and traitors so long as they were still alive. You have allied yourself with our enemies. They kept us in subservience and misery, and you have assented to it. You have been held by the enemies of our sex, because they have bought you. You have taught us how to dissipate our strength, in order that we should not employ it. All our deeds, all our strivings, have been fruitless. You have condemned us, damned us, to barrenness, so that we might not be admitted to your privileges, neither to yours nor to those of your twelve Lightbringers. Did you imagine we had not seen how zebus propagated themselves? Man is only an animal of the same kind. There are masculine animals and feminine animals, and the masculine are there for the feminine, as the feminine are for the masculine. The women you have made into goddesses, but us into uncleanly animals miserable even among the animals.

"It may be that Mukalinda is our father. If so he is a bad father, perhaps not to his daughters, but nevertheless to his sons. Well for us that his temple has been burned down. His sons will not build it up again. A son is what his father is; if not, the procreative force of a god is less strong than that of an animal. Against this Mukalinda we will wage war, god against god, in the strength of our godhead. What need have we of your light, ye Lightbringers? In ourselves burns the true, divine light. From you, too, our master in many arts and our foster-father, I have for long derived no light. Nay, you stand in my light. I say your notions are womanish. In the stillness of my exile I have weighed them. The aim of procreation and of birth is not woman. Man alone is the aim of birth. That is my truth, for which I stand. The banner which I would plant on the ruins of the Temples of the Bona Dea and of Mukalinda would carry, worked in fire, the inscription: Man. It is not true that man's use of force is an unworthy thing. Where there is force there is force. How can power not be where it is? Is Fate, then, not power? The fire-spitting Mont des Dames, you have taught us, lifted this island out of the sea. Did it do so by persuasion? Not once would the Holy Mothers admit us to the festival of the dedication of the brides, as if they thought Mukalinda would be dishonoured through us. Now we will instruct them who we are. We are afraid neither before gods nor men.

The old musty era of stagnation is no more. The new time has begun: our time. In reality what are we to-day but a wretched, forgotten, contemptible, shrunken dust-heap of humanity? Our drums, our voices, can scarcely be heard. They are swallowed up, like the noises of ants, in the immensity of nature around us, a stillness like that of the grave. We would set free our vital powers and people every valley and height. And, Father Phaon, I am he who will propagate himself on the ladder of the generations to the farthest heaven. The roar of the voices of my people will drown the sound of the surf round our coast; the smoke from their chimneys will make the furnace of Mont des Dames appear like a wretched cottage fire. I shall be king over Mont des Dames, over the island, over the ocean and all the lands of the earth."

"Since when, then, has the world existed, my dear son?" enquired Phaon.

Bianor replied: "Since I was born to a knowledge of myself."

"Not longer? Only as long as that?"

"Not an instant longer," exclaimed the Rebel.

"Indeed. You know but little of the world."

"I know only one world—my own," cried the other.

"Before your time—is this what you mean, my son —the whole world was filled with spiritual darkness, perverted desire and evil fulfilment?"

"Yes," said Bianor, "that is what I mean."

"But you are still very young, my good son."

"I have lived for seventeen years," exclaimed the

Rebel, "and in the first of them—reflect what that means—life was given to me. How many living experiences in that year alone thronged in upon me through all my senses! Admit the experiences of these seventeen full years, and deny that they signify something monstrous beyond computation, to add to which would be almost impossible."

"And yet, as regards experience, I am far in front of you, my son."

"Your experience is of no help to me. Experiences, which one does not experience oneself, are none."

"Well," said Phaon, "do what you must."

With the fire-raising in the temple precincts and its echo in Manland there had set in almost simultaneously in both halves of Île des Dames a kind of anarchy, whose early stages, regarded from a higher plane, might have been likened to the first flashes of lightning in a period of thundery spring weather. While Mother Egli, as was natural, took the revolt and its results tragically, and the hump-back, Fräulein Auguste, read more than ever her Thomas à Kempis, the worthy and inseparable soul-mates Rodberte and Anni lost nothing of their calm and cynical cheerfulness.

The artist said: "God knows, now I have a desire to live! For twenty years I should quite candidly have given out my old Adam as totally dead. But now if I pleased I might conclude from all manner of mad dreams that it is lifting up its head again. But do not let us talk about it. For, in truth, bulls might become shy when two old scarecrows begin to gossip."

Clips full when for the stray
On sky   Cell first full
                      Crooks full
              will me the clips
                    all sign all
                         Chose

Rodberte said she had really seen only once a scare-crow in a field, and it would perhaps be better in all respects if one restricted oneself in such comparisons to an object which one was absolutely certain fitted such a risky analogy.

Never had rebels or conquerors a lighter task than that of the Manlanders led by Bianor. The young girls, whom wild enthusiasm had turned into mænads, greeted them on the narrow pass to the isthmus, be-tween Golfe des Dames and the open sea. Truly the procession which from that point steadily grew was very different from that which had recently been seen in the temple grounds. Like a storm wind they came, girls and youths mingled together, raging through the night, illumined by countless wildly swinging torches, veiled in thick and flaring smoke. Wild leaping was seen, and cries were heard of limitless intoxication. Apparently the rage against Motherland boiled still more wildly in the renegade Daughters of Heaven than in the rebels. In the grey of morning, stamping, shout-ing, raving, they reached the first of the settlements, where immediately all the remaining girls joined the rout. The dancing, shrieking, pressing and butting forward were contagious. It sucked irresistibly all who were young into its vortex, aggrandising its power by their renunciation of resistance. Soon nobody but Bianor knew what was happening around and within him. And Bianor himself was horrified by the uncanny power he had unchained. But to arrest it was now unthinkable, and he, too, was hurried on, like a boulder in the bed of a torrent in flood.

Rigid with astonishment and pale with terror the mothers came out before their doors. They wrung their hands, they implored, they cried to their sons with tender, maternal words, but the raging of the forward-rushing throng did not abate. Rather it increased and ever became more terrifying. It could now be seen that those dancers, that leaping throng, those yelling, shrieking, whirling bodies, could no longer be in their senses. And if one had ever thoughtlessly used the expression, You have been stung by a tarantula, so now one would have thought in truth that this illimitably abandoned crowd had been thrown into this state by the bite or sting of a poisonous insect or reptile.

The girls and youths had seized everything which could add to the noise; these were seized now by the children as well, down to the tiniest. Tambourines, triangles, and fifes rattled, groaned, and tinkled in wild confusion. Leaving the youths aside, where now could be found among the girls any remnant of their good breeding? Gestures of boundless obscenity, expressed as completely as dance and wild movement could, were displayed by them with a like blind shamelessness. In the beginning they had roused their mothers to anger, but wrath was chased away by pity and anxiety when it was seen that, under the influence of the dæmonic force of an unchained desire, the throng no longer possessed any power over itself.

Soon they had left the settlement once more behind them, and the mothers who still retained their senses breathed more easily. Before the breath of the driving tempest houses and shops here and there were going up in flames and smoke. Not a few of the Holy Mothers, too, had been unable to withstand the power of the madness which seized upon them from all sides. When the wild spring lightning had passed over the settlement and was raging up Mont des Dames one was astounded to see here and there between the now silent houses one of the Mothers suddenly drawn into the delirium and torn, leaping and flying, after the Bacchanalian rout.

On this very morning, the Manland banner was planted by Bianor in the deserted temple grounds: a rag of cloth with the inscription: Man.

But the disorder rolled on. There were now no bounds to it. Phaon, who had reached the temple grounds without being observed, watched it rage farther up Mont des Dames. If any one had discovered him it would possibly have gone with him as it went with Pentheus, who was torn to pieces by mænads.

Phaon's way now led him swiftly by a descent known only to himself to a small harbour impassable by any other way from the land, where an exceptionally well-built sailing boat lay at anchor. It was furnished with provisions, water, and all that was needed for a month's expedition. Dagmar-Diodata was busy stowing various objects in a very efficient way, using the available space to the best advantage. She greeted Phaon with cheerful gravity, and he began to take part in the work.

For a long time they waded from the beach to the boat and back, and while they were occupied in this way few words were spoken. In the evening they made a fire on the volcanic sand.

Down here Phaon and Diodata met day after day in the following weeks, without their hiding place being discovered. In truth they had planned a flight, but it seemed to Phaon that the right moment had not yet come.

The Golfe des Dames and particularly its superb beach became in the following weeks the stage of that god who is the earliest of all. As everybody knows, he prefers clear moonlit nights to day. It was as if he had laid a snare and caught in it indifferently, as hunters catch wild animals, the storm troops of Manland and the Bacchic throng of girls. Over the bay and its shore hung night after night, spread under the moon, the sultry and intoxicating twilight of his mystery. One could hear women's voices cooing, trilling, exultant with longing, and gloriously rolling voices from manly throats breaking into a tumult of joy, in the inexpressible ecstasy of beauty enjoyed. The plashing of oars was heard, and the spreading smoke-branches of Mont des Dames, lit up from below, seemed only to exist for the sake of its reflection on the smooth surface of the salt inland sea, in which it was glorified.

Phaon himself came under its spell. Although he carried in his heart all the sweetness and heaviness of farewell, he had a deep desire to observe for the last time and without being seen the life which he had fashioned. Like a hunter he glided from tree to tree in the shadows cast by the moon, concealing himself whenever he heard voices or footsteps. As often happened with this strong and serious man in the noblest moments of his life, joy and pain were now indissolubly mingled in his breast. But both were stronger than ever before.

What was it, then, that made him tremble? It was himself. It was his own incomprehensibly rich mystery. From the palm and eucalyptus thickets broke the call of a conch. It was his breath which had summoned that sound from the conch. A deep masculine voice laughed. The sound came from a little fire which flickered on a point of land. "Is it not my laughter," thought Phaon, "which has sundered itself from me so that it might have a life of its own? Or is it *not* my laughter? Then verily there would be nothing of mine in me. Then would my own self not be mine. Then it would be only an empty self that has flared up in me, which exists only to receive and render back a Something, and to recognise that it is not mine."

Strewn here and there burned the fires of love. They lighted up more or less brightly the great encampments of nightly pleasure. In the radiance of one of these, leaning against a breadfruit tree, while flower-crowned maidens danced round him, the chief Rebel was standing. Then said Phaon half-loud:

"You fool!" exactly as one blames oneself for a stupid thought.

Thereupon he strode through the lights and the dancers to Bianor, and the Rebel wept for a long time on his breast. But Phaon disappeared as quickly as he had come, and Bianor scarcely knew whether he had suffered from a hallucination, or the incident had really occurred.

Phaon regarded the new Manland banner long and pensively. "This reality," he said to himself, "signifies truly little in our reality. As symbol it signifies much. What has happened and happens even now is simply one of the eternally recurring acts of nature, whereby from time to time, she sweeps away from her all that is artificial. After all, this whole island is the product of man's superficial instinct of play. Or is this instinct, gay and superficial, quickly finished and impermanent as its creations may seem, not so superficial after all? In the end deep and shallow are but words whereby, in busying ourselves with spiritual things, we denote something which is neither deep nor shallow. For shallow we can always substitute the word joy, and for deep the little word grief. But final grief is unattainable in art, for art in its deepest deeps is still joy. No art, then, without superficiality; no art without joy. Our heaven, the holy worlds of the future, must either be inhabited by divine children at play, or they will not repay habitation. For a heaven in which omniscient sages shall sit round with wagging heads and I myself will be such a sage—for that at any rate I do not yearn.

"All those young pairs raging in the fires of love do but cast themselves in blind certainty into the glory of superficial enjoyment which unlocks to them the ultimately possible deeps of pleasure. Here we have, perhaps for the first time in our life's phantasmagoria, a reality which is real even though all those dancers, those blest hunters of pleasure, are encompassed round by phantastic clouds and each by his particular dream. Yet every one is alone; every one would reach his own isle of the blessed. I find it hard to leave Île des Dames," thought Phaon. "But what can I do? In no other way can I sunder myself from the spirits I called forth. Into the corner with you, broom! This is where my respected, good Prächtel would say: 'Oh, don't mention it!'— If it were possible to perceive external reality, which is not possible (for one can only have weaker or stronger perception), then it would be impossible for me to tear myself away from those I have created, whether they be well or ill created. It is hard enough for me as it is. And to tear myself away, too, from the mothers I have given them is a hard task for the sensitive heart. I shall guard myself securely against meeting any of them again alone.

"In our eternal Spring this momentary event is but a spring tempest. And, Bianor, what are you then truly —you, my beloved, untamed, tameless son? When in due time we gave Bianor his name the learned Rodberte said it might signify something like, the primal procreative power of matter."

About this hour the Golfe des Dames rang with an unutterably melodious symphony in which pain and joy seemed blended in a harmony which could never end. One could not tell how far this sound could be heard. But the holy anchorite Laurence, who was sitting in silence before her cave, heard it, and it entered into her heart. Sighing deeply she lifted her heavy head so as to hearken to the distant sound. "At last I have attained," thought she, "to participation in those unearthly, super-terrestrial tones. Can they have fallen down here from the planets? Can they perhaps have fallen from Mercury, which of all planets is nearest the sun? And in listening to these harmonies am I indeed beginning my journey thither?

"It is said that Mercury turns ever the same side to the sun. The other is buried in eternal night beneath mountains of ice. Yet some scientists believe that, between the burning wastes and dreadful light of the one side and the eternal ice and darkness of the other, there is a broad, everlastingly serene zone, irrigated by the thawed waters of night, green and blooming to the verge of the eternal waste, and bathed in everlasting light.

"If this music comes from thence then, just as scientists can demonstrate by the spectroscope the presence of this or that gas, I could predict from it that in the blest, life-giving zone of Mercury, too, pain is not an unknown greatness. But was it not clear to me even as a child that pleasure and pain are but two sides of one and the same thing?   And yet I must ever desire pleasure, even if thereby I must also desire pain.

"Or does the music come perhaps from Uranus, where the mysterious gas of Jupiter is found?   That planet is of all planets the farthest from the sun.   Perhaps it is one single, monstrous, suspended, grey ocean. Four moons circle round it in their strange courses. Immanuel Kant, who attained nearer than anyone else to the source of Being, seems to have had an intimation that, in spite of its remoteness from the sun, that planet might possibly nourish higher forms of life than any of the others. A life compacted of finer and more mobile elements of matter."

And, weary and ripe for death, the noble Laurence could not refrain from pondering whether grief and regret over loss, salt and bitter tears, were not known, too, in that twilit world. Whether even in it, that watery wilderness over which the sun shone but as a tiny star, the consciousness of the pain of the universe did not brood like the spirit of God over the waters, a God who experienced in himself to everlasting all the despair and anguish for some irreparable loss.

No, that music was confident and full of hope.   It might rather be the music of a brook of paradise freed from night and ice, and knowing that forever and ever it would water the soil of an Eden.

-C 326 ꜿ-

On the morning after his meditation on the meaning of the Manland banner, Phaon awoke not by Golfe des Dames but by the Lake of the Birds of Paradise. He noticed that not far from him Dagmar-Diodata was sitting among flowers and pensively weaving garlands of them. As he looked, the unicorn lifted his head close by her, snorting through his nostrils while grass hung from his lazily-moving jaws.

Never at any time that Phaon found himself up here did he know how he had reached the crest. Even now as he still battled with the effects of sleep the sun rose over the brim of the ocean. He sprang up. There had rung in his ears as it were a command to do so.

And he went whither he had first seen the solitary lady walk, who was his mother. And again in holy silence she approached along the avenue.

But even as he saw her Phaon abruptly turned away. He beheld Laurence, who laid her left hand on his shoulder. But immediately the apparition vanished.

About the same hour Mucci Smith clambered down the walls of rock in her bast shoes from the temple grounds, to bring the day's ration to the noble hermit Laurence. She found the priestess of the Great Mother sitting upright, lighted by the first sad radiance of the approaching sun. As, filled with a vague fear which she could not fathom, Mucci Smith went nearer, it seemed to her that the noble lady was still asleep, her back leant against the rocks of the cave entrance. She was completely naked. But her loosened and still dark hair flowed down like a robe over her breast and shoulders, and gathered in a pool on the ground.

"This is no sleep," Mucci thought in a lightning flash. With frightful, unfathomable, open eyes Laurence stared into the sun.

At once Mucci knew what she had to do. The body of the dead woman was still warm. Weeping, with gentle fingers Mucci closed the dead eyes.

And once more Phaon did not know how he happened to be in the sailing boat, which rocked with him and Diodata in the night on the open sea. He greeted the fire from Mont des Dames. The anguish of parting pierced his breast.

How terrible, said he to himself, that we must remain eternally separated from those very beings whom we have fashioned, and love most. The anguish of this intuition is so great, and would be so fearfully magnified by every attempt to avoid parting, that to lighten it only flight is left to us.

As these thoughts coursed through Phaon's mind he felt on his breast and in his ear a sweet and tender breath, which formed the name of Rukminî. In the next moment he saw a girl riding on a zebu who with wild cries urged her rearing animal from the shore of the secret and deserted harbourage into the waves.

Then Phaon gripped the helm with firmer hand, and the breezes of freedom swelled his sails.